AN EMPIRE FOR RAVENS
The Twelfth John the Lord Chamberlain Mystery

Reed and Mayer's outstanding 12th whodunit set in the sixth century CE takes John the Eunuch, a worshipper of the sun god Mithra and former lord chamberlain to Emperor Justinian, from Greece, where he has been in exile from Constantinople, to Rome, which is under siege by the Goths. General Felix, one of Justinian's emissaries, has summoned John to help him deal with unspecified troubles. His arrival is viewed suspiciously by the general in charge of the Roman garrison, Diogenes, who dispatches a courier to determine whether Justinian knows that John has left Greece. To John's further dismay, he learns that Felix has been missing for days, and he races to find him in the city's labyrinthine catacombs. His explorations uncover a dead man, stabbed with an ancient knife used in ritual sacrifices. The cleverness of the plot and the solution to the murder are among the series' best.

—*Publishers Weekly* (Starred Review)

The twelfth John the Lord Chamberlain Mystery "places the reader in the middle of the turmoil of sixth-century Rome and into a tense historical mystery."

—*Kirkus Reviews*

MURDER IN MEGARA
The Eleventh John the Lord Chamberlain Mystery

"Meticulous research makes this historical series set in the Byzantine Empire a joy to read. Admirers of Steven Saylor and Lindsey Davis will enjoy exploring this ancient world."

—*Library Journal*

"...John, who's solved many mysteries for the emperor in Constantinople, finds that digging into corruption, past secrets, and misdeeds in a small town is every bit as dangerous as the intrigue of the emperor's court. John's 11th case combines historical detail with a cerebral mystery full of surprises."

—*Kirkus Reviews*

"If you are unfamiliar with this engaging series, where have you been? You are lucky. It is easy to get caught up with the story. The authors' wonderful research and writing skills clue you in with no trouble at all."

—BookLoons

"Their narrative is barbed with questions about every motive, about every danger and about every possibility, and with each question the screw is tightened once again but (as if for counterbalance) the dialogue often has a poetry of its own."

—Eric Barraclough, *The Reluctant Famulus*

TEN FOR DYING
The Tenth John the Lord Chamberlain Mystery

NINE FOR THE DEVIL
The Ninth John the Lord Chamberlain Mystery

"More complex and colorful than any Byzantine mosaic, *Nine for the Devil* by Mary Reed and Eric Mayer, will sweep you back into the cruel intrigue-ridden court of the Emperor Justinian, where treachery and murder linger behind every shadowed column of the imperial palace in Constantinople."

—Robin Burcell, *New York Times* bestselling author

"Twisty plotting, fabulous dialogue, and aristocratic backstabbing drew me into this clever plot (Who killed an Empress who showed no signs of being murdered?) and I could not stop reading until I watched master problem-solver John dance his way out of the deadly wrath of his grieving emperor."

—Jerrilyn Farmer, bestselling author of
the Madeline Bean mysteries

"The puzzle is challenging enough to keep readers searching for clues, but the triumph of the authors lies in their spot-on recreation of the political and bureaucratic climate of the times."

—*Publishers Weekly* Starred Review

"The authors once again make the Byzantine Empire vibrant and nuanced."

—*Library Journal*

EIGHT FOR ETERNITY
The Eighth John the Lord Chamberlain Mystery

"Reed and Mayer bring the time of the Nika Riots in Constantinople to vivid life in this eighth installment in their series, capturing the burning city, the mob mentality, the panic in the castle as the rioters come ever closer, and the effort to convince Justinian to use whatever methods are necessary to keep his throne. A must for followers of the series."

—Sue O'Brian, *Booklist*

"Subtle, well-drawn characters, from the ascetic John to the capricious and enigmatic Justinian; deft descriptive detail revealing life in the late Roman Empire; and sharp dialogue make this another winner in this outstanding historical series."

—*Publishers Weekly* Starred Review

"Historicals have a proven track record of presenting unforgettable protagonists like John the Lord Chamberlain. His military background gives him that unflappable air, and his high intellect provides him with the means to solve whatever Justinian needs. For readers who can't wait for the next Laura Joh Rowland or P.C. Doherty mystery."

—*Library Journal*

SEVEN FOR A SECRET
The Seventh John the Lord Chamberlain Mystery

"Solving the crime involves navigating the mean streets of Constantinople, and as always in this series, the authors bring those streets to vivid life. This isn't one of those superficial mysteries that use historical trappings to cover up a weak story; it's a compelling crime novel that happens to be set in another time and place."

—David Pitt, *Booklist*

"Once again convincing historical detail and strong characterization help drive a riveting plot. Fans will be pleased to know that while the title is based on the last line of the verse on which the series is based, the authors plan to send John to Italy in an eighth volume."

—*Publishers Weekly*

"The authors get everything right in their latest historical. The story is fast paced, the tensions between characters well portrayed; the ending leaves the reader clamoring for more."

—*Library Journal*

SIX FOR GOLD
The Sixth John the Lord Chamberlain Mystery

"As usual the authors write precisely and gracefully, maintaining a perfect balance between historical atmosphere and old-fashioned mystery. The setting, sixth-century Byzantium, is still fresh, still full of wonders and weirdness. And, like Lindsey Davis' Falco series, there's an agreeable mixture of drama and comedy. Fans of the series will be overjoyed."

—Booklist

"Set in plague-ridden sixth-century Constantinople, Reed and Mayer's captivating sixth John the Eunuch novel opens dramatically as John, lord chamberlain to Emperor Justinian, flees "excubitors" (i.e., palace guards) in the Hippodrome...Filled with quirky characters, including a bee seller and a magician, this fresh entry with its intriguing details of Egyptian culture reveals further depths to the most clever John and his family members. A helpful glossary rounds out the book."

—Publishers Weekly

"A busy historical mystery with an engagingly wry tone. Many detours, but getting there is most of the fun."

—Kirkus Reviews

FIVE FOR SILVER
The Fifth John the Lord Chamberlain Mystery

Winner, Glyph Award for Best Book Series

Nominee, Bruce Alexander History Mystery Award

"In a John the Lord Chamberlain novel, the mystery is only half the fun. The other half comes from the delightful supporting characters (in this case, a shady antiques dealer, a bookseller, and a poet, among others) and the crafty way in which the authors discreetly sneak in little nuggets of historical information. The historical-mystery series that stand the test of time are those that put story first and research second. This is one of those series."

—*Booklist*

"Not just a chilling backdrop, the plague that runs rampant through the city, afflicting rich and poor alike, is linked to the murder. The conflict between Christians and pagans adds further weight to this sterling historical page-turner."

—*Publishers Weekly* Starred Review

FOUR FOR A BOY
The Fourth John the Lord Chamberlain Mystery

Nominee, Bruce Alexander History Mystery Award

Best Little Known Series, *Booklist*

"The authors aren't professional historians, but their historical mysteries are sharper, more realistic, and certainly more enjoyable than many written by professionals...This installment of the series is as devilishly convoluted as its predecessors, and fans will relish the extra thrill of seeing how John was launched on the career that eventually finds him working as Justinian's Lord Chamberlain. At some point, every great series needs an "origin story," and this one's a real corker."

—*Booklist* Starred Review

"Written with humor and pathos, this superior historical is sure to please existing fans and send new ones in search of the rest of the series."

—*Publishers Weekly* Starred Review

THREE FOR A LETTER
The Third John the Lord Chamberlain Mystery

"Return with us now to sixth-century Constantinople (A.D. 539, to be precise), where two politically important, eight-year-old twins are key players in Emperor Justinian's plans to resurrect the crumbling Roman Empire...Characters in the John the Lord Chamberlain novels don't spend time telling each other things they already know, for the benefit of the reader: Reed and Mayer educate us in more subtle ways, and we're having so much fun following the story that we don't even realize we're learning things. An excellent entry in an excellent series."

—*Booklist* Starred Review

"The details of daily life, from food and food preparation to the care and writing of manuscripts, enhance the action. And the ongoing struggle between Christianity (Justinian's state religion) and the pagan rites that play a central role in the plot is particularly well drawn...those who appreciate strong historical backgrounds and solid plotting will get their money's worth. The Byzantine mosaic art on the jacket is a real plus."

—*Publishers Weekly*

TWO FOR JOY
The Second John the Lord Chamberlain Mystery

"This is a very intelligent novel; its examination of the nature of belief and faith (and deception) is as insightful and well reasoned as some book-length nonfiction treatments of the same subjects. Add to that a rich and fascinating setting, a solid mystery, and a few surprises, and you have a novel that will capture the interest of anyone who picks it up. If the perfect historical mystery is one that uses the past to let us see the present from a new angle, then this is darned close to being the perfect historical mystery."

—*Booklist* Starred Review

"A fascinating historical, with glimpses of eunuchs, slaves, politicians, and prostitutes, this sweeping adventure is suitable for all collections."

—*Library Journal*

ONE FOR SORROW
The First John the Lord Chamberlain Mystery

"The twists and turns of the plot are skillfully constructed, and the writing is highly readable. Fans of Lindsay Davis and Stephen Saylor in particular are in for a treat when they discover the work of this talented husband and wife team."

—Martin Edwards, award-winning author and editor of the British Library Crime Classics

"Rich in period detail, expertly paced with compelling, complex characters, *One For Sorrow* is one of the most resonant, pleasing novels I've read in a long time."

—Mark Terry, author of *Blood Secrets*

"Painting an enticing picture of sixth-century Byzantium, Reed and Mayer ably evoke court intrigue and the conflict of religious beliefs in the Christian capital of Constantinople...the authors gracefully intertwine John's personal history and the traffic in holy artifacts with the early history of Christianity."

—*Publishers Weekly*

An Empire
for Ravens

An Empire for Ravens

A John the Lord Chamberlain
Mystery

Mary Reed & Eric Mayer

Poisoned Pen Press

First Edition 2018

10 9 8 7 6 5 4 3 2 1

Library of Congress Control Number: 2018940612

ISBN: 9781464211102   Hardcover
ISBN: 9781464210655   Trade Paperback
ISBN: 9781464210662   Ebook

Poisoned Pen Press
4014 N. Goldwater Blvd., #201
Scottsdale, AZ 85251
www.poisonedpenpress.com
info@poisonedpenpress.com

Printed in the United States of America

Prologue

"Praise Mithra, Lord of Light. Mithra the unconquerable. Mithra the ineffable."

As the man in the lion mask reached the end of the roughly hewn passage and turned the corner, the chants from the mithraeum faded. He pulled up the mask. His wild beard made his broad face look only slightly less ferocious than a lion's.

The man drew a deep breath. It was easier to fill his lungs with the cool air than it had been behind the mask. An oil lamp in a wall niche dimly illuminated burial recesses in the tunnel's walls, each sealed with a slab bearing the name of the deceased. Beyond this spot the lamps were not maintained but the catacombs snaked on interminably, a Stygian maze.

The man turned another corner, paused, and listened. There was only the utter stillness and silence of a place where time has turned to dust. Satisfied no one had followed him away from the ceremony, he walked through the trembling light of another lamp into deepening darkness.

He would not like to spend eternity down here, wrapped in a shroud, locked away in a compartment chiseled from solid rock. He tugged his beard, as if to reassure himself of his own corporeal existence.

"Felix."

At first he thought the voice was in his imagination. A thin, dry rasp, the shifting of bones. Then as his eyes adjusted a robed and hooded figure coalesced from the inky blackness where the tunnel intersected another. For all Felix could make out, the hood of the speaker might as well have been empty. The figure was bent, as if with age. It matched the ancient voice. Yet there was something else about the voice, something unnatural. Had, in fact, someone seen him slip away from the mithraeum and taken another route to intercept him?

"How do you know me?"

"Everyone in Rome knows about you."

"What are you doing down here?"

There was a faint, distant rattle—a rat nosing through old, brittle grave wrappings, or perhaps a dry laugh. "I often wander Hades."

"This isn't Hades."

"Are you certain of that?"

Chapter One

The mounted Goth soldiers spotted the mule-drawn wagon just outside Rome. Staying on back roads, John and Marius, disguised as farmers on the way to market, had hoped to get closer to Rome and then find a way to slip into the besieged city.

That was not going to happen now.

John pulled his sword from under the seat as Marius got the mules turned around. The swine they were hauling milled around or stared out over the wagon gate. One of them let out a weirdly human shriek. Blood spurted from the spear in its neck. The rest of the pigs went wild with terror.

The Goths were gaining ground fast.

Without a word, Marius thrust the reins at John and scrambled over the seat into the back of the wagon. He slipped in its filth, fell, and crashed through the panicked swine. Risking a glance behind, John saw Marius open the gate.

The pigs exploded out of the wagon onto the road, squealing, screaming, and grunting, scrabbling for footing, blundering into one another. The Goths tried to veer aside too late. The writhing landslide of enraged flesh slammed into their horses, panicking those that weren't knocked down.

Marius, who had almost been swept into the road with the pigs, clung to the gate and began to pull himself back into the wagon. He might have succeeded except that the mules, frightened by the explosion of noise behind them, swerved suddenly. John's hand blazed with pain as the reins were torn from his grip. The wagon, relieved of its load, accelerated with a lurch. Marius lost his hold and fell.

Clinging to the seat with one hand, his other clenched around the hilt of his sword, John prepared to leap after his friend. Then he saw Marius crumpled in the dirt, already surrounded by four Goths who had disentangled themselves from the chaos.

There would be nothing John could do.

The mules bolted off the road, across ruined vineyards, in the direction of the Appian Way, reins dragging over the ground, far out of John's reach. He hung on as the wagon lurched and rocked wildly. Every moment he kept his grip took him further from the Goths.

More of his pursuers extricated themselves from the swine. Two horses and several pigs lay on the ground. Marius had not got to his feet. Some of the Goths had remounted and as the figures dwindled behind the wagon, John made out one gesturing in his direction.

It wouldn't take horsemen long to catch up with the tiring mules.

The wagon had entered the fringes of a cemetery alongside the Appian Way. The mules zigzagged between tombs of marble, travertine, and brickwork, structures shaped like towers, pagan temples, or massive square tombs decorated with statuary and bas-reliefs of aristocratic families, tombs displaying the names of the deceased incised into enormous plaques, reminding John of the signs of shops along the Mese in Constantinople.

He glanced back as his pursuers drew nearer. As he prepared to leap, a corner of the wagon caught a low obelisk, bringing it down and flinging John to the ground.

He found himself staring into a lichen-bearded marble face identified as Publius Attius. He raised his head to peer over the side of the toppled obelisk. The wagon was already lost to view amidst tombs and cypress trees, but he could hear it rattling and banging. Had the Goths seen him fall? The horsemen raced straight toward him and he ducked down. The hoof beats veered away, avoiding the obelisk and continuing on past.

He stood up. It wouldn't be long before the Goths overtook the wagon and realized John must be somewhere in the cemetery. He had managed to retain his grip on his sword, for what that was worth, outnumbered as he was. The tombs all around offered no hiding places. What he needed was a large mausoleum he could enter. Those tended to sit beside the road, the better to be admired by travelers. He glanced around. Rows of umbrella pines, shade for marching legionnaires in the old days, clearly marked the Appian Way's location. Cautiously, he moved in that direction.

He heard angry shouts. The Goths had found the empty wagon.

Dodging around a rough-barked pine he looked up and down the road. Not far away sat a brick pyramid guarded by an army of spear-like cypresses. He ran towards it. Hooves clattered along the highway as he reached the base of the pyramid. He saw only a smooth slanting brick wall. More shouts. Had they spotted him?

He sprinted around the pyramid and came to a columned entrance, guarded by a snarling stone Cerberus, a peculiar design for a Roman tomb. Perhaps the deceased had served as an official in Egypt. The wealthy could afford their whims, even in death.

He stepped inside. There was a cry. A ragged figure rushed forward. John raised his sword but the man stumbled by and outside.

John blinked, trying to adjust his eyes to dimness. The interior was an empty brick box. Whatever it might have contained had long since been looted. A faint odor of smoke filled the hot air. A small fire burned in the middle of the floor, throwing shadows against the bare walls.

The sound of horses grew louder, then stopped. "I saw movement there. He must have gone into this monstrosity," someone shouted.

There was no place to hide. John retreated into the darkest shadows in a back corner just before a Goth appeared in the entrance. John tightened his grasp on his weapon. It was an automatic response to danger. He had no intention of rushing armed men by himself. Having served as a mercenary, he had no illusions about the effectiveness of such a rash maneuver.

He sidled along the wall to a low archway on his right. His foot found a step. He started to descend as quietly as possible.

But not quietly enough, because there was another shout and the ring of nail-studded soles on stone.

John went down the stairway in a controlled fall. At the foot a glimmer of light showed a corridor. Rounding a corner, he entered a chamber lit by a wall torch. A massive sarcophagus sat there. Roman and Egyptian gods in bas-relief jostled for space on its sides like a crowd of foreigners in the marketplace at Constantinople. This was the tomb of a pantheist.

John dodged behind the sarcophagus. As he did he noticed a carving of his own god, Mithra, slaying the sacred bull.

He took it as a good omen, just as a spear flew overhead.

Goths poured into the chamber.

Another corridor led off from a side wall. One of the soldiers got there before John could reach it. He drove his sword into the man's thigh. The man went down to one knee with a shrill scream. John leapt past him into a corridor, its rough-hewn stone walls lined with burial niches covered by plaques inscribed with names and dates. More than one bore Mithraic imagery.

Might he encounter a living worshiper down here? Was this catacomb still in use? Was that why the torches were lit?

Did the caretaker reach this place via the mausoleum on the Appian Way or could it be accessed from the city?

He had no time to ponder. He heard running footsteps behind him. The echoes made them sound like a charging army. John grabbed a wall torch and turned down a side corridor, then another. As he ran he knocked torches from their holders. They hissed and flared on the floor, then went out, leaving a trail of darkness in his wake. Before long the torches ceased. The upkeep of the catacombs here apparently extended only a short distance.

It was impossible to say how many different routes the sub-terranean maze presented. The moment the sound of pursuit began to diminish, new footsteps sounded nearby. The Goths must have split up. John increased his pace, heard shouts in front of him. He'd been cut off.

He swung his torch around. Could he pry one of the plaques off a burial niche and hide there?

The torchlight vanished into a dark, rectangular hole above him.

A ventilation shaft.

John placed the torch in an empty bracket, jumped, found a handhold, and pulled himself up. The rough, crumbling bricks lining the shaft allowed him to climb out of sight. He clung to them as the Goth search parties met directly below him. They milled around, shouting at each other. Where had their quarry gone? John held his breath. If someone thrust a torch toward the opening in the corridor ceiling, the light might reach him, but none of Goths looked upwards. The consensus was he had slipped away down a passage they had missed. After a short time they left.

John waited. When the silence remained unbroken, he finally allowed himself to shift his grip, easing his aching muscles. The shaft which allowed fresh air into the tunnels might provide a way to escape. He started to climb into its darkness. He could see no light above, but surely it could not be night yet?

Tree roots had found their way through the brickwork and John used them as an uneven ladder. But before long the roots started to crisscross the narrow shaft. John squeezed his way through the thickening obstruction until at last he could go no further. Exploring the darkness with one hand he found only a solid mass of roots and earth. At some point in the past the ventilation shaft had become blocked.

By the time he climbed back down into the corridor his lungs burned and he leaned against the wall, catching his breath. At least the Goths had not returned. So, for now at least, he had escaped them, if not the catacombs. Taking his torch, he looked up and down the corridor.

"At least I know exactly where I am," he murmured, reading the inscription on the wall. "Right in front of the resting-place of Aurelia, sweet daughter who retired from the world, aged fifteen years and twenty-seven days."

John had lost his position as Lord Chamberlain to Emperor Justinian, been exiled to Greece, yet nevertheless left for Rome. Now he might forfeit his life in these catacombs. But he had reached late middle age so that even if he did die here, Fate had treated him more kindly than fifteen-year-old Aurelia.

He pondered what to do next. It would be foolhardy to return the way he'd come. Even if the Goths had stopped searching for him, they might be lying in wait. There was nothing to do but plunge deeper into the labyrinth and hope he would come to an unblocked ventilation shaft or an entrance other than the one he'd used. There would surely be other entrances. During the years when their religion was outlawed, the Christians who carried out surreptitious burials and ceremonies in the catacombs, provided themselves with escape routes in case of need. Nevertheless, as he moved deeper into the tunnels, John found himself breathing hard, chest constricted with anxiety. It felt too much like plunging into a black, bottomless pool. Perhaps there was no other entrance, after all. Perhaps the tunnels descended down and down, straight into Hades.

The cool air created a musty shroud clinging to John's face. There were no sounds except the soft grating of his own footsteps and the occasional hiss or pop of his pitch torch. No scuttling of rodents, no faint murmur of a breeze, or dripping of water. The corridors were filled with oblivion emanating from the thousands of dead all around. John felt that if he stopped, stilling the sound of his footsteps and extinguishing the torch, he might simply vanish into oblivion himself.

He wondered if Marius had survived and what the Goths would do to, and with, him if he had. What was Cornelia doing at their estate in Greece? In a few hours she would be preparing for sleep—as John would be doing, if not for his damnable sense of loyalty. But what else could he do after Marius arrived with a letter from Felix asking John to come and assist him in Rome? An old friend was in trouble. If he had stayed in Greece, neglected his duty to Felix, he would not have slept well for a long time. At first Cornelia had reminded him that as an exile he was not permitted to leave the Megara area. In the end, though, she had given up her attempt to dissuade him and urged him to go. She said she would sacrifice nightly to the Goddess for his safe return.

Carved from soft rock, the passageways rose, fell, widened into chambers, narrowed until the walls almost brushed John's shoulders. Here and there burial niches lay open, the uneven floor below littered with bones and desiccated scraps of burial garments.

John paused to rest. His mouth felt full of dust. He had tried to keep going in the same direction, but it was impossible to know whether he had succeeded. There was nothing to take his bearings by. He guessed he was very deep in the maze.

He knelt and put his face close the floor, hoping to feel a draft that might indicate an opening to the outside, but the air was still.

Then he heard a sound. Or was it only his imagination?

No. There was a shuffling up ahead, where the passage branched.

Cautiously walking closer he saw a flicker of light disappearing around a turn in the left-hand corridor. Someone else was down here with him. Someone who knew his way, if John were fortunate.

He followed the light until, coming around a corner, he was startled to see a robed, hooded figure. He ducked out of sight.

Should he accost the man and ask for directions to the outer world? Perhaps it would be better to simply follow. Unless the man was lost like John, he must be going somewhere.

John laid his torch on the floor. If he lost sight of his unwitting guide, he'd be left in total darkness, but he couldn't risk the man spotting the light behind him and running off.

Following was not difficult. The hooded figure shuffled along slowly, his long garment dragging, leaving a snail trail in the dust. His gait and bent posture suggested advanced age. Sometimes his hand shook, making torchlight on the walls tremble. He never turned around but continued resolutely forward. When he came to intersections, he went one way or another without hesitation.

Then he turned a corner and vanished.

When John rounded the corner, the light was gone.

Groping in the dark, John found a rough wooden door. On the other side, stone stairs led up into darkness.

At the top was the tiny enclosed confines of an armarium, albeit with a close-fitting stone door turning on a central pivot.

Pushing it open, John saw dim, shimmering light. It glimmered at his feet and crawled more faintly over distant walls and ceilings and rows of tall columns. The door he had just come through was in the side of a column. As his eyes adjusted he realized he was standing on a walkway surrounded by water. A few narrow beams of sunlight entering overhead illuminated water which reflected light off the walls. He was in the middle of a cistern.

But was he inside the walls of Rome?

Chapter Two

John felt a chill, a sense of being watched. He looked up into a pair of demonic eyes.

It was just a sculpted creature on the capital of the column he stood beside. A gigantic toad? Decayed and half-covered with lichen scales, it was difficult to identify. No doubt the column had been scavenged from an ancient pagan temple. The bowels of every city were filled with ancient gods, once worshiped, now condemned to menial labors in a Christian empire.

John shut his eyes and willed himself to remain calm. The water on all sides made him anxious. He feared deep water. The smooth, sinister surface gave no clue to what it concealed.

He spotted his guide proceeding along the walkway. John followed carefully. In places the walkway had crumbled. One misstep and he would find himself falling through the reflections dancing across unknown depths.

What had the man he was following been doing in the catacombs? Was he responsible for keeping torches lit in the distant reaches near the Appian Way? Or was John not so far from the great road as he imagined? Perhaps he was being led straight into a Goth encampment well outside Rome. There was no way to tell where the twistings and turnings of his journey through the underground maze had taken him.

The hooded figure moved from one interconnected walkway

to another, moving in and out of shadows. Did he know he was being followed?

At last he reached the edge of the cistern and disappeared through an archway guarded by a mismatched pair of granite lions. Still trailing behind, John came to the base of a stone stairway leading upwards.

He ascended silently. His heart was beating so loudly he had to remind himself that its thumping was only audible to his own ears. The stairs ended at a doorway through which he could see the empty nave of a church. His guide was nowhere to be seen. He crossed the nave and peered through a tall window. Beyond a bare courtyard, on the other side of a low wall, lay a city street lined with partly ruined tenements.

"Welcome to Rome. You are in the Church of Saint Minias," came a voice.

Turning from the window, John saw an ancient creature in a chair borne by four husky slaves, accompanied by armed men. The ancient's legs looked withered where they showed below sumptuous garments. His face was dark with age, a shrunken and wrinkled apple.

"I am the Holy Father," the man proclaimed. "For years I begged on the steps of this very church but now, as you see, I have assumed my rightful place."

Before John could respond, he was struck in the stomach by the hilt of a sword. As he attempted to catch his breath, the guards dragged him away.

"We must trust the Lord to protect our immortal souls," the Holy Father called after him. "Our flesh is for us to look after."

More accurately, the Holy Father believed that flesh was best protected by the secular authorities, given John was led from the church and handed over to a pair of soldiers stationed outside. Finally, he had arrived at the destination he and Marius had hoped to reach by a more straightforward route.

General Diogenes, the man in charge of the garrison at Rome, had set up his command on the southeast corner of the Palantine Hill, in what had been part of the imperial palace before Constantine moved the capital of the empire to Constantinople. He confronted John in a semi-circular domed porch fronted by pillars giving a view of the Caelian Hill, bristling with mansions and churches, to the east, and overlooking the Circus Maximus to the south. Beyond, past the city walls, John could see roads leading into the former center of the empire, the vast cemeteries spreading from the Appian Way, ruined villas, and ravaged fields. Here and there smoke rose, betraying Goth camps or activity.

The general turned from consulting maps nailed to the back wall, partly obscuring the frescoes there. "I'm happy to see at least one of our churchmen is cooperating with the army by sending a suspicious stranger to me." He gave John a brief, cold smile.

"My reception was more violent than I would expect in a church."

"Basilio's a deluded former beggar. The true Holy Father is still in Constantinople as a guest of the emperor, discussing their theological differences."

"Vigilius is Justinian's prisoner, if we are being honest."

The general shrugged. Of late middle age, he had the look of a member of an old Roman family and the build of an athlete run to fat. Had his patrician nose been broken in battle or a drunken fight at a tavern? John imagined he was a man with a long and honorable career but most likely not as much honored as he would have preferred, since at present he was merely overseeing a garrison in a besieged city.

Aging and disappointed generals were often still ambitious and, with their time running out, not always to be trusted, John reminded himself.

"I was summoned here by Justinian's emissary, General Felix," John said. "His aide, Marius, brought me this document."

John handed Felix's letter to Diogenes, who eyed it with obvious suspicion.

"Where is Marius? I wish to question him about this communication."

"Captured by the Goths. I could not help him, but managed to escape and make my way into the city."

Diogenes scanned Felix's letter. "Easily forged as an excuse to ask questions and expect answers."

John produced from the pouch at his belt the imperial seal he had surreptitiously carried with him into exile.

Diogenes waved it away. "Stolen."

"That would not be so easy a task. As you well know."

Diogenes ran a finger absently down the side of his nose. An old habit, perhaps. He must have checked a thousand times to see whether it was healing straight. "So you may be an excellent thief. Or perhaps a spy. Is the true story that Marius deserted to the Goths and is telling them all they wish to know about our defenses?"

"Certainly not. I just hope he is still alive. Do you have any reason to suspect Marius of disloyalty?"

"None at all. Except that he accompanied Felix from Constantinople. Who can say what intrigues might be hatched at the imperial court?" Diogenes offered a smile even icier than before. "But I don't need to tell you that. You know the court. You are John, former Lord Chamberlain to the emperor. You are supposed to be in exile in Greece. One of my men, who served under Felix as an excubitor in Constantinople, recognized you. I am of a mind to have you locked up to await execution for leaving Greece."

"That would be unwise. I am here on important business involving Felix."

"You expect me to believe that?"

"If you choose not to, you will have to answer to Justinian."

"It was Marius who delivered Felix's letter to you. Am I supposed to imagine Marius had orders directly from Justinian?"

"Felix is Justinian's emissary. Everything he does is imperial business."

Diogenes tapped nervously at the side of his crooked nose. "Hemmed in by Totila and his Goths out there, and now I have a man who should be in Greece asking questions likely to bring all manner of troubles on my head if I give answers that I later regret."

"My only purpose is to assist Felix. Do you know what sort of trouble he writes about?"

Diogenes shook his head.

"Then I will have to ask him myself. Where can I find him?"

The general's eyes narrowed and he stared at John speculatively. "You don't know? Felix has been missing for two days."

Diogenes pointed towards a vast, sunken enclosure running alongside the portico through which he was leading John. "When Domitian ruled, it was a remarkable garden with menageries of wild animals. Now, as you see, it's just a vast overgrown tangle of vegetation. Here's the door to my quarters."

Sunlight streamed in through tall windows overlooking the erstwhile garden.

"It's said there are still lions in the garden, descendants of Domitian's specimens. They have lairs in there and come out to hunt rabbits and birds and whatever else makes its home in the undergrowth."

"You are skeptical?"

"Once or twice, while trying to sleep, I thought I heard a distant rumbling, a muffled roar. But I was half asleep, still dreaming. There may be foxes down there, however. Foxes hide everywhere, don't they?"

Diogenes invited John to sit at a long wooden table in his dining room, which had once served as a conservatory, judging by the ceramic pots piled against its walls. A servant brought in wine and small portions of duck cooked with olives.

"We have enough supplies for now, but it doesn't hurt to be

frugal," Diogenes remarked. "Were you lost in the catacombs long? Some have gone into them and never returned."

John took a sip of wine and said nothing.

Diogenes continued, "Long enough to enter them outside the city and emerge in the cistern beneath Saint Minias, then." His tone of voice conveyed his feeling it was a story many would not believe.

"What is the situation in Rome?" John asked. "How many men have you garrisoned here?"

Diogenes gave him a suspicious look. "I can tell you that because it's common knowledge. About three thousand."

"And Totila?"

Diogenes shrugged. "Who can say? His ranks swell every day. He's probably recruited more deserters than I have men. And he can pay his soldiers, which I am finding difficult."

"Will you be able to defend the city, general?"

"I believe so. Four days ago we held off a series of forays against the walls. I suspect Totila was simply testing our defenses and the real assault will begin soon." Diogenes shook his head and sighed. "Not a day passes when I fail to remember that I walk the same streets the immortal Julius Caesar walked. And what will my legacy be? I came, I saw, I avoided being conquered?"

They had finished their meal. A servant took away the duck bones and refilled their wine cups.

"And now, what about Felix? You said he was missing. When did you last see him?"

"He told me he was going to visit Archdeacon Leon. He's the man who has officially taken over Vigilius' duties. A troublesome man, Leon. In fact it was because of him that Justinian sent Felix." He leaned forward. "It was this way…"

When John had been escorted away, Diogenes returned to the portico.

"Viteric."

"Yes, sir?" answered the young soldier who resembled a statue of Hercules dressed in armor, except for his dark beard, which was still barely more than shadow.

"I'm assigning you to assist the man just brought to me. I've sent him to lodge in Felix's house. He implies he is here on the emperor's business, to assist Felix. Which now means helping to find him."

"He should start looking in Totila's camp, sir."

"You may be right, but if his story is to be believed, he could be of great help to us. From all I've heard, he's a shrewd man. Not to be trusted, however. A eunuch."

Viteric looked as if he would have spit except one does not spit at the feet of a general. "What help would you expect from such a man?"

"This is the man known in the capital as John the Eunuch. He once served as Lord Chamberlain to Justinian."

"That kind have a way of intriguing themselves into powerful positions."

"He fell out of favor rather recently and was sent into exile. Of course Justinian often changes his mind. I'm sending a courier to Constantinople to determine whether the emperor knows his former Lord Chamberlain has left Greece. The trip there and back shouldn't take more than three weeks, and until then I wish you to keep an eye on everything he does, everywhere he goes, everyone he speaks to."

"And if it turns out he did not have permission to leave Greece?"

"I'll have him executed on the spot."

Chapter Three

As twilight deepened and night drew on, John followed Viteric through grass-grown streets. Some of the buildings lining the way tottered half-demolished, others looked untouched. In the distance an occasional shout and once a scream shattered the night air. A ragged fellow armed with a stick detached himself from the darkness and approached the pair, but scuttled away as soon as Viteric and John drew their swords.

"When General Diogenes returned my weapon, he told me I would need it," John said.

They continued on. Small fires twinkled on patches of wasteland and in the shelter of walls. Shadowy figures outlined by firelight crouched over steaming pots.

"At present that's in hand, sir," Viteric said in response to a question about food supplies. "Looking to the future and based on previous sieges, however, those who remain in the city have begun cultivating as much land as possible. There's a man who's planting nettles in his garden."

"An unusual choice of crop," John observed, having guessed that Viteric would be reporting everything John did and said to General Diogenes.

"It's been said his humors are deranged by his experiences but the common explanation in the taverns is since people ate boiled nettles during the last siege, he is preparing for the same eventuality and planning to sell his crop when food becomes scarce. It's even whispered, since he will sell for a high price, he may well recover much of the fortune he lost in the last looting of the city."

And what would he do with the fortune in a city reduced to eating nettles, John wondered. "If Totila fails in his assault and lays siege, how long until we are eating nettles, Viteric?"

"Months, sir. The storehouses are full and the fields are planted with wheat."

"I didn't realize there were many fields inside the walls of Rome."

"There are now. When Totila captured the city the last time he spared the public buildings but reduced much of the city to rubble. He declared he intended to turn Rome into a cattle pasture but General Belisarius persuaded him against it. As it was, he forced the entire population out and dragged the aristocrats off into captivity, leaving the city to the owls and ravens. Then he left to campaign in the south. Belisarius re-entered the city, repaired the walls as best he could, and invited the population to return. A few did. The desperate, the destitute, those with no other place to go."

"This is where I will stay? General Felix's house?" It was located off the street called Sandalarius. Behind the house rose what appeared to be a rectangular mountain of brick. The Temple of Rome, Viteric told him. Past the temple lay the Roman Forum.

John stepped over toppled columns.

"Don't worry, sir. The building is habitable. But…"

John gave his guide a questioning look.

"I shouldn't say anything. I'm not superstitious. However, despite it remaining intact, unlike the buildings on either side as you see, it's commonly rumored it is a house on which Fortuna frowns."

"And in what way does Fortuna frown? Aside from the fact that its last occupant has vanished?"

"That's part of it. General Conon lived here before Felix. He was killed in the house by his own troops. They had not been paid for some time and finally mutinied. Belisarius straightened it all out, but now…well, Diogenes was hoping Felix would bring funds from the emperor."

Viteric knocked on a stout door and a pale face peeped out. "Oh, sirs, is there news of the master?"

"None yet, Eutuchyus. For now, this is your new master," Viteric replied. Turning toward John, he added, "I have been told that Eutuchyus was Conon's steward. He still serves as steward but there are only two other servants and a cook. With such a small staff, Eutuchyus assists with everyday chores as necessary."

Eutuchyus simpered and bowed. He was slender and long-limbed with hands as delicate as those of a woman. A eunuch, neither man nor woman or even angel as some believed, the sort of being that John despised, despite his own condition. For were not those creatures castrated before puberty different from himself who was mutilated after reaching manhood? At least the steward was not drenched in perfume as some were, not that it would be likely to be found in the devastated city.

"My needs are simple, Eutuchyus, so your duties will be light," John said. "We will consult on that tomorrow."

John tossed and turned on the bed once occupied by Felix. Despite his exhausting day and desperate need for sleep, he could only fall into a light intermittent doze. He kept recalling the final stages of his journey to Rome. Hearing that the city had been surrounded by the Goths, he and Marius had left ship south of the city. It had been John's idea to purchase a wagonload of pigs. From all reports Italy was filled with wandering armies. Posing as farmers on the way to market gave them a plausible reason to be traveling whoever they might encounter.

Contending armies had rampaged across Italy for more than

a decade. Now the birthplace and former center of the Roman Empire was a landscape of death. Yet the combatants continued to fight over the corpse. In the dark he imagined he was still enveloped in the ripe smell of swine mingled with the dry odor of ashes as they passed farmhouses gutted by fire. Fields were scorched or lay fallow, populated by the skeletons and carcasses of cattle, sheep, and goats. Whatever had not been carried off to feed the military had been devoured by carrion birds to be seen alighting nearby or startled into flight but always returning to the rich pickings awaiting them.

There were human remains along the roads also, but few travelers, mostly refugees with wagons or donkeys laden with household goods, sometimes only a sack on their backs, fleeing one battlefield, most likely to find themselves in another.

The sun shone brightly and birds sang, yet an invisible cloud of dread lay across the ruined landscape, a sense that whatever monster had caused this destruction might lie in wait over the next hill.

"So this is what Justinian seeks to reconquer," John had murmured. "An empire for ravens."

He did not think for long about Felix. If he knew his friend, his absence meant he had been detained by a lady or was recovering from a drinking spree. He worried mainly about Cornelia and the others left on his Greek estate. What if Justinian paid a spy in Megara to keep an eye on him? Would the emperor choose to make John's family pay for his disobedience in leaving Greece?

Yet, from the moment Marius arrived with his plea from Felix, there had been no real doubt about John's going to Rome. Cornelia knew John would never desert her, but she also knew that he would never forgive himself for abandoning a friend. In the end it was she who insisted he go.

She would have insisted, even if he had not downplayed the risk he was taking. Then again, she surely realized that he would try not to worry her. She certainly wouldn't want him worrying about worrying her.

He smiled faintly to himself. It sometimes seemed he and Cornelia understood each other so well there was no need to talk. They could almost hear each other's thoughts. Now, if only they could communicate over distances, across the hills, and the terrible sea. Perhaps in time…

Having finally been clasped in the arms of Morpheus, at the darkest hour of the night he was awakened by the sound of stealthy footsteps. He slid out of bed, grasped his sword, and crept out into the hallway.

He cautiously prowled the corridors. Eventually he stumbled upon Eutuchyus, huddled in a corner of the kitchen.

The steward admitted to hiding after hearing faint noises during the night. "It was the shade of General Conon returning, sir."

John could hardly conceal his disgust at such cowardice. "It was more likely to be your master Felix returning."

Eutuchyus' white hands fluttered. Was it fear or was he making the sign of the Christians? "Oh, sir, I fear if General Felix returns, he will also return as a shade."

Cornelia walked along the ridge overlooking the sea and wondered if John had reached Rome safely and what had been waiting for him there. Long ago they had parted and he had not returned. For years she had been torn between cursing him for deserting her and mourning his death. Their daughter was nearly grown when they met again by chance in Constantinople and she learned the truth, that he had been captured and sold into slavery by the Persians.

He was a different man, no longer a simple young mercenary but Justinian's Lord Chamberlain, when for so long she had imagined him either dead in a battlefield grave on the Persian border or a hardened, rootless wanderer.

Now he had gone again to an uncertain fate.

She felt too old to bear losing him a second time.

She did not look much different than she had when she was young, still slender with dark hair and sun-browned skin, but she sometimes felt as if she were a hundred years old.

For a while she sat on a fallen pillar in front of the small, half-ruined pagan temple where she and John often came to talk. Then, restless, she made her way to the opposite end of the estate, to the house John had given to their former servants, Peter and Hypatia.

Hypatia, almost comically younger than her husband, came out to meet her, scattering chickens pecking in the grass. "Mistress, is there anything I can do for you?"

Cornelia didn't bother to point out she was no longer Hypatia's employer. "The villa seems empty without him."

"If you need any help…"

"You and Peter have your own work to do."

Cornelia accompanied her into the nearby meadow. Hypatia sought out the spots where her chickens nested and put the eggs into the basket she carried. Bees darted amidst the wildflowers in the grass.

"Have you seen that stranger on the road again, Hypatia?"

"The one who was loitering beside the gate yesterday? No. Probably just a wandering beggar."

"I worry John was being spied on."

"If there's trouble coming," Hypatia said, "the master should never have left. He put you in danger."

Although Hypatia continued to use the term mistress, this was clearly not a sentiment she would have dared to share when she was still serving Cornelia.

"If Justinian finds out about John leaving, he will take action against John, not me."

"I wouldn't be so certain. The emperor can be merciful one day and cruel the next. Hurting you is the worst thing he could do to the master." Hypatia bent to lift a hen off its eggs. The hen clucked in outrage.

"I wasn't unhappy when John was exiled," Cornelia said. "I thought we had put palace intrigue behind us. He always said he wished to return to the countryside and live simply. However, he is not a man who will abandon his friends."

"No. He'd never do that. But some friends are more trouble than they're worth. From what Peter tells me, the master was always saving Felix from himself. He carried him home from the tavern when he was too inebriated to stand, consoled him over doomed love affairs he had no business getting into in the first place, helped pay off his gambling debts. He even extricated him from a plot he got involved in against Justinian. And what did Felix do for the master in return? Peter says he did his best to get him to drink too much."

"Peter told you all that?"

"Isn't it true?"

"Oh, yes."

"Then why should the master race off to his aid again, under such dangerous circumstances? Why does he value this friendship so highly?"

"Maybe because Felix has always treated John as a friend, not as a political rival or the Lord Chamberlain, not as..."

Not as only half a man, she had been about to say, but it was not something one ever said aloud. Eunuchs were common at the imperial court but most considered them as a kind of race apart.

"Well, it isn't for me to criticize, mistress. But I am sorry you have been left in such a difficult situation. Did he arrange to let you know when he reached Rome?"

"How could he, under the circumstances? He may have had to turn back, as far as I know. He could be sitting at the kitchen table at the villa when I return." Tears came to her eyes as darker possibilities forced their way into her thoughts.

"I'll keep my ears open in the marketplace. If I hear any news—ships due to arrive from Rome, for instance—I'll let you know immediately."

"The marketplace knows practically everything, and often before it happens. I—oh!" Cornelia gave a start as a nearby bush rustled.

"A weasel! The locals say it's a very bad omen!" Hypatia gasped.

Chapter Four

Archdeacon Leon sat at a table in the library of the Lateran Palace, the papal residence. His sharp-beaked nose almost touched the parchment of the codex lying in front of him. He was alone, except for the souls of all those clerics who had used the library in the past. Here, where they had meditated so deeply and reached out to God so fervently, their thoughts and prayers seemed to linger, suspended in the musty air, invisible until some Biblical verse, some flash of insight, illuminated and revealed their presence like the dust motes tumbling in the sunbeams slanting through the windows.

"Blessed are the peacemakers," Leon read in a voice as quiet as a turning page. Did his failing eyes discern the letters on the page or did he only see them in his memory?

The past was so palpable that when he lifted his watery gaze, he was almost startled to find the room empty, its shelves and wall niches and cabinets all but bare of the leatherbound codexes and ancient scrolls that had once been the pride of so many popes, until the invaders came, looting and burning again and again.

Leon had hoped to die in the Holy Land but here he was, ending his days in a city once again surrounded by barbarians. What more was there for them to destroy?

He looked around. What had disturbed his reading?

There. A light tapping at the half-open door. His hearing was leaving him too.

"What is it, Matthew?"

His private secretary advanced, sending dust motes fleeing. "Father, a man wishes to speak to you but will only say it's a delicate matter."

"Has he no name?"

"He refuses to give it, but I believe I know who he is. He looks very like an official I saw in a procession when I was in the delegation to Constantinople for the funeral of the empress. I was told then he was Justinian's Lord Chamberlain. Not long afterwards he fell from favor and was sent into exile."

"Since he's here, he may have been reinstated. Be careful what you say to him, Matthew. It's always wise to be cautious when talking to officials close to the emperor. Send him in."

The elderly archdeacon's senses were fading but his mind was as sharp as ever, even if more prone to reveries than it once had been.

Matthew ushered John into the room. After the usual exchange of greetings, Leon asked whether John had any objection if his secretary remained to take notes. "It helps my recollection, if needed."

"None. I am in Rome in connection with Justinian's emissary General Felix."

Leon saw an unusually tall, slender man. His bearing identified him as a person to be respected but his narrow face was as sun-browned as a farmer's. "I shall endeavor to assist you. Meantime, if you will take a seat? My apologies it is merely a bench, but most of the furniture has been carried away, if not burned along with everything in our library."

"I noticed the scorched wall and a fresco depicting a man reading," John replied.

"It's said to represent Augustine." Leon sighed. "So much trouble, so many tragedies, for so long. We are lucky to have walls and a roof. Men at war loot. Each time it is the same. They strip the city of everything that glorifies either God or the emperor, from statues and sacred vessels to the humblest artifacts and the clothes from the backs of the poorest. A century ago, before the Goths were laying sieges, when the Vandals rampaged through the city, their leader even ordered the imperial copper cooking pots transported to his capital."

"Yet each new conqueror finds goods to be looted."

"The faithful have replaced our treasures more than once, only to have them stolen in turn when the city was overrun again. The church took to concealing its sacred possessions, although some have still not been found. It grieves me to say it is entirely possible some of the flock who assisted in their concealment returned to excavate them later. At present many such church possessions are buried until the current trials are past, although we may have to dig them up to sell in order to purchase food if the siege lasts long enough to cause those who remain in the city to starve."

John observed that during a siege food would be more valuable than gold and silver.

Matthew coughed and Leon felt the light touch of his secretary's hand on his sleeve. He blinked as if coming awake. "Forgive the ramblings of an old man, sir. You said you were here in connection with Justinian's emissary?"

"Yes. General Felix told General Diogenes he intended to visit you."

"He did visit. Matthew can show you his notes, but I can give you an outline of our meeting. We spoke at length and he told me Justinian had chosen him to dissuade me from attempting to arrange a surrender to the Goths. I had put this suggestion to Diogenes, who agreed to send a message to his superior Belisarius, currently in Constantinople. Naturally, as a fighting man, Diogenes made it plain that unless ordered to do so by a higher authority, he would not agree to my suggestion. I had the distinct impression Felix would not have accepted it either. Also that he did not care for performing diplomatic work, not having the smooth tongue of professional liars."

"He can be blunt," John admitted.

"I sense you also disapprove," Leon replied. "However, I say to you what I said to him and to Diogenes. I will continue to press for surrender to preserve what remains of the city and save many from death by slow starvation or outbreaks of disease, in which case a quick death on Goth blades, should that happen once the gates are opened, would be preferable. On the other hand, it may be the Goths would allow residents to leave the city in safety."

"I was told the city could hold out for months without fear of starvation, that the storehouses are full and the fields are planted in wheat."

"Did Diogenes tell you that? The general has been hoarding food for the garrison. The population is already half-starved because of it."

John wondered if that was so. "So you were not swayed by Felix's entreaties?" he said. "How did he react?"

"He was displeased and agitated. Clearly he would much rather have faced me in a sword fight than wage a war of words."

"That certainly would agree with his humors. Did you discuss anything else?"

"No. I think we were both more than happy to get away from each other."

"Did he indicate where he intended to go next? Was he to report back to Diogenes immediately?"

Leon shook his head. "He said nothing on that subject." He felt that the tall man to whom he was speaking was poking, prodding, measuring him with his keen gaze.

John thanked Leon and took his leave.

"He will be back," Leon told Matthew.

When his secretary left the library, Leon tried to resume reading but he could no longer concentrate. The comforting spirits of the past had fled, leaving him by himself in the present in a city on the precipice of disaster.

•••••

Fate was against John. He had been thinking about his interview with Leon, wondering whether the archdeacon was as yet aware that Felix had been missing for two days, when he realized suddenly that he was lost. He should have had no difficulty navigating back to the house in which he was staying. Descending the Caelian Hill with its many churches, all deserted now in the depopulated city, he kept the Palantine Hill in sight, knowing it was south of his destination. Unfortunately, the streets curved and branched, and here and there were blocked by craggy barriers of rubble or charred piles where burning buildings had caved in. It was impossible to maintain a straight route.

He was sorry he had taken advantage of the clothing at the house to discard his pig farmer disguise and make himself presentable to the archdeacon. Dressed in costly garments he must appear an inviting target for the rough characters lounging around, eyeing him speculatively. He wondered momentarily if the clothes belonged to Conon. They didn't fit too badly and Felix was shorter and much broader than John.

He had not been attacked yet. Even when he wandered the streets and alleys of Constantinople he had rarely encountered any trouble. There was something about him, the way he carried himself, that seemed to discourage predators.

He found himself in the same long, rectangular area he had passed through already. He had mistaken it for the Roman Forum. He realized now that it was another because he could not see the Temple of Rome near to Conon's house. Admittedly, a vast basilica occupied one end of the forum; its gilded roof blazed beneath the sun. He glanced at it and a dark image of the sun drifted across his eyes until he blinked it away.

John had not passed anyone who looked trustworthy enough to ask for directions. This forum, cobbled with blocks of white marble, was populated only by statues of once-famous poets, generals, and statesmen. What would they have to discuss were they alive?

He was pondering which direction to try next when a man appeared from behind a marble philosopher.

"I beg your pardon, sir. May I be of assistance?"

The speaker was a middle-aged man with a stout body perched on a pair of incongruously skinny legs. He wore a charioteer's leather helmet which had the appearance of having been trampled on by several teams of horses.

John judged him harmless. "Could you could tell me where I am?"

"This is the Forum of Trajan. You must be new to the city?"

John nodded.

"Seeing the sights while they still remain to be seen?"

"What I most wish to see is the house where General Felix lives. It is near the Temple of Rome."

"Oh, I know that area very well. Let me show you the way."

John thanked Mithra that Fortuna had relented. "Thank you. I was beginning to feel a kinship to Odysseus with all my wandering around."

"A well-traveled friend of yours, is he? Well, sir, you just follow me."

The man scurried off, his legs scissoring back and forth energetically beneath the rotund body.

"This is the way to Sandalarius. The house you want is nearby," John's guide said, as they passed through a colonnade at the northeastern end of the forum. "You are a friend of General Felix, sir?"

"I am." John was curt. He did not intend to answer any further questions about his business or the reasons for his own presence in Rome. However, nothing further was said.

Instead his garrulous guide embarked upon a story about Trajan. "Remember this, sir, as you walk about our ravaged and lawless city. There was a time when Trajan, setting off to battle, stopped to grant an audience to a poor widow who prayed to him for justice on those who had murdered her son and was granted it. If only any of our leaders would pause what they are doing today to hear a prayer for justice."

Chapter Five

Delivered back to his house by the obliging stranger, John couldn't help wondering how he was going to find Felix in a strange city where he couldn't even find his own way home.

Viteric came out to meet him. "My apologies that I did not accompany you, sir. I was summoned to a meeting with my superior and when I arrived you had already left."

John brushed past him in silence. Viteric had almost certainly been reporting the little information on John he had to offer. So far. He managed to remember where the dining room was located. It looked out onto a central garden that had been dug up to grow crops during a previous siege. A few formerly cultivated flowering shrubs had re-established themselves amidst weeds growing around animal pens at one end. The pens were empty. Felix hadn't been looking ahead. John would have liked to have had a couple of the pigs he and Marius had transported.

Almost before he and Viteric were seated, Eutuchyus appeared with wine, arriving so silently one might have thought the steward barefoot.

"You visited Archdeacon Leon?" Viteric asked.

"How would you know?"

"You were seen."

John wondered if it was Viteric who had seen while spying on him but kept the thought to himself. "What do you know about Felix, Viteric?"

"Nothing, sir. I only saw him occasionally when my superior wished to speak to him. Marius would have been the best person to consult. He was Felix's aide."

John sipped his wine. There must have been oceans of wine abandoned by aristocrats fleeing the city, ripe for the looting. "I questioned Marius extensively on the way to Rome. He knew nothing useful."

"Or didn't want to tell you?" Viteric suggested.

"That is possible," John admitted. When it came down to it, what did he know about Marius? He had not been in a position to seek information on the man. Diogenes had confirmed that he had arrived in Rome from Constantinople as Felix's aide. He wasn't an imposter, at any rate.

"There was gossip in the barracks that Felix wanted to rush through the gates and attempt to drive the Goths away. Diogenes believed venturing forth would be suicidal."

That haste to engage the enemy sounded like Felix, John thought. Too often impetuous. "Did the two men work well together?"

Viteric's lips tightened. "That is not for me to say, sir."

"No, it isn't." John rose and ordered Viteric to return to the barracks.

"But sir—"

"I shall send for you if I need you."

Viteric departed with ill-concealed reluctance. It struck John his main problem with his aide was not going to be summoning Viteric but avoiding him—he who was Diogenes' eyes and ears.

John wanted to search the house without Viteric peering over his shoulder. It was an unusual house, a sprawling villa that must have once belonged to a wealthy family who over the years had constructed additions haphazardly.

John explored, trying to sense some sign of the Felix he knew.

What would that be? He had rarely visited Felix's mansion in Constantinople. Usually it had been to help the excubitor captain safely back through the dark streets when he had downed too much wine. Had Felix left traces on his living space? It was not likely. He was a military man, a creature of barracks and encampments. He had no use for the niceties of domestic life.

What might he have brought with him from Constantinople? One couldn't transport many belongings and everything that he wanted—which is to say a military command—was waiting for him in Rome.

There would be no religious displays because, like John, Felix was a Mithran, an adherent to a proscribed pagan religion who necessarily must keep his beliefs secret.

More often than not, John had been with Felix in the streets and taverns of the capital as they undertook some investigation on behalf of the emperor. Although they had never fought side-by-side on the battlefield, they had faced death together more than once. They had come to trust each other with their lives. There were few bonds stronger. So far, that trust had never proved futile and John was determined not to be the one to fail in his obligations.

Before long John turned his search to the room Felix had appropriated for his bedchamber. It was decorated by a colorful fresco showing the kidnapping and return of Persephone. Had his old friend suddenly developed an interest in Greek mythology? More likely he had admired the depictions of the semi-clad Persephone. Her legend hinged on her sudden disappearance The irony was not lost on John.

There was clothing in chests, and placed underneath some tunics, perhaps for safekeeping, a codex. Puzzled, John picked it up. Felix read little, although he had once taken to perusing Cassiodorus' *Gothic History*, enthralled by visions of a time and place where a warrior might still aspire to power without the need to cope with an emperor. This text was history as well.

Book One of Julius Caesar's *Commentaries on the Gallic War*. The leather cover was worn slick. John opened the codex and saw written: "May he who steals this volume from Diogenes be cast out from the light of God and wander in darkness forever."

John hoped Felix had borrowed the volume.

Eventually, John found an unlocked box in a desk. He laid out the contents of the box on the bed. Among other things there was a silver fibula in the shape of a dolphin and a matching ring made of silver and amethyst.

Perhaps his friend subscribed to the belief, held by some, that such a gem guarded against intoxication? Here was a note of private purchases, some of them made for a woman unless Felix had taken to wearing necklaces and fine silks. Such luxuries must be expensive in this long-beleaguered city. John read over several sheets of parchment, most of them copies of orders issued by Diogenes.

There was also a passionate love letter from a woman who had not signed her name and John came close to blushing as he read it, not so much because it embarrassed him but rather that he felt embarrassed for Felix. And worried. He knew only too well how these affairs usually ended for his friend.

The letter-writer was another person he could consult, one who might well have useful information.

Whoever she might be.

And given Felix's eclectic taste in women, she could have been anyone from a high aristocrat to a prostitute.

He sensed movement behind him and looked round.

"Excellency…" The woman who stood in the open doorway held a ceramic platter. She was sinewy and brown-skinned. Dressed in a brown tunic she might have been preserved in a smokehouse.

She introduced herself as Maxima, the household cook.

"What is it?"

"Honey cakes, sir. I had enough honey left for one last batch."

"And where did you obtain honey?" John gestured her to put the platter on the desk.

"Eutuchyus brought home a pot a couple of days ago. Seems it was buried in the ruins of a bakery, sir."

She hesitated at the desk and John asked if she had something further to say.

"Oh, sir. It is a pleasure to serve you, a true Roman. I am from a venerable Roman family. We've been engaged by the greatest households for generations. It is a terrible thing when even high army officers are Germans. It isn't right for Romans to serve Germans."

The cook was referring to Felix. Could her dislike of Germans extend to doing them harm? Many crimes went unnoticed or were ignored when daily life was a scramble for survival. John put the thought aside for later examination. "I can assure you, Felix is as good a Roman as I am, and by my accent you can see that I am not German." He didn't bother telling her he had been born in Greece. He picked up a honey cake. "I can tell just by looking at these you have had much practice in cooking them. Were they also favorites of Conon?"

Maxima said she did not know as she had only recently taken up her current position. "When offered the opportunity to cook for master Felix I hesitated, sir. Not just because he was a German. Except for Eutuchyus, all of the servants were executed when the soldiers came for Conon. What if master Felix were to suffer the same fate? But we must take our chances and trust heaven to guard us in these hard times, and so, needing work, here I am."

"Is there more you wish to say?"

"I have a complaint to make, sir."

Finally, John thought. She was about to reveal why she had brought the platter of cakes to him. It was remarkable how often the real reason someone wished to talk was revealed only as they were about to leave. He invited her to state her difficulty.

"Someone has been stealing our food for days. Most recently it was our last loaf. One of the servants is a thief, sir."

"There are only three others living here, Maxima. Which do you suspect?"

She flushed with anger and her voice rose. "I cannot say, sir. But someone is creeping around the house at night stealing the very bread from our mouths. That's bad enough, but who knows what other mischief they may get up to in the dark hours?"

John responded he would look into the matter and dismissed Maxima. He ate a honey cake. It was a strange coincidence that his favorite sweet would be offered him in such circumstances. Munching, he pondered why a house steward would be digging in a ruined bakery.

Licking his fingers, he pushed the platter aside.

He must make haste with his investigations. Based on their recent conversation, Diogenes had struck him as a cautious and suspicious man. Were he Diogenes, he would immediately attempt to confirm John's mission was as he had stated, which would involve sending an inquiry to Constantinople.

It should not be difficult to get a single courier out of the city. Once he reached Greece, where the imperial post road still functioned, it would take only days for a messenger to reach Constantinople. Allowing time for the answer to return, providing the courier could by then find his way back into the city, John calculated he had three weeks or less to locate Felix and help him resolve whatever difficulties had driven him to ask John for help.

When Justinian discovered John had left his place of exile… well, there was little point thinking about that while there was work to done.

• ● ● ●

"You wished to see me, sir?" Eutuchyus' pale moon of a face was apprehensive.

They were in the kitchen. Two rabbits lay on the table with a bunch of carrots and several onions, which the steward informed John were the ingredients for a stew for the evening meal. Nearby, out of sight along the corridor, Maxima was singing as she dusted, an endeavor John thought fruitless but which reminded him of his servant Peter, who had always carried out the same task to the accompaniment of quavering hymns.

"Sit down, Eutuchyus." John took a seat on the other side of the table. One advantage of his exile was that he had no longer had to deal with these ambiguous creatures who swarmed around the imperial court.

Eutuchyus sat primly and looked warily at John over the dead rabbits.

"I wish to know about your master's life here," John said curtly.

Eutuchyus blinked as if he'd been suddenly struck.

"Proceed," John ordered.

"Yes, sir." The voice was reedy and almost too soft to hear but John felt no inclination to lean closer. "He was a stern man who spent much of his time out and about, even in the worst weather."

"Why do you say 'was'? The last time I spoke to you, you feared Felix would return as a shade. He has not been missing for long. Is there some reason you do not expect him to return?"

"No, sir. Forgive me. I was merely speaking of him with respect to his absence. But I am afraid for his welfare because Rome is dangerous and he is not yet familiar with it."

"That would explain this." John showed Eutuchyus a hand-drawn map of Rome he had found in Felix's box. It was the kind of map that might be used for military purposes.

"Yes. He spent a good deal of time studying that."

Felix had not made any marks on the map, however—no indications of any destinations, for example. "Did he ever ask you for directions to a specific place?" John asked.

"No, he simply studied it. As master, he never told me where he was going and was often vague about when he might return."

The air was becoming hotter, heavy with the earthy smell of carrots along with the sharp odor of onions. Flies buzzed. One landed on a rabbit and Eutuchyus brushed it away with a look of disgust.

"This is a wicked city," Eutuchyus continued in little above a whisper. "The devil creeps about where emperors once walked."

John wondered how someone who was devout, he assumed by the cross inlaid with colored glass swinging from a silver chain around Eutuchyus' neck, could consider the city that housed the head of the church wicked. But perhaps Eutuchyus was a different sort of Christian than Archdeacon Leon. The Christians had as many sects as the Roman pagans had gods.

"Did your master say anything to you about his mission?"

"No, sir."

"You did not notice anything, documents perhaps? Did you overhear conversations that gave you an idea about what he was doing?"

Eutuchyus' cheeks reddened. "I do not eavesdrop on my master, sir, nor do I inquire into things that are not my business. The apostle Paul teaches us that whatever role we are assigned in life, we are to do our jobs honestly and to the best of our abilities as if we are serving the Lord himself, for so we are."

Evidently Eutuchyus was wary about those who looked at his kind with suspicion.

"You said your master spent much of his time out and about? During what hours?"

"All hours. The master did not appear to have a schedule. More than once he was away half the night."

"And after being away half the night how did he appear when he returned?"

"If you mean had he been to the taverns, I think not. At home he drank less than many."

John was happy to hear that Felix had apparently been controlling his weakness for wine, if this statement was to be believed.

Eutuchyus added, "The master was generally kind to us, sir. However, he did not attend church and there was…but it is not my place to say…"

"Go on," John ordered.

Eutuchyus looked uncomfortable. "Well, sir, he unfortunately fell into the snares of a low-born woman named Clementia. Yes. I often said to the other servants his sins with her would inevitably lead him to a bad end. As for Clementia, sir, she is a mere servant."

John asked where Clementia could be found.

"She will not be difficult to locate, sir," came the reply. "She still occupies her former master's house on the Sacra Via. He was a senator, one of those unfortunates carried off by the Goths. No doubt he has already met an unimaginable fate in their hands."

Eutuchyus' gaze went to the dead rabbits on the table. "I do hope you like rabbit, sir. Maxima found some recipes when we were rearranging the house for master Felix. Most of them involve rabbit."

Chapter Six

The house of the unfortunate senator was a short walk from where John was living. The street called Sandalarius brought John to the massive oval Flavian Amphitheater, where gladiatorial games had been held during the glory days of the empire. Then the Via Sacra led downhill to the Roman Forum. The senator's two-story mansion sat behind a high brick wall across from a hill surmounted by a structure seated on a massive base faced in travertine, with a line of gray, granite columns along the side overlooking the street—the Temple of Venus and Roma, Eutuchyus had told him. Clementia might as well cross the street and live at the temple, the steward had added with a sly grin.

Judging from the way the young woman presented herself, Eutuchyus may have been right, John thought, as he was led to her by a couple of hulking German guards. The senator's servant was plump and black-haired with gray eyes. She wore a long, pleated white gown with gold stitchery belted at the waist and caught in under her bosom. A pearl necklace encircled her throat and her hair was bound with a gold band. The servant appeared to have helped herself to her mistress' wardrobe and her artificially flushed cheeks and ruby lips showed she had not hesitated to pilfer her employer's cosmetics as well.

John realized that while he found her merely plump, Felix would have considered her voluptuous.

She met John in the shade of the garden peristyle. Glancing around as he passed through the building John had noticed the house appeared all but untouched by Rome's troubles. Although the fountain in the atrium was dry, the garden had been kept up perfectly. Roses laden with blossoms and heavy with bees drooped in its strongly scented air. Marble statues from mythology stood dotted about among a riot of bushes displaying varying colors of the flower sacred to Venus.

John opened the conversation by indicating he wished to speak to her about General Felix.

Clementia scrutinized him, a slight smile on her full lips. "Is there word of Felix, sir?"

John shook his head. "I hoped you might have news. I understand you were close to Felix and visited him regularly?"

"It's true I keep in touch with him. He's well placed and has promised to let me know if he hears anything of the master and his family. I'm taking care of their home while they're gone. And keeping it safe." She glanced at the two guards who had remained, lurking in the shadows nearby.

"I've been given to understand your relationship with Felix is more personal."

Clementia laughed. "Oh, my! I assure you we're not having an affair. Felix is old enough to be my father, after all. I know very well who told you that. It was Eutuchyus, wasn't it? We all know what eunuchs are, gossips and liars and quick to put a knife in ordinary people's backs." She made a stabbing motion. "They're all like that, sir. Don't believe a word of what he says."

John, who did not put himself in the same category as Eutuchyus, was not offended. "Even so, is it not true you were a frequent visitor?"

She moved close enough so that John could smell her perfume. Or rather her mistress' perfume. Giving a glance toward the guards she leaned forward with an almost flirtatious gesture, and tugged gently at his robe. "Come to the other side of the garden where we can speak more freely," she whispered.

They followed a stone walkway through the rose bushes while Clementia waved fretfully at bees which seemed to find her scent more pleasing than that of the roses. She stopped in front of a marble Venus who had been decapitated.

Clementia giggled. "The goddess of love lost her head. Very appropriate, don't you think?"

"Felix has not been in touch for any reason?"

Clementia drew her lips into a pretty pout. "You're a shrewd man, I can tell. There is another reason I consult Felix now and then. I need his assistance on a matter causing me increasing anxiety, sir. The fact is, I am now almost at the end of the money the master left in my keeping. Soon I won't be able to pay guards to protect the house. They are fine and faithful men, though one drank too much one evening and thought he was beheading an invading Goth rather than Venus. But if I can't pay them, they will find an employer who can."

"How did you expect Felix to help you?"

"He is an emissary of the emperor, isn't he? He knows great men. He is a great man himself and great men are wealthy. I'm sure my master will gladly pay off any loan once he returns."

John thought it unlikely the senator or his family would ever set foot in Rome again, or even that they were still alive. He wondered if their servant, dressed in borrowed finery, ruling over a mansion, really expected them to return and how she would cope with falling back into her former position if they did suddenly reappear.

He watched her pick a rose and bury her upturned little nose in its petals. Yes, she was certainly the sort of woman Felix would find attractive.

"When did you last see the general?" John asked, struck by both the informal way in which she referred to Felix and her frankness in confessing her hope of obtaining money from him. In his view the two put together supported what Eutuchyus had told him.

"Three days ago. And now, I am told he is gone. Do you think he ventured outside the city and was captured? Or killed?"

"Did he say that he intended to leave the city?"

"No, but he was impatient with the way things were going. He didn't like the idea we might be imprisoned inside Rome for a long time. A soldier should not hide behind walls. It was better to die with a sword in hand, or so he said on more than one occasion."

"But he had not made any plans?"

"None that he shared with me."

She sounded sincere enough but John was not convinced. If she had not been disguised in borrowed aristocrat's clothing, he might have been more inclined to believe her.

She grasped his arm and looked up at him urgently. "You don't think he's come to harm? Surely you will be able to find him, Lord Chamberlain!"

John looked at her sharply.

"Have I said something wrong? Felix told me all about you, sir. He said you had caught any number of criminals and traitors."

"Don't let the information go any further," John said. "It would be unwise."

"Yes, sir. Except…"

"Yes?"

"Well, it is all over the city already, that the Lord Chamberlain has arrived in Rome."

Shadows crept silently across the city as John left the senator's house to return to his temporary lodgings. What should he make of Clementia's remark that everyone in Rome knew who he was? Was it any more believable than anything else she'd told him? She knew who John was, thanks to Felix talking too much.

His journey took him past a fountain into which water sluggishly flowed. A ragged man with one leg leaned on the lip of its basin, drinking. There was a tavern nearby across from the Flavian Amphitheater. Of the tavern's scant number of patrons, more sat outside than lounged at tables within. Conversations were muted and slow and faces showed exhaustion. John placed them as laborers, except for two husky men with cropped hair and military boots. They were in the middle of an argument over their game of knucklebones as he approached. A half-empty jug of wine beside them helped explain their lively if profane discussion.

"That's three times I've rolled the dog," cried the man who had a scar running from cheekbone to jaw. "No one's luck is that bad. These bones aren't fair!"

"They're the same ones I'm rolling. Put another coin in the pot. Those are the rules."

The scarred man pounded the table with his fist, scattering the bones which, despite what they were commonly called, were, in fact, made of glass. One fell to the pavement and skittered to a stop at John's feet. He picked it up and returned it to the players. "An excellent game for a man Fortuna smiles on, my friends. Provided he avoids over-familiarity with the embrace of Bacchus while playing!"

"You are correct, sir," slurred the scarred man. "So I dare not invite you to participate!" He nudged his companion in the ribs and gave a raucous laugh before sliding off his bench onto the pavement as smoothly as an eel spilling from a net.

The companion prodded the motionless body with a boot, eliciting nothing but a muttered curse. "You must excuse my friend. He doesn't like to lose, and I've already won a paltry sum. Paltry but half his month's pay."

"Didn't I see the two of you coming away from a senator's house as I approached?

"That's right. We work there. I'm Gainus. We were coming off duty. I remember you now. I said to my friend here, 'There's a military man if I ever saw one.' A new recruit to the garrison?"

John shook his head.

The heavily intoxicated guard had fallen asleep, so John stepped over him and took his seat. "What can you tell me about your employer, the senator's servant?"

"I'm not one to betray my employers, sir."

John pushed a coin across the table. "You indicated she does not pay well."

Gainus set his hand on the coin without hesitation. "She pays better than some in this benighted city. But not as well as you."

"She claims she is in charge of the senator's house."

"That is so." Gainus picked up the coin and turned it around, admiring it before stuffing it into the pouch at his belt.

"She is certainly an attractive employer."

Gainus chuckled. "None of us would mind being permanently posted to her bedroom."

"What kind of woman is she?"

"She thinks highly of herself, sir. She can squeeze into her mistress' clothes but her morals are a little loose. She loves the knucklebones." He made a throwing motion.

"Placing herself in the hands of Fortuna you mean?"

"And not only Fortuna's hands."

John picked up one of the glass bones, tossed it into the air, and caught it on the back of his hand. "This is how we played with them when we were children. An innocent game."

"But we are not children any longer."

John tossed up two bones and caught both of them. "Has Clementia been visited by a man called Felix?"

Gainus looked thoughtful. "I don't know the names of all her visitors."

"He's a German, a big bear of a man with a bushy beard."

"No one like that. You may be thinking of Hunulf. He became, let us say, a favorite of Clementia soon after she hired him as a guard. A young man. A large German fellow. He left weeks ago because he was dissatisfied with the pay. I'm not so sure he didn't compensate himself with a few items of value when he left."

John asked Gainus if he knew where Hunulf was currently working.

"Probably for someone who pays better. He came to Clementia after working for Basilio at Saint Minias church until the old fraud halved his wages. Before that he deserted from the army over lack of pay, and he wasn't alone."

John wondered if Gainus was referring to himself. "Why wasn't he arrested?"

"If Diogenes arrested every deserter, he'd have to put half of the able-bodied men in Rome into custody and he'll need them when Totila attacks, whether they're officially part of the army or not. Diogenes is just happy the whole garrison hasn't risen up to murder him as they did in the case of General Conon. If Hunulf comes to grief, it'll be because he's a Mithran."

John expressed surprise. Evidently Gainus had had enough wine to loosen his tongue when talking to a stranger.

"Diogenes is determined to stamp out Mithraism in the ranks," Gainus explained. "Most think he's trying to curry favor with Archdeacon Leon. Romans and Goths have the weapons, but it's the church that rules people's minds."

John said nothing. He couldn't help thinking it was ironic that Diogenes had unknowingly sent Felix, a secret Mithran, to deal with the archdeacon. He gathered up three bones, tossed them upwards and caught all three.

"You have excellent reflexes for a man your age, sir. But let's try a different game."

The inebriated man near John's feet twitched and groaned.

Gainus took out the coin John had paid him and set it on the table. "A small wager."

John matched the coin with one of his own. He tossed the bones and they clattered as they bounced on the tabletop. Gainus stared at them in consternation. "You rolled a Venus! There's no beating that. You're a lucky man."

John retrieved the two coins and left, hoping Gainus was right, for Felix's sake.

The single oil lamp in the bedroom cast its feeble imitation of the fires of Hell across the fresco of Persephone in the underworld. It made for a confused picture of the afterlife, John thought. Did the dead either burn in eternal flame or rejoice forever in the light of their god as Christians believed, or did all alike wander through the gloom of Hades, as some pagans supposed?

He picked up the codex of *Caesar's Commentaries*, which he assumed Felix had been reading, and leafed through it. He tried to read to distract himself for a while, but it only made him worry about Felix, who had likely dreamt of conquering Gaul himself. More than five centuries after the beginning of the empire, long after Rome had reached the zenith of its power, Gaul was free to be conquered again. Felix would have been pleased to be part of the effort, but Justinian was having enough trouble just taking Italy back.

So why was Felix missing? Was he really sleeping off the results of a drinking spree somewhere or had he taken some rash, foolish action in aid of the emperor's cause? Had he decided to go ahead and do whatever it was he had summoned John to assist?

Not that it was very clear why he had asked for John's help. Did Felix know John had arrived in Rome? If he did, why hadn't he been in touch yet?

John realized that a general would make a valuable hostage.

He was tired. His thoughts were floating around, unmoored from reason. Suddenly he was aware the lamp had gone out.

Had it been blown out? Had he dozed?

He looked around the dark room. The darkness at the foot of the bed seemed denser. A figure stood there, motionless.

"Felix?"

There was no reply but John was certain he could make out his friend's bushy beard and bulky form.

He lit the lamp with the striker.

As light flared, the figure vanished.

John decided he must have gone to sleep and when he woke his imagination had painted a shadow with his friend's image.

Chiding himself for seeing things, he blew out the lamp and settled back to sleep again, still worrying about Felix.

Chapter Seven

The gold solidus in General Diogenes' hand flashed in the sunlight. "Would you care to wager on the next race, Lord Chamberlain?"

John declined.

Diogenes looked disappointed. "Your friend Felix never passes up a wager, especially on the chariot races."

A crowd of gods in marble and bronze filled the imperial box high above the race course at the Circus Maximus. Hundreds of years before, when the emperor attended the races, he was considered another of the Olympians, though flesh and blood. Now no additional god sat in the special place, only a general, a soldier, and a former Lord Chamberlain.

When Viteric arrived at John's house that morning bearing a message from Diogenes, John had immediately hoped there might be news of Felix. Instead, he had been invited to the races in terms that sounded more like an order.

He had obeyed reluctantly. He had no time for chariot-racing with Felix still missing. The previous night's vision of Felix—nothing but a dream he'd had while only half-awake—still clung to his awareness, a black fog making him uneasy for no discernible reason.

John sat with Diogenes at the front of the box, while Viteric stood discreetly behind. The stands could have accommodated thousands but there were only hundreds present, most of them soldiers, clustered in the lower tiers nearest the track. Thin cheers drifted up to the three onlookers. The distant rattle of the chariots and the crack of the charioteers' whips echoed around the empty expanse. It was a far cry from the tumultuous races John had attended at the Hippodrome in Constantinople, despite that the Circus Maximus was half again as large as the Hippodrome.

"It's good for morale," Diogenes remarked. "My men enjoy it and some of them race in their spare time."

Rome had been turned into a city of phantoms. The senate had been deported. The Goths outside the walls might attack at any moment. Yet the races went on. The Roman way of life was not yet dead.

"Do you attend the races with Felix?" John asked.

"No. But I run into him every time I go. He invariably suggests a wager."

"And usually loses."

"At least he enriches me, even if he does vex me."

"It sounds as if you are not on friendly terms."

"I wouldn't say we are unfriendly. His mission here is ambiguous. Awkward for everybody. He hasn't been very forthcoming. He did not arrive with orders putting him under my command. Julius Caesar once said he would rather be first in a village than second in Rome. These days, being first in Rome isn't much different than being second in a village, but I'm not going to be second in Rome, either to Felix or to Leon."

"You told me Felix was sent to deal with Archdeacon Leon, to stop him from agitating for peace negotiations with Totila."

"Ostensibly, but what was he up to all the time between his talks with Leon? When I asked he said he was assessing the situation to report back to the emperor. When I pressed him about when he was due to report back he told me he was awaiting orders."

Awaiting orders to take over command of the Rome garrison

from Diogenes? That was what the general feared, John thought. "What about his aide, Marius? Did he reveal anything?"

"He never met or even spoke with anyone except for Felix, so far as I know. No one in the city knew a thing about him." Diogenes leaned forward, hands on the parapet to watch two chariots come flying down the course toward the finish line. The racer wearing the color of the Blues won and Diogenes grimaced and looked over his shoulder. "You have won our wager, Viteric."

Turning back to John, he said, "I'll have to stop gambling until Felix returns."

"How is the search going?"

Diogenes absently rubbed the side of the crooked nose in his noble face. "By this afternoon my men will have made inquiries at every tavern and whorehouse in the city. A few years ago that would never have been possible. Rome is much diminished. Even vice is dying out."

"Is it possible Felix accomplished his mission and has left to return to Constantinople without notifying you?"

"If he has, we will soon find out."

Yes, John thought, Diogenes would find out when the messenger he had doubtless sent to the emperor to inquire about John returned. If Justinian's emissary to Rome had returned, everyone at court would know it. "Would Felix have any reason to keep out of sight?"

It was getting hot. The bulky general was sweating profusely. His face was flushed. "Are you suggesting Felix imagined he had reason to hide from me? That I threatened him?"

"I was thinking of those who collect debts by forceful means. Of gambling losses."

Diogenes shrugged. "Who can say? Commerce of all types continues here as best it can."

"Where do you think he is? In hiding with conspirators, planning to raise a mutiny against you?"

"You are the one he asked for help, Lord Chamberlain. You are more likely than I to know the answer to that."

"As I told you, Felix did not specify what type of help he needed or why he needed it. Perhaps you don't believe me?"

"I've seen the letter. It offers little basis to compel you to rush to Rome."

"Felix is my friend. An old friend."

Below, the starting gates sprang open and the next race began. Six chariots jostled to position themselves next to the spina in the middle of the track. An elderly man who had stationed himself alone, far up in the stands, could be heard bellowing his support for the Greens.

"I hear you have been out in the city alone, Lord Chamberlain. Rome is a dangerous place these days. Most of those who returned here were desperate, and remain so."

"Have you visited Constantinople? It is a dangerous city too and far more populated than this one."

"Nevertheless, I insist Viteric accompany you. I will provide more guards if you think it necessary."

"I've always preferred to conduct my business alone. I don't like to be surrounded by an escort. There is safety in anonymity."

"That may be, but if you're ambushed and killed by some ruffian, I shall have to answer for it."

The chariots were on the opposite side of the track, mostly concealed from view by the monuments, statues, and obelisks decorating the spina. The sparse crowd was cheering but the cries of seabirds circling overhead were louder. John glanced back to see Viteric, now seated against the rear wall, apparently concentrating on the race but overhearing everything being said.

"It was Belisarius' idea to bring back the races," Diogenes went on. "Do you recall years ago how the Goths offered to make him king? I've had no such offer. Pity." He smiled to show he was joking.

"Are you expecting an offer?"

"Certainly not! Totila is a brilliant general and the Goths are loyal to him. But short of replacing Totila, the Goths may be willing to make arrangements with Romans who are inclined to make them."

John asked him if he had anyone specific in mind.

"Archdeacon Leon."

"Leon told me Felix's visit was an attempt to persuade him from continuing to press for a surrender."

"Leon can be very persuasive. Tell me, is Felix a particularly religious man?"

John ignored the question. "So, in your opinion, is it possible Felix may be convinced he should act as a go-between for Leon and Totila, despite his orders from Justinian?"

"I didn't say that. I'm just searching for possibilities in a chaotic situation, Lord Chamberlain. Alliances can shift. I am sure a man who has held such a position as you realizes that. A general needs to concern himself not only with the battlefield but also with the changing political situation, and when an emissary of the emperor shows up out of nowhere, that changes matters. It is necessary to remain flexible."

John had the impression the general was sounding him out, wondering if John might be inclined to shift his loyalty away from the emperor or Felix and give it him. Why had he asked whether Felix was religious? Simply gauging what effect a Christian leader's argument might have on him? Or did he know or suspect Felix's pagan beliefs?

Archdeacon Leon had not mentioned Mithrans, but Gainus, when John interviewed him outside the tavern, had.

"I was told there are secret Mithrans in the ranks. Is that true?"

"Archdeacon Leon thinks it is. If I could actually identify any, they'd soon be eliminated."

"Do you suspect there are Mithrans?"

"Yes."

"And they might be sympathetic to the Goths?"

"The Goths are heretics also."

"But Christian ones."

As the sun warmed the walls and the marble and bronze gods decorating the imperial box, the air grew stifling. The sound of hoofbeats drifted up from the tiny chariots which blurred and melted, visions in a dream, as they raced through waves of heat rising from the track. John had the impression he was looking down into Rome's glorious past from a great height.

"Mithraism is a military religion," John replied. "There will always be fighting men who are Mithrans."

"Not in a Christian empire."

"Had you considered rooting out Mithrans might lead to problems with morale?"

Diogenes gave a nervous wave of his hand. "I'm more concerned what Archdeacon Leon will think if I don't clear them out. The church runs Rome and has for many years. It's the church the populace respects."

John thought there wasn't much left of Rome to run and not many inhabitants aside from the garrison. Apparently, Gainus had been telling the truth about Diogenes' animosity—at least officially—toward Mithrans.

The two leading chariots approached the turn at the end of the spina, marked by a platform supporting three gilded, conical pillars. The Green team's driver veered to the inside. The Blue's driver attempted to cut him off. Even up in the imperial box John heard the screech of a wheel hitting the platform. Then the Green's chariot turned over. The panicked horses dragged it away, spilling the driver onto the track as the trailing chariots bore down on him.

Instantly, a figure emerged from what John had supposed was a small columned temple on the spina. The man leapt onto the track, scuttled to the disabled charioteer, and dragged him away as the remaining chariots thundered past.

Something about the rescuer struck John as peculiar. His movements suggested those of a large spider, because of his bulbous body and skinny limbs. He didn't resemble the sort of man to be leaping from temples and pulling charioteers to safety.

John strained to see. It looked as if the man was wearing a charioteer's leather helmet.

It was the same man who had shown John the way home.

The population of Rome was, indeed, small.

Chapter Eight

When the races ended John announced he was returning home to rest, claiming he was still feeling the effects of the long journey to Rome. Despite his protests, Viteric insisted on accompanying him so John was forced to waste more time walking all the way back to the house and pretending to retire to his room before resuming his investigations.

In case Viteric was watching the house, John left by the back door and returned to the Circus Maximus. The Church of Saint Minias faced the Forum of the Bull near the western end of the racetrack. An unattractive pile of bricks, the church cast its shadow over the graceful circular peristyle of the now-closed Temple of Hercules. John wished to speak to the self-styled Holy Father, Basilio, who had greeted him upon his entry into Rome and promptly turned him over to the authorities. Before he entered the church, he paused to admire the bronze bull displayed in the forum. Although the statue had probably been erected in past centuries to mark the place as a cattle market, the bull was sacred to John's god Mithra. He murmured a brief prayer for fellow Mithran Felix. In a Christian empire, pagans took their objects of veneration where they could find them.

Armed guards intercepted him at the entrance to the church. Inside, a building project looked to be well underway. Marble blocks were being pried from the floor and workers were tearing down a wall in one of the side aisles. The sounds of hammering elsewhere rang hollowly in the nave. The guards led him around the work area to the sacristy.

Basilio sat at a table polishing a badly dented silver chalice. Other than faded frescoes, the room was austere. Over the door hung a wooden cross, and a few damaged sacred vessels, whose exact purposes were a mystery to John, occupied largely bare shelves. An open chest revealed threadbare vestments. The garments Basilio wore were of better quality.

The aged man looked up from his work. "The Lord Chamberlain, I believe. We weren't properly introduced at our first meeting."

Basilio invited John to sit. He took the indicated stool, the only other seat in the room apart from Basilio's chair which lacked its cushion. He wasn't certain how one was supposed to greet a man who imagined himself to be the pope, and was happy Basilio didn't appear determined to stand on ceremony.

"Young girls are not reliable," Basilio said, screwing his face up in displeasure, accentuating its deep wrinkles. "It's part of their flighty nature. And Veneria has taken flight."

John raised his eyebrows.

"I see you are puzzled. Veneria is a young woman who took care of chores like this but now she has gone off and left the Holy Father to polish his own chalice. Still, even those of us in high positions must remain humble and the Lord gives me strength to do whatever work is necessary. Now, what is your business here? Has Diogenes agreed to lend me some of his men, as I requested?"

"No. I am unaccompanied."

"Pity. Next time a stranger comes crawling out of my cistern perhaps I will not send him to the general."

John remembered too well his shock at emerging from dark tunnels only to find himself surrounded by water. "A cistern is an odd place for an entrance to the catacombs."

"A secret entrance," Basilio replied. "My church holds many

secrets. It was built on the site of a pagan temple and at some point, while the original structure was still in use, its worshipers must have created that entrance. I knew where it would be found, although I can barely see." Basilio squinted at his reflection in the gilded interior of the chalice, narrowed his eyes, and lowered his face until his nose was almost inside the bowl. "Age robs us of the ability to see the physical world even as our vision of the spiritual grows keener."

The equally poor-sighted Archdeacon Leon might have voiced a similar sentiment, John thought. The elderly men held opposing religious beliefs but their contrary gods visited the same physical sufferings on them. John hoped he would not be subjected to a sermon. He muttered a vague assent and Basilio continued.

"Just by keeping my ears open I learned amazing things while I was a beggar on the steps of this church, a church my father had helped to keep in repair. I thought the Lord was punishing us when my family fell upon hard times, but not at all. For you see, beggars are invisible and even priests careless in their conversations, thinking because we are destitute, we are also deaf. So I overheard matters the church—or those who falsely call themselves the church—have hidden for centuries. Truths, if you will."

"I am also looking for the truth," John put in. "I am seeking information about one of your former employees. Hunulf."

Basilio frowned in thought.

"A big German, I am told," John offered.

"Oh, yes. A bit taller than you and much broader. He's the one Veneria ran away with."

"You are certain? The man I'm talking about served with Diogenes."

"He's the one. The garrison is infested with Germans."

"And he is involved with this young woman, Veneria?"

"I am sure about it. I once found them in this very room pretending to examine the frescoes, hoping I would not notice their disarranged clothing."

John examined the paintings. The largest depicted the life of the church's titular saint, a military man who converted to Christianity, was martyred by beheading and, according to legend, picked up his head and walked away. A second, clumsily done, showed the judgment of Solomon. Set in the reception hall of Solomon's palace, it struck an anachronistic note in that Solomon was clothed in a billowing toga. A statue of Thanatos with a raven perched on his shoulder sat on a gilded column near Solomon's throne. The god was pointing out a not-quite rectangular window toward what the painter had rendered as a structure with only three sides.

John noted the raven, the lowest Mithran rank. Another sign from his god, right here in the temple of the Christians' god?

"I see you are admiring them," Basilio was saying. "Beautiful, are they not? As for Hunulf. He was one of our guards but left some time ago to work for a notorious woman called Clementia. Even after that, he still continued to pay Veneria visits. I couldn't help notice her wearing expensive baubles, quite inappropriate for scrubbing floors. They had to be gifts from Hunulf. I hate to speculate how he got them."

"Hunulf visited her here?"

"More than once I saw him skulking about outside, waiting for her to finish her work. That they could not meet at her home seems to me to show her family did not approve of their liaison. I made it plain a number of times this was also my opinion, for I felt responsibility for her as a straying lamb, not to mention we cannot countenance sinning in a woman connected, however tenuously, with the church without some effort at reform."

"Indeed. You say Hunulf went to work for the woman Clementia?"

"So Veneria confided in me just before she suddenly left. She said she was afraid Hunulf would desert her for this other woman. It is possible her decision was strongly influenced by that fear. The young can be headstrong. So now, until I find a replacement for her, I do my own polishing." He gave a dry chuckle.

•• ● ••

Basilio made his way toward a dusty-leafed beech behind the church where another old man sat in the shade removing dirt from a pile of carrots. The man's fingers were as twisted and knobby as the carrots. He worked slowly.

"Don't rise, Martyrus," Basilio called as he approached. "I want to talk to you."

"As you wish."

The two ancients made a strange contrast. Basilio's skin sagged with wrinkles as if it had grown too big for the skull beneath, while Martyrus' skin was desiccated, cracked parchment drawn tight over the bone.

Basilio lowered himself awkwardly onto the marble bench, wincing as he did, picked up a carrot, and brushed off clinging soil. "My bones are aching today."

It was the result of too many years sitting in open doorways and in front of public buildings in all weather, importuning passersby for coins or a scrap of bread. He knew the steps of Saint Minias Church better than any man alive, knew the hours when the cold winds were likely to blow across them, and the daily procession of the sun and shadows which had governed his own movements.

During his years as a beggar, he had prayed and pondered deeply, and the Lord had inspired him. Now he lived inside the church, but he could still feel his past in his joints.

"I have some willow extract left," Martyrus said. "I won't be able to replenish the supply when it is gone. As long as the Goths surround us, I can't get to the trees by the river. I shouldn't have dug up my medicinal herbs to plant vegetables."

"We may need the vegetables," Basilio replied. "I had a visitor," he added. "The Lord Chamberlain. He asked me about Hunulf."

His companion gave him a glance. His eyes were clear and as black as two newly polished stones. They might have been inserted into the old face just yesterday. "Hunulf was a trouble-maker, if ever I saw one!"

"I cannot say I am unhappy he has gone. He was always creeping around in a suspicious manner, not to mention Veneria told me he is a man of violent humors. At the same time, even though he is gone, he is still causing trouble, given I would prefer not to talk to a man asking difficult questions about people who go away and don't return. I was afraid my visitor was accusing me of having a hand in their disappearances."

Martyrus nodded. "You told him Veneria had vanished?"

"Yes."

"Perhaps the pair have just run away together."

"Just so long as they don't come back here. I didn't like being questioned by the Lord Chamberlain."

They worked in silence until Martyrus remarked, "Contributions to the church have dropped off the past few weeks."

"Should I hold more services?"

"I don't think that would help. The faithful have only so much to give."

"Do we still have enough to pay the guards? That's the important thing. If we aren't able to keep hold of the church…"

"The people are preoccupied with the Goths. They rightfully fear an assault is coming. Even if that fails, the siege will continue."

"It is difficult to distract even the faithful from such worldly concerns."

"We need something to rekindle their enthusiasm. Faith is like a fire, it burns down and has to be prodded once in a while."

"Yes. I will think about it. It may be an opportunity—"

He was interrupted by a distraught man who raced around the corner of the church. He stopped, gasping for breath, in front of the two ancients. "We've seen that shade wandering the catacombs again! My men dropped their tools and ran!"

Basilio climbed to his feet with a grunt and patted the visitor on his shoulder. "My son, you are mistaken. Tell your men to have faith in the Lord. The blessed departed do not wander about. They are all at rest. But you should not be. You have work to do. Get back to it."

This did not placate the workman. "It is the work of the devil or demons!"

"Would the Lord allow demons to play and terrify the righteous beneath His holy church? Now gather together your men and reassure them. There is much work yet to be done."

The man went off reluctantly. Basilio sat again and continued cleaning carrots. "Demons do not worry me," he went on. "This Lord Chamberlain does. I didn't like it when he emerged from the catacombs and I like it even less now that he is asking pointed questions. Do you think he was really lost down there?"

"The workmen might just be imagining this spirit. It may be nothing more than shadows."

Basilio gave a snort. "Ugh! A worm!" He shook the worm off his hand, stood up, and stamped on it.

At least that problem was quickly solved.

Chapter Nine

Leaving the Church of Saint Minias, John wondered whether the vanished servant Veneria had actually run away with Hunulf or simply gone back to her parents' home. He would need to visit the family. The glint of the lowering sun on the Tiber caught his eye. He made his way through a weedy maze of toppled pillars, the remains of a porticoed street, until he came to the riverbank. The brownish waters gave off the stench of the effluvia dumped into it, although not as strong as it must have been when the city still thrived.

Two men were dragging something through the shallow water. By the time John arrived, they had wrapped what looked like a body in a canvas sheet. One of the men, short, broad-shouldered, and completely bald, stamped mud off his boots and greeted John warily.

"Yes, it's a corpse," the bald man confirmed in reply to John's query.

"A man," added his companion, a nondescript fellow with a scraggly beard. "Big, a soldier, going by the way he's dressed. Too bad for us. Men don't wear jewelry."

"Quiet, you fool," snapped his colleague.

"We work for the authorities," the other put in. "Can't leave corpses lying around."

"Few enough of them now," his companion complained. "Not

like during the siege when bodies blocked the streets. Plenty of jewelry back then."

John's gaze fell on the large belt buckle in the speaker's hand.

"The authorities do not compensate us well. They expect us to tax those who use our services. This one owes us more than this belt buckle, given how much trouble he was to haul in."

John wasn't worrying about whether the men were looting bodies. At the words "big soldier," he couldn't help thinking of Hunulf or Felix. He stared down at the bulk hidden beneath the sheet and for one sickening instant was sure he recognized his friend from the outline of his build alone.

"I wish to take a look at the face."

The two others exchanged questioning looks.

"You don't want to, for I can tell you are a man of some refinement."

"I'm a man who has been on battlefields. Uncover the face."

As John bent down to see, his heart seemed to leap into his throat.

The face was fat and beardless. Not Felix.

No, not fat, John corrected himself, exhaling in relief as he straightened up. Just bloated from being long in the water. As far as he could make out, the face was that of an older man so he was not Hunulf either.

The scavengers lifted the corpse into a handcart. Faint moans and sighs issued from the body as gasses escaped.

"Where are you taking this man?"

"During the last siege they set up a mortuary in the Baths of Decius," answered the bald man. "They haven't been used for their original purpose in years."

"I shall come with you. I am searching for someone."

Both men nodded and smiled.

The bald man rubbed his sunburned scalp. "Oh, I see. That's reasonable. Well, I mean, there are some who just like to look at the dead."

"And some want us to uncover the women," added his companion.

They set off across the forum and climbed the Aventine Hill. The streets were deserted except for a couple of stray dogs who sniffed the air and followed them hopefully. The baths were a complex of ponderous buildings. Entering the main building, they walked down a wide hall, leaving muddy bootprints and cart tracks on the elaborate mosaic floor. They were observed by painted marble statues so ancient that the colors were mostly worn off, as if they'd just been in the baths for a good scrubbing. Halfway down the hall they turned through an archway presided over by an infant Hercules carved from basalt.

The main bathing pool, long since dry, had been turned into a mortuary. Cadavers in various states of putrefaction were laid out on the tiles, some wrapped better than others. The bald man and his bearded companion carried their burden down the steps into the pool, turned it over to the attendant, and left.

The attendant's large white beard made him resemble a weary Greek philosopher. "Can I be of assistance, sir?"

"I am looking for a man who is missing."

"Very well. But I must accompany you. Everybody who comes here says he is looking for someone but most are really looking for what they can find on the bodies."

"I am surprised there is anything of value left on them by the time they arrive here," John remarked, thinking about the men who had pulled the body from the river.

"It can happen. Some time back there was a young woman with an expensive necklace. It had slipped down into her tunica, which is how her family identified her. If not for the necklace… well, she had been in the water for quite a while."

A thick haze filled the pool where water had once been, smoke from bowls of burning, scented oil placed amidst the neat rows of bodies. Still the heavy stink of death was overwhelming. The air was filled with the buzzing of flies.

"Are you looking for an adult?"

"Yes."

The attendant walked briskly past a row of smallish bundles, bent, and pulled a sheet away from a face John, thankfully, failed to recognize. Some of the corpses stared sightlessly up at the smoke through opaque eyes. Others' faces were little more than scraps of flesh hanging to the skull. Each time the attendant pulled a sheet aside, John's stomach lurched and his heart raced. Flies rose in a cloud, their fat bodies hitting John's face, before settling back down in a swarm over the features John was attempting to identify.

"You should have seen the crowds we had here during the last siege, sir."

Up and down the rows they went. To John's growing relief, all were strangers. Why had he imagined he'd find Felix here? No one had seen him for a few days. That was all. And yet, as he'd walked to the makeshift mortuary, he had become convinced that his friend's body would be lying there. The mind had the bad habit of fixing upon the worst possible outcomes.

John silently thanked Mithra as they approached the final corpse. The attendant lifted the cover.

The first thing John saw was the huge, bushy beard. Then he noticed the bear-like body.

He suppressed a gasp. The face was largely gone. White bone showed through the red ruin of the flesh.

"Is this who you are looking for?" the attendant asked.

John squeezed his eyes shut, opened them again, steadying himself. "No. It can't be. The man I am looking for hasn't been missing long enough for his corpse to have decayed to such an extent."

"This is not decay, sir. The dogs had been at him."

John wasn't sure if the deafening buzz he heard was in his head or only the flies. He scanned the wrapped body. "Could you lower the sheet more?"

The attendant complied. The corpse was dressed in laborer's clothes and, though his build was large, he was not as broad as Felix. Then again, didn't the dead always look shrunken, as if something vital had escaped?

"It isn't the person I am looking for."

"I will not say I am sorry. Most of those who come here legitimately searching for someone would prefer not to find them."

It was an uncharitable thought but John wondered if the attendant was less concerned with bodies being robbed as with them being robbed before they reached his care? He recalled his companion had told him about a young woman identified by her jewelry.

So perhaps he was honest. Or simply hadn't checked her tunica closely enough.

He thought about Basilio's former servant who had worn jewelry while scrubbing the church floors.

"This young woman who was identified by her jewelry, do you remember anything else about her?"

"I recall that her parents were distraught. Even more than usual, I mean. I've become used to it most of the time but this pair…the father was cursing the Lord and crying out for justice for Veneria."

Veneria! Basilio's former servant! Mithra was assisting him today, John thought.

A short walk brought John to an abandoned tenement at the base of the Aventine Hill just south of the Circus Maximus. He recognized it from the mortuary attendant's description. It loomed precariously over the buildings lining a dead-end alley. It was the place where Veneria's family has asked for her body to be sent. Even on the sunniest day John doubted much light could penetrate the gloom of the passage, which was hardly wider than a man's shoulders.

Now darkness had fallen. John entered the reeking black maw, his sword at the ready. It was the perfect place for an ambush. There was an eerie sense of people hiding nearby, waiting for an opportunity to strike, a feeling familiar to him from numerous forays along similar and equally foul alleys in Constantinople. However, given only one family now lived in this particular location—or so he had been told—perhaps it was peopled with the spirits of former residents. It reminded him too much of the solid darkness of passages branching away from those he traveled as he escaped from the catacombs.

He did not believe Felix was dead and thus had set his boots on the seven-runged ladder leading to Mithra's realm. However, Veneria, a possible source of information, was dead. Veneria, who had worked for the churchman Basilio, and may have run off with Hunulf, who also once worked for Basilio and was later employed by Clementia. Hunulf, who the gambler Gainus hinted had been involved with Clementia, the same woman Eutuchyus claimed was having an affair with Felix. Did the convoluted string of rumors—as likely to be false as true—form a link between Veneria and the disappearance of Felix?

When he reached the door to the five-story wooden building, he could see it was even more ramshackle than he'd expected. Given how it was tottering on its foundations, he wondered why anyone would live there. As a former fighting man, John knew a narrow approach with only one end open was easily defended, and in this desperate city perhaps that was the explanation.

The door had served as a common entrance to the apartments within. Now it was locked. At the sound of his rapping, a window above him opened. A man held out a lantern and examined John's upturned face by its flickering light.

"What do you want?"

John identified himself and informed the man at the window he was willing to pay for information. The man clattered downstairs and unbarred the door.

Beckoning John in, he hastily barred it again. "What sort of information do you think I have to sell?"

His words echoed in the empty passage. The air was malodorous, a mixture of rotted fruit and dead rats. Even so it was not quite as unbearable as the atmosphere in the mortuary. The bright lantern blinded John. As his eyes adjusted, he made out a rotund figure with oddly thin legs and a charioteer's leather helmet.

"You are the one who showed me the way to my house when I was lost," John said. "And I saw you leap onto the racetrack this morning."

"Yes, sir. I'm Aurelius. Normally, I repair chariots, but these days we all pitch in to do anything we can to keep the races going."

John wondered why the man continued to wear the leather helmet even at home. Was he bald and vain? He followed him into a room which must have been enlarged by knocking down partitions between apartments. It was decorated and furnished with a motley array of scavenged items—a big couch with torn upholstery, wall hangings burnt at the bottom, a small statue of a goddess, the bust of a statesman without a nose.

"You will excuse my wife if she does not join us. We lost our daughter recently. My wife is upstairs weeping. She's been weeping ever since the funeral. We had to bury our daughter in a temporary grave inside the walls. It's been a nightmare."

"I'm here because of your daughter."

Aurelius eyed John warily. "You are staying at General Felix's house, where General Conon once lived. You must be an official. Have the authorities finally decided to take notice of my daughter's death?"

"Not exactly. I am searching for the general, who has vanished. Finding out what happened to Veneria may help me find him."

Aurelius stamped the floor and cursed. "So he is the villain who led her astray?"

"What do you mean?"

"What do I mean?" He strode over to a cabinet and drew out a necklace. It flashed and sparkled in the lantern light. "Gold and pearls and sapphires! Where does the daughter of a man who repairs chariots find the money for such jewelry? How does a servant girl earn such money? It was on her body when we found her at the mortuary."

"I am told she was involved with a former soldier."

"Military pay is low at the best of times, never mind about these times. There must have been someone else, someone wealthy and generous, sir. Some high official or other. A general, an emissary from the emperor."

Felix's roving eye might easily be caught by any attractive woman, but John couldn't imagine him murdering one. "I'm not aware of any such connection between General Felix and your daughter."

A forlorn-looking woman drifted into the room like a shade and came to stand beside Aurelius.

"My wife," he said putting an arm around her shoulders. "This man has come to help us, to look into Veneria's death."

She looked at John with hollow, haunted eyes. "You could help us? How? My husband says you told him as he helped you home that you have not been long in Rome. The authorities wouldn't pay attention to me when I begged them to search for her. To them she was nothing, not worth bothering about. If it had been a person of their own class, it would have been a different story."

"She was a fine girl," put in Aurelius, stroking his distraught wife's gray hair. "She worked hard. She promised her mother and me we would all soon have a better life. I suspected she had strayed, but these days what are we to say about that? We all do what we must to continue living. Yet the wages of sin are poor, it seems, for here we still are, and poor Veneria is dead."

"When did you see her last?" John asked him.

"A week ago. After she left Basilio." This elicited a sob from his wife. "Now, there…" He patted her shoulder reassuringly.

"Did she tell you her plans?"

"Not really. She—"

"She was going to run off with a military man," blurted out Aurelius' wife. "Such men are trained to kill. They quarreled and he killed her!"

"Did she identify the man?"

"No," said Aurelius, "and we didn't like to ask."

"Did she ever speak of a man called Hunulf?"

Both shook their heads.

"Your daughter promised you a better life. Did she ever bring money home?"

"Only small amounts, amounts she might have obtained honestly."

It had occurred to John that the necklace found on Veneria's body must be worth a fair amount. She might have stolen it. He continued questioning the pair but learned nothing of interest. According to them Veneria was an industrious young woman who dreamed of a happy future but had worked for bad employers and become involved with a bad man.

John promised to do what he could and left.

Aurelius lingered in the doorway and shouted down the alley after him. "Justice, sir. All we want is justice!"

Chapter Ten

John lay in bed, sleepless, Aurelius' shouts for justice still echoing in his mind. Justice was what everyone wanted, yet everyone wanted something different. When, as a young mercenary, he had inadvertently wandered into enemy territory while seeking silks for his lover, been captured by the Persians, castrated, and sold into slavery, that must have seemed eminently just to the Persians. Perhaps a Christian—Archdeacon Leon, for example—might also consider what John had suffered a just punishment for a sinful relationship. From John's perspective it was an injustice. And now, who at the court of Constantinople would dare say that Justinian had not meted out justice by sending his former Lord Chamberlain into exile? The emperor was the very source of justice, but John, having served Justinian loyally for more than twenty years, did not consider the action just. Fortunately, John, unlike many—including Aurelius—did not expect justice, or at any rate did not expect others to administer his personal idea of justice. Was it even possible that anyone could deliver to Aurelius whatever it was the bereaved father would consider justice for his daughter's death?

John tried to stop his musings from racing around in circles like chariots at the track. As soon as he thought he had succeeded, the starting gates flew open again. He had attended Plato's Academy in Athens and run away from his studies to fight as a mercenary, so it was no wonder he tried to send his philosophizing into retreat. What did philosophy teach, after all, except that there were no answers? And a man could not live his life as if there were no answers. Perhaps those who had never bothered to think deeply about things were better off.

His friend Felix had never read philosophy. He read histories, read about what men had done, rather than what they had thought about.

It occurred to John that another day had passed without word from Felix. It seemed increasingly unlikely Felix's absence was the result of a drinking binge. He would have surely returned by now.

John rolled over, opened his eyes, and looked toward the window, hoping for some sign of daylight, the welcome end of a sleepless night. But there was only darkness. The room was unfamiliar, perhaps part of the reason he couldn't sleep.

He listened to hear signs of life in the streets beyond or the song of a predawn bird. Instead, he heard a thump from above followed by the sound of scraping. Padding to his door, he opened it a crack. The hall was dimly illuminated in light from an unseen lamp in another corridor.

A shadow disappeared around a corner.

John followed, treading as silently as possible, ready for sudden ambush.

There was a burst of noise from the direction of the kitchen. The crash of something knocked over. Shouts, then a high-pitched shrieking.

John sprinted through the doorway and saw Eutuchyus cowering beside the overturned kitchen table, clutching a bleeding hand and screaming as his assailant stood uncertainly in front of him. The knife-wielding attacker was a boy on the edge of manhood, slight of build.

John easily disarmed the boy. When he tried to bite, John slammed him down into a chair.

Seen up close, he wasn't merely slightly built but rather emaciated. John could have circled his wrist with one hand. The boy's face was drawn and his eyes sunken, giving him a look of precocious worldly wisdom. He was also none too clean.

"He tried to kill me!" Eutuchyus thrust a shaking, bleeding hand toward John.

John pushed it away. "It's nothing but a shallow cut."

Eutuchyus stared at John resentfully. "This is the thief who has been stealing our food, master. I lay in wait for him. He might have murdered us all in our beds."

"He is only a hungry boy, Eutuchyus."

"A hungry boy armed with a knife!"

"To cut my food with," snapped the boy. He spat in Eutuchyus' direction.

"Go to your room and see to your hand," John ordered the steward.

The boy smirked as Eutuchyus slunk away.

John turned the table upright and set out a plate of leftover rabbit stew. The boy ate quickly but in a controlled fashion. The plate cleared, John was rewarded with a grin and a nod. A confident young man then, John thought, and not afraid of me. He asked his visitor for his name.

"Julius. I live near here."

"Where?"

Julius waved his hand. "In the abandoned house next door. I hide there in the daytime and come out to forage for food at night."

It was possible Julius was telling the truth. There was no reason for anyone to enter the semi-destroyed building next door, so he would be fairly safe from discovery. If spotted, he could easily run off. If cornered, he was equipped with a weapon, and a well-sharpened one at that.

"How did you get into this house?" John asked, thinking of the building's stout doors barred at night.

The visitor shrugged. "You might say I dropped in from heaven. One of the upper windows does not close properly. It's easy to use it as an entrance if you don't mind climbing up on the roof and letting yourself down on a rope."

That explained the light thud and scraping John had heard. He reminded Julius it would be far safer to enter an unoccupied house.

"True, but there's no food in houses where nobody lives. I assure you I am most careful to be as quiet as possible. See?" He raised a foot wrapped in scraps of linen.

"You are alone?"

"I've been alone a long time," Julius replied in a matter of fact tone. "What do you intend to do with me now?"

John admitted he had yet to decide. He asked Julius how he had come to be living by himself in a ruined building in a largely deserted city.

"It was easy. I ran away from home to join the army. My parents wanted me to study. What's the use of that? I wanted to fight. But when I reached a Roman camp, they said I was too young. I decided to try my luck elsewhere. Never got wherever elsewhere was, because I was caught by the Goths. They're everywhere."

"Indeed."

"They gave me to one of their noblemen. Ha! Nobleman, they called him. As if a barbarian can be noble." Julius spat again. "He used me like a slave."

John had to stop himself from smiling. The boy's tale was so like his own. "And how did you get away?"

Julius shrugged. "One night I slit my master's noble throat."

• ● ● ● •

"Stay here? But you can't let that filthy little beast stay here, sir!" Eutuchyus fluttered around the kitchen like a wounded butterfly. "It disgusts me to get anywhere near that boy!"

"You don't have to get near him, just serve him the meals you serve me."

This morning, for John, that meant bread and cheese with a cup of watered wine. He was having a difficult time choking it down, not because he favored more elaborate fare, but rather because Eutuchyus' wailing had begun to irritate him. The steward was intolerable. When he wasn't complaining in that grating voice, he was gliding around, silently, always appearing out of nowhere.

"Serve that little thief? Why do I need to? He's been helping himself all along. Stealing from us brazenly while we slept!"

Losing patience, John banged his cup down on the table. "You speak like a frightened woman! You're afraid of being murdered by a child?"

Eutuchyus' lip trembled. "But, sir, he admitted he slit his master's throat."

John stood up, eyes angry. "You were eavesdropping last night."

"No, sir. I mean, yes, but…but…I didn't mean to hear…"

"You are a liar. You don't really believe the boy killed anyone, do you? It was merely bravado. Boys are all like that at his age. I shall overlook your comments this time, but Julius will stay. If I hear more complaints, you won't. Now get about your business."

Julius strolled into the room as if he'd lived in the house for years. "Good morning, sir."

By daylight, Julius looked even thinner than he had in the dim lamplight.

"You can have my breakfast," John told him. "If you want more, Eutuchyus will provide it, although I suppose you already know where our supplies are kept."

"Yes, sir."

"And Eutuchyus will show you where the bath is."

"I know where that is too."

He knows this house better than I do, John told himself. "Before you eat, though, Julius, I want you to do a job for me."

Suddenly the boy looked wary.

"Leave the house carefully, without being observed. There will be a guard somewhere outside. Distract him. Throw a stone, yell. Lead him away."

Julius brightened. "Certainly, sir." He raced off on his mission. Emaciated as he appeared he was not lacking in energy.

John waited.

Before long he heard the muffled sound of something hitting the house. From the back of the house came the sound of a man shouting and a boy laughing. There was the faint slap of running feet.

So Viteric had had enough sense to guard the escape route John had used the previous day. As he peered out the front door, John hoped Viteric had not been given an assistant.

Chapter Eleven

There was no one stationed at his front door as John left. It might be Diogenes feared being too obvious about spying on the house, anxious about putting John on his guard. Or maybe he felt he couldn't spare more than one man.

Although John was unfamiliar with the city, he arrived at the wall with no problem. It was built of red brick. A wide, crenelated walk awaited him as he emerged from one of the sturdy towers set at intervals. None of the guards he met on the way up challenged his presence, despite his civilian garb. It must be true that everyone knew who he was. Or rather everyone knew who he had been—Lord Chamberlain rather than a man in exile. And just as well, given it meant he could ask questions freely and expect to be given answers.

If he knew the right questions to ask.

Once on the walkway he scanned the countryside spread below. Next to the Appian Way lay a large encampment of Goths. It was excellent tactics, he thought, to camp next to a well-paved road, making it easy to move troops quickly, whether advancing or retreating. Smoke rose, thin fingers probing a deep blue sky, an augury of another hot day. He could make out men cooking their morning meal. Closer to hand, he could distinguish, half-screened by trees, the peculiar monument through which he had entered the catacombs while escaping into Rome.

Footsteps behind him announced the arrival of a trio of tired soldiers, evidently going off duty after serving in the night watch.

"Salutations!" John said with a nod. "All is quiet, I see."

The tallest of the three stayed behind as his colleagues disappeared into the tower. Returning the greeting, he continued, "True, sir, but there's bound to be an assault soon."

"The city is well fortified, isn't it?"

"Belisarius repaired the walls but whether we have the numbers to man them, who can say?"

He was a lanky youngster, only a couple years older than Julius. His shoulders were broad but his body had not filled out yet.

"You fear the Goths might attack multiple locations at the same time?"

"That's right. The garrison, even augmented with civilians, would be hard-pressed to keep them out. Also, there are spies in the city, seeking information useful to their masters."

"How do you know I am not one of them?"

"Everyone has heard about your arrival, Lord Chamberlain."

"So I gather."

"Word gets around fast."

"And you trust me?"

"You are a friend of General Felix. He is an admirable man and that is good enough for me."

"Then you know him personally?"

"He spent a lot of time with the garrison, sir."

John wondered what Felix had been doing. He couldn't picture his friend trying to persuade the garrison to rebel. He was an ambitious man, although none too prudent. In the past he had allowed himself to be drawn into some unfortunate ventures, but John could not see him hatching such a plan personally. "The general mentioned he was a friend of mine?"

"Yes, sir. We were curious about him coming from Constantinople. He said he'd been captain of the emperor's excubitors and even knew the Lord Chamberlain and had drunk wine with him far into the night on many occasions."

John wanted to ask how much had Felix drunk before revealing that. He refrained. "What is your name?"

"Cassius."

"What did Felix speak to the garrison about, Cassius?"

"Our defenses. Like us, he feared we might be overwhelmed. He said that if the Goths discover how weak we are and coordinate their attacks in the right fashion, the ravens will have rich pickings. Those were his precise words."

John had the impression Viteric was scrutinizing him closely, watching for his reaction and grasped the opportunity. "I was just pondering what you said about those who work inside the city to betray it. There's even a rumor Persians are serving in the garrison."

Cassius frowned. "Persians? I don't think so. Next, you will be telling me my comrades at arms supposedly include lions and fools who run with the sun. Rumor, sir, only rumor. And rumor ever has a lying tongue, as is the case with most women."

Persians, Lions, Ravens, and Runners of the Sun were all ranks of Mithraism, which was an all-male religion. Cassius was a Mithran.

John made a certain sign and the other nodded. "Mithra is my lord. You are in need of assistance? How may I render it to a fellow initiate?"

"I am thinking about Goths," John replied. "I know they could get into the city via the catacombs if they had a guide. If they did, then the person who guided them would be betraying Rome and well paid to do it. Has anyone you know been displaying sudden wealth?"

"No, sir."

"When did you last see Felix?"

The young man shuffled his feet, opened his mouth and then closed it. An expression of panic crept across his face. "I don't know. That is, I can't be certain."

Had it suddenly occurred to Cassius how foolish he'd been speaking about Mithra to a near stranger, when his commanding officer and the church in Rome were intent on stamping out what they considered a sacrilegious cult?

"How can you not be certain when you saw Felix last?"

"I thought it was Felix but I couldn't actually recognize him, sir."

"A big German with a bushy beard? How could you mistake him?"

"He was masked. We all were masked."

John understood immediately. "When did this Mithran ceremony take place?"

"Last week. Sir, I—"

"Don't worry, Cassius. I am not a spy for Diogenes or anyone else. I want you to take me to the mithraeum."

When Viteric saw Julius throwing rocks at the house, he yelled at him to stop. Julius took flight and Viteric followed, drawing his sword for effect. He certainly didn't need a sword in a fight with a child.

The child was faster than Viteric expected. Viteric chased him around a corner and down an alleyway, gaining very little ground before he realized he'd been lured away from his post. Cursing himself, he raced back.

There were seldom many people on the streets of the depopulated city and it wasn't long before he located John heading in the direction of the city wall. He kept his distance to avoid being seen.

Once on the wall, John fell into conversation with a soldier. Hiding behind a pile of crates holding supplies, Viteric couldn't hear what was being said. He did catch the man's name. It appeared from their manner of meeting that John and Cassius did not know one another, but Viteric couldn't be certain. Spies would naturally act circumspectly.

Abruptly John and the soldier started to move off. Viteric prepared to follow.

"Viteric."

One of Diogenes' commanders was striding toward him.

"Yes, sir."

"I want you to a convey a message to General Diogenes." As Viteric fidgeted impatiently his superior launched into a long series of complaints about the inadequacy of supplies on his sector of the wall. Viteric kept looking over his shoulder but by the time the commander finished, Viteric had lost sight of John.

He stared out across the countryside beyond the wall, fuming. Should he try to find John again?

He decided instead to ask about Cassius. The first three men he questioned professed not to know a Cassius. The fourth admitted he was acquainted with the fellow only after Viteric drew his sword.

"Why are you interested in him? Is he in trouble?"

"He might be. You might be too, if you don't tell me everything you know."

The soldier backed up against the parapet in alarm. "Who are you to be questioning me?"

"I'm General Diogenes' aide! Now tell me about Cassius."

Access to the mithraeum lay beyond two inconspicuous locked doors in obscure hallways leading off an armory beneath one of the towers on the wall. Cassius lifted a grate in the floor of a musty underground hallway. Though few would have noticed, John saw that the metal was less rusty than it should have been, the result of being regularly handled. Below, instead of a sewer, steps led downwards.

They descended to a rough-hewn catacomb, similar to the one John had traversed on his way into the city. Cassius handed John one of the two torches he had lit above. "This is a Mithran burial place, dating to a time before our religion was outlawed. There are others."

"Do these catacombs connect with those of the Christian dead?"

"I wouldn't be surprised. The Christians kept enlarging their catacombs for hundreds of years. It's not as if they were working from plans. They must have tunneled into other catacombs by accident."

John was thinking of how the tunnels he had come through could be entered from outside the city. Was this another way out of—or into—the city?

On the way Cassius had told him that the previous week Mithrans had held a ceremony to celebrate a brother's advancement to the rank of Lion. Cassius said he supposed Felix normally attended ceremonies but with the celebrants being masked, it was impossible to say for certain.

John well knew how Mithrans were at pains to respect each other's anonymity during religious ceremonies. They were there not as the individuals they were in everyday life but as warriors in the army of Mithra where all that counted was the rank which they had attained in service to him. John was a Runner of the Sun, the second-highest rank, while Felix, a Lion, was also high up the ladder of initiates, only two rungs below him. However, it would not be unusual to find a general, newly admitted to the Mithran ranks, as a lowly Soldier while a bricklayer might have risen to the exalted rank of Persian.

According to Cassius, this particular ceremony had been held the night before the morning Felix had failed to return home.

Where had he gone? John had assumed he had been on a drinking binge from which he was still recuperating. That would have been like Felix, unfortunately. But would he have gone straight to a tavern with Mithra's admonitions to lead a pure and austere life still fresh in his mind?

Was it possible that the reason Felix had not been seen in

Rome since the ceremony was because he had left the city via the catacombs?

John shivered. These rock passages were chilly.

The two men plunged into the maze. Soon the flickering light from their torches revealed a series of wall paintings repeated at intervals. Crudely rendered, should Christian mourners have chanced to see them, the pair of torchbearers depicted, one holding a torch up and the other down, would offer the comforting thought that the extinguished life of their loved ones would rekindle after death. To the initiated eye, however, they were immediately recognizable as Mithra's attendants, their Phrygian hats mirroring that worn by the god.

Cassius had said there were other Mithran catacombs. John did not reveal that he had entered through another one, near the Appian Way, similarly decorated with Mithraic symbols.

"Don't worry," Cassius said. "We are following the torchbearers. We can't get lost."

For what seemed like hours they turned right and left along a dizzying array of corridors, with others branching off them. Then they turned a corner and passed under an archway.

A long, low-ceilinged room opened out before them. A representation of Mithra in the act of slaying the sacred bull was painted on the wall of a recess at the far end. Benches facing each other across a narrow aisle completed the furnishings of the sacred space. It was familiar to John as a smaller version of every mithraeum in which he had worshiped, from Bretania to Constantinople.

As the men entered, they bowed their heads to an altar carved from the rock below the painting.

"As you have seen, this mithraeum is not easy to find, sir. We pass on its location to adepts who arrive with fresh troops, although there haven't been any of those lately and there aren't likely to be any more in the near future. Many Mithrans are entombed hereabouts, but we carve their resting places from the rock around us by our own sweat rather than engage fossors,"

Cassius explained, referring to those whose profession it was to cut out burial niches for the Christian dead.

John paced around, directing his torchlight into nooks and crannies. The ceiling had once been a magnificent blue studded with stars. Now sky and stars were mostly obscured behind clouds of soot. He sensed Cassius' gaze following him. He probably wondered why John had wished to come here. John wondered that himself. Partly it was because it was the last place he knew Felix had been. But something else had drawn him. An indefinable feeling.

Why couldn't he put his finger on it?

"Where does that passage lead, Cassius?" He had returned to the entrance to the mithraeum. He pointed out an opening in the wall of the tunnel by which they had entered.

"It goes further into the catacombs. There are a few more burials, then empty tunnels, some collapsed in spots and others ending abruptly, probably where work stopped after Mithrans could no longer conduct legal burials. But no one goes there. There's no reason to, sir."

John stepped into the darkness beyond the opening. "All the same, I'd like to explore a bit further."

The catacombs here looked no different than those he'd just been through.

Suddenly John lowered his torch and pointed down. "The dust has been disturbed."

The faint scuffs might have been footprints. What else could they be? But whether of a single person or more, it was impossible to be certain.

He followed the marks to an intersection where they turned to one side.

John cautioned Cassius and moved on more slowly.

He stepped on something, had to steady himself against the wall to avoid falling. He looked down into the face of a lion.

A Mithran ceremonial mask.

John's heart began racing.

A spear-throw away, a body huddled against the foot of the wall.

With difficulty John turned it over. It was as heavy and lifeless as a boulder.

His torch illuminated the familiar bushy beard.

"General Felix!" It was Cassius who uttered the words.

John swallowed the bile that rose in his throat, squeezed his eyes shut, and said a silent prayer to Mithra. Then he willed his hands to stop trembling and, while Cassius stood nearby, searched his friend's corpse. He did so quickly and efficiently, knowing he was going to vomit before long, his vision blurred by a red mist of fury. He found nothing but a few copper coins and a scrap of parchment bearing a scribbled list of names in Felix's pouch.

"We will need to move him into the city," Cassius said. "Once he's found there, the authorities will consider his death the result of a brawl or robbery, never knowing where he was really found."

"Yes, you're right." John could hear himself speaking far away, as if he were observing a dream. It was necessary to keep the existence of the mithraeum secret.

There was a knife embedded in Felix's chest. The silver hilt was elaborately worked. It appeared to be a ceremonial knife.

How many times in the course of their work together had John and Felix thought they were on the verge of a violent death? And yet each time death had seemed imminent, even unavoidable, they had escaped. Each had saved the other more than once.

But not this time.

John bent and yanked the knife from the body.

The engraved hilt seemed to burn his hand. The blade's edge glinted darkly, evil in the sparking torchlight. The hallway faded around him, Cassius vanished, and John felt he were standing alone with Felix, in a place beyond either death or life.

He ran his finger along the blade. His blood glistened, mingled with and gave life to Felix's blood.

"Old friend, I swear by Mithra the blade that took your life will take the life of your murderer."

Chapter Twelve

Wrinkling her nose, Clementia tossed the wool cloak on the floor. It was a military cloak, smelling of sheep. It shouldn't have been left here with her things.

She resumed spreading her wardrobe on the bed for inspection. The bed sat on silver feet shaped like the paws of a wild beast. The only other furnishings in the bedroom were a green marble lampstand supporting a statue of Eros from whose right hand descended a silver chain attached to a bronze lamp, while a plinth of matching marble displaying a sculptured head of the young god stood opposite a fresco of the Graces dancing in a flower-strewn clearing in a wood.

A rustling caught her attention. She looked out the window into the garden. There was movement at the far side of the thickly planted roses. Through the leaves she glimpsed a tanned arm. Someone was crouched behind the shoulder-high bushes.

A momentary pang of fear struck her. It's only one of the guards, she told herself.

The figure moved away stealthily without revealing itself.

Why would her guards be skulking around, trying to hide themselves from view? For that matter, how had they allowed a stranger into the inner garden?

She called out for them.

There was no immediate response. She scanned the garden

without spotting the intruder. But a tall trellis in one corner swayed.

Clementia moved away from the window to the doorway and shouted down the hall.

The only answer was a clatter of feet. From where? The roof!

"Guards! Guards!"

After an eternity a husky fellow came puffing down the hallway.

"Gainus. Where have you been? I could have walked to the forum and back since I first called you."

"My apologies. Three or four men attempted to enter the house. We only heard you after we stopped them."

"You didn't stop them all. One got into the garden."

"That's impossible!" Gainus' face clouded. "Wait! It may have been a feint designed to allow the ruffian you saw and others to get inside, ambush us from behind, cut your throat, and then loot the house."

Clementia paled. "These men you fought, where are they now?"

"Bleeding in their den. We ran them off without injury ourselves."

Clementia stared at Gainus incredulously. "Why didn't you kill them?"

He shrugged. "We foiled their scheme. Only one man got past us and he didn't cut your throat."

"No one should have got past! I don't need to pay anyone to give every beggar and brigand in Rome free access to my house!"

"Mistress, in all fairness, it's a very large house and the guards are few. Another left this morning to find greater compensation elsewhere."

"You are compensated well enough for failing to do the job I hired you to do, Gainus. Don't let this happen again."

Clementia dismissed him. She was furious. What business did he have trying to terrify her with stories about ruffians wanting to cut her throat? Was the whole incident nothing more than a ploy for higher pay? Had the guards really been fighting off would-be intruders or sitting around drinking wine in the atrium? She had heard no sounds suggesting a brawl, despite her window being open. Besides which, she would have expected any attack to be carried out during the night hours, not in broad daylight.

Nevertheless, the whole thing made her uneasy. Would her remaining guards have staged such an elaborate scene unless they were paid rather than just threatening to leave?

Was she no longer as safe here as she had foolishly assumed?

John sat on the cold floor of the catacomb, his back against a marble slab, and stared numbly at the sprawled body of his friend. Soon that body would be no more recognizable than the bones he supposed were moldering within the tomb behind him. Torchlight shivered over the corpse, lending it a spurious illusion of life. Didn't the broad chest rise and fall almost imperceptibly to draw breath? Didn't a finger twitch? Didn't Felix's lips briefly curve into a smile?

No. Nothing moved but the shadows.

Cassius had gone for help. John chose to wait here. He'd had some vague idea of spending a few final moments communing with Felix. He wanted to ask him what woman had got him into this? Or what ambitious scheme? What losing charioteer? What jug of wine?

But Felix was gone. John knew well enough that the man inhabited the body. The body was not the man. His friend's spirit was now ascending the ladder through the seven celestial spheres, unchained from the physical world.

John's own worldly journey was not yet over. He ran his fingers over the elaborately decorated knife hilt, imagining how it would jerk in his grasp as he drove the blade into the man who had murdered Felix.

He stared into the darkness beyond the torchlight as if the heavy air might retain some ghostly impression of the murderer. He had searched the area meticulously finding nothing but a confusion of footprints in the dust and a large amount of dried blood. More than he would have expected.

Cassius was taking a long time.

What did John know about the man?

Could he be trusted?

For all John knew, Cassius might have abandoned him here, or sent men to arrest him.

Finally he heard footsteps. He jumped to his feet, sword at the ready. Cassius arrived accompanied by two others, fellow Mithrans. They had brought a large piece of canvas. Wrapped in it, the corpse might be any sort of goods.

"We'll hide him until dark, then leave him on the street, raise an alarm, and disappear," Cassius said.

John nodded his assent. It would be an undignified end for a man who had served as captain of the emperor's excubitors.

Archdeacon Leon's hand trembled as he drew the knife nearer to his watery eyes. "How did you obtain this?"

"I found it," John replied, omitting to specify the exact location and why he had been there in the first place.

"Indeed? I shall be interested to hear more." Leon scrutinized the weapon.

"I have the impression it's old," John remarked. "Its decoration is suggestive of ritual use."

Leon laid the knife down. The two men were standing in the library at the Lateran Palace, where they had met before. Then, John had believed he was searching for clues to the whereabouts of a missing friend. Now his mission was much grimmer.

"You are correct, Lord Chamberlain," Leon replied. "It is a ceremonial knife of the type used to make offerings to the gods in pagan times. See, clearly this is Jupiter's thunderbolt engraved on the hilt, although overlaid with a deeply engraved cross. I am not an authority on those old gods, but given the juxtaposition, I believe this is a relic and fortuitous circumstances have conspired to see it returned to the possession of the faithful."

"You think it may be connected to a martyrdom?"

"Yes." Leon reached down and traced the cross on the hilt. "The apostle Bartholomew was flayed while still alive. It might have been used for a terrible death of that kind. Later, a Christian graced it with a cross." He fell silent, looking thoughtful.

John wondered if he were contemplating the scene of Bartholomew's death. It seemed strange it would be the first thing to come to the archdeacon's mind. Why not a simple stabbing or throat-cutting? Death by torture seemed to play a surprisingly large part in a religion that preached love and fellowship.

Leon might have read the meaning behind John's frown because he added, "When we think of martyrs, we remember how our Lord sacrificed His Son for us all. We draw great comfort from such thoughts in these times that test our faith. At any rate, this is surely a stolen relic. You will recall I mentioned to you not so long ago that many of our hidden treasures have not been found and I felt it possible those who assisted in their concealment returned to steal them. I am grateful to you for returning it."

Leon's fingers continued to trace the hilt as if seeing details his aged eyes could not. Was he more concerned with the religious significance of the knife or its value should it need to be sold to buy food for the faithful? What would the cleric think if he knew the blade had taken the life of a Mithran, the devotee of an officially proscribed religion, as the Christian martyrs had been?

John picked up the knife. "I shall return it in due course."

"But Lord Chamberlain—"

"My apologies. I have need of it for a while."

Chapter Thirteen

John examined the scrap of parchment he had found on Felix. It was well creased, suggesting he had carried it with him whenever he left his house. Thus, the note had been important. Dirty marks on the parchment showed it had been handled frequently.

He was seated on the edge of the bed Felix had slept in until a few days ago. He furrowed his brows again over the smeared list written in Felix's bold hand: *Sergius, Lucinius, Nilus, Optatus, Junius, Bassus.*

And *Diogenes.*

What could this collection of people represent? Had Felix been investigating a matter with no connection to his official business? Or had Diogenes not fully informed John about Felix's mission? In either case, were these persons of interest in whatever he was investigating? The presence of Diogenes' name was the most immediately intriguing. Was it possible the garrison commander was involved in some wrongdoing and the others were his associates?

Until he obtained more information, John decided, he would keep the existence of the parchment from Viteric, who would be sure to report to Diogenes. If Diogenes was involved in something unsavory, John might find himself under lock and key.

He folded the note and put it in the pouch at his belt, then went to the kitchen, hoping to find something to eat. He had no time for formal dining arrangements.

Julius was there, gnawing a chunk of bread, more like a feral animal than a child. He started when John appeared.

"Don't run off, Julius. Sit down on this stool. I want to talk to you."

The boy regarded John with undisguised suspicion but did as he was told.

John hunkered down beside him. "Are you getting along with Eutuchyus?"

Julius sneered.

John wasn't surprised. It was easy to see Eutuchyus resented the boy's presence.

"You would probably like to return to your parents. When the siege is over, I can help you find them."

"My parents are dead."

"Are you sure? How could you know that?"

"I know. They're dead." There was flat finality to his tone. They were dead as far as he was concerned was what he meant. John could understand that. When he'd run off from Plato's Academy to become a mercenary he had considered his former life and everyone in it dead.

"Your room is to your liking?"

"Better than sharing a leaky ruin with rats and smelly cats."

"But you spent a certain amount of time foraging in this house."

Julius did not reply. His gaze darted around as if looking for the best escape route.

"I only want to know what you saw here," John went on.

"I didn't see anything. It was always after dark. I only visited the kitchen and the storeroom."

"Did you ever see anyone?"

"No. Everyone was asleep."

"You didn't hear people talking?"

Julius shook his head.

"You lived next door. There must have been people coming and going, visitors?"

Before Julius could answer there was the clatter of running footsteps and Viteric burst into the kitchen.

"The Goths are attacking!"

• • ● ● •

John followed Viteric into the street, which was filled with civilians running for the city walls. They were armed with whatever they could lay hands on, including kitchen knives and axes.

John had ordered Julius to remain in the house but he knew very well the boy would find his way to the battle.

When they reached the top of the wall, the massive size of the Goth force was plain to see. Countless archers, foot soldiers, and cavalry, and in the front ranks, a vast array of scaling ladders alongside rams. More fearsome than all the rest, leading the way, were siege towers, immense wooden structures, taller than the wall, drawn by teams of oxen. They reminded John of mobile tenements but housed fighters and weaponry.

Viteric led him to Diogenes' command post. The general eyed John suspiciously. "Do you know anything about this assault?"

"Of course not."

"Can you use a sword well, Lord Chamberlain? I imagine at the emperor's court, treachery is wielded more often than steel."

"I have fought on many battlefields," John replied coldly.

Diogenes turned away. "Don't let him out of your sight, Viteric."

"Are you afraid I'm going to open the city gates, general?" John asked. "Or stab you in the back?"

"It may be you've stabbed me in the back already."

An armored man pushed his way through the confused crowd of civilians surrounding the post. "Sir, the Goths are advancing from the north also!"

Diogenes cursed. "There aren't enough men to cover the whole wall. Totila has more ladders than I have men. Spread these civilians out. They can deal with the ladders."

"What about the siege towers, sir? The catapults are in place."

"Hold off. Go and organize the rabble."

John heard orders shouted.

Monsters out of a nightmare, huge Cyclops menacing the city, the towers continued to advance behind their straining oxen.

Transfixed by the sight, John didn't see the soldier fall ten feet away. He only heard the scream. By the time he turned toward the sound, the man was on his back, an arrow protruding from his chest.

Another arrow hissed past John's ear.

Diogenes, hit, clamped a hand on the suddenly bloody sleeve of his tunic. "Their archers aren't in range yet. Where are these coming from?"

Viteric leaned out over the parapet looking right and left, oblivious to two more arrows that passed by without finding a target. "Over there. Under that pine tree!"

A lone archer had crept to within a stone's throw of the wall. He stood with his back to the tree and unleashed another shaft as John spotted him.

"Get down, general! He's targeted you!" cried Viteric.

"Ballista!" shouted Diogenes. "Eliminate the bastard!"

The men manning the ballista winched it, aimed, and loosed the huge bolt. It was a perfect shot. Traveling at tremendous speed the thick arrow caught the archer in the stomach, passed through his body, and pinned him to the tree trunk. He spasmed, shrieking, then was motionless, held upright by the shaft.

Diogenes' eyes might as well have been shooting bolts at John.

Surely the general didn't suspect John of giving away his position in some fashion? The archer could just as easily have been aiming at John.

Totila's army continued to advance, and for a time, the crowds on the battlements fell silent as they looked on, almost in awe. Finally, however, as the siege towers loomed larger and larger, there was a swell of mutterings and curses. What was Diogenes waiting for? Did he want the Goths to be clambering over the walls before loosing the first arrow?

The general flexed his injured arm, walked to the parapet, and readied his bow. "Men," he shouted, "watch what I do and then do the same."

He let an arrow fly. It struck one of the oxen hauling the siege towers in the neck. The beast bellowed and crumpled to the ground.

Instantly, a swarm of arrows enveloped the ox teams.

The thunder of their terror and death agonies filled the air. So must the roar of the Great Bull have reverberated through the cosmos when Mithra slew it.

The towers came to a halt.

Realizing what had happened, the Goths launched their assault, unleashing a storm of arrows at the defenders on the wall.

Keeping as much of his body hidden as possible, John peered down, intent on what was happening. A number of men were advancing, one arm hooked into long ladders and the other holding their shields over their heads. Rows of Goths marched behind them, flourishing their weapons and screaming insults and threats at the city defenders.

A ram moved toward a nearby gate. Incendiaries poured down on the wooden tortoise sheltering it and, as the roof caught fire and collapsed, the Goths who had been underneath fled, screaming, rolling on the ground, trying to put out their blazing clothes.

The Romans laid down an unceasing fire from bows, ballistae, and catapults, but by virtue of the enemy's overwhelming numbers, ladders soon reached the walls. Civilians dropped rocks on the climbing soldiers or pushed the ladders away. An old man wheezed and strained at one ladder until an arrow embedded itself in his neck. As he fell back, two children replaced him. His blood spurted over them. They seemed not to notice. Their expressions were fierce and fearless.

They were not old enough to respect death, John thought. He rushed to their side and helped push the ladder over. The children stared wide-eyed and laughed with delight as Goths crashed to the ground. It was all an exciting game.

One fighter calmly polished his blade on the sleeve of his tunic. His gaze went to the sword in John's hand. "Don't worry, sir. The archers won't be able to get them all. There will be some left for us, and soon."

As he spoke, a helmet appeared. Its owner clambered the rest of the way up the ladder, striking down a chubby man in a baker's apron who tried to fend him off with a broom. More Goths followed.

John charged toward them.

He wished Felix were at his side. This was what his friend had wanted—to see battle again, a sword in his hand, face-to-face with the enemy. Then again, had Felix been in charge, he wouldn't have waited on the walls as Diogenes had. He would have launched a preemptive sortie.

He saw Viteric step into the melee.

As John fended off a sword stroke, Viteric's blade flashed past his side, slicing into the assailant's arm.

John dodged a new attacker, ducked down, and brought his sword up under his opponent's chin. He felt the sickening momentary resistance of bone against steel then a hot rain of blood spattered his face.

He caught a glimpse of Viteric glancing at him, his expression indecipherable.

He had no time to think, only to react. The din was unbearable. The clashing of blades, shouts, curses, the screams and moans of the wounded and dying. The air smelled of blood and death and smoke.

John was stepping over bodies. It was becoming difficult to find safe footing.

His boot slipped and he went down. When he raised his head he was staring into the ashen face of a corpse.

Felix.

Chapter Fourteen

Dogs barking and the sounds of voices in the street had drawn Clementia out of the senator's house. She had clutched at the iron bars of the gate in the high brick wall and watched the noisy ragtag procession surging along the Via Sacra, every man, woman, and child brandishing a makeshift weapon.

So the Goths were storming the walls? Where were her guards?

"Gainus," she shouted. There was no answer.

Clementia called again. By now the crowd had passed and her voice echoed loudly across the empty graveled courtyard.

She ran back inside and searched up and down deserted hallways, finding only the ancient cook sitting in the kitchen, calmly presiding over her boiling pots. "All gone to the city walls. The evening meal will be ready for them, if they come back. I might be cooking for Goths, for all I know." She struggled off her stool and rattled a ladle around in the bubbling pots.

"But what will we do?" Clementia cried.

"Wait to see who shows up."

"How can you be so unconcerned?"

"I'm an old woman, mistress. What do I care who I cook for? Goths need to eat too."

Clementia retreated to the garden and huddled on a bench. The tumult from the walls could be heard clearly. It sounded not unlike the crowd noises which sometimes drifted from the Circus

Maximus or the Flavian Amphitheater. If the Goths fought their way into the city, the fate of a young woman found alone was not hard to imagine. Would she be safer if she took to the streets, looked for a hiding place?

Her guards could have at least warned her they were leaving. Perhaps they had no intention of returning even if the Goths were driven off. Maybe the army would find a way to pay them after this. Pay them better than Clementia could.

She got up and paced through the rosebushes. Her fear blinded her to both their beauty and the pain inflicted by their thorns.

Perhaps she should go to the walls. At least she would know what was happening, instead of having to wait while her heart raced faster and faster. Before long she'd be ready to race screaming into the street.

She could hear dogs howling all over the city. The noise from the walls rose and fell. Periodically there was a brief outburst from one direction or another. A melee? A breach in the wall? There was no way to interpret it all from the sheltered garden.

Staring up into the bright blue rectangle of sky overhead she saw wisps of smoke.

Something clattered on the tiles over the peristyle behind her. Alarmed, she whirled around, remembering the intruder who had exited over the roof.

A rooster peered down at her through beady, uncomprehending eyes.

She took a deep breath.

She'd been deserted. Her guards had run off. No one had come to her aid. Everyone in Rome who could be was at the walls. Who had that intruder been? What if he decided to take advantage of the situation and come back now?

General Diogenes pulled the sheet over Felix's face. "Well, Lord Chamberlain, whatever trouble Felix was in he's out of it now.

Which means that your mission is concluded, though I fear unsuccessfully."

The Goth assault had been repulsed, at least temporarily. The dead were being taken away, the wounded given attention.

"I wish to find out why he vanished."

"What's the point? In the end he died on the wall, as was his duty."

John concealed his chagrin. Diogenes must have known from even a cursory glance that Felix had died days before the battle. For some reason it suited him to pretend otherwise. An excuse to get rid of John? To prevent further investigation? Or was the general really that blind?

"Go home," Diogenes advised. "Like General Felix, you have fulfilled your duty."

"It might be dangerous to find my way through the Goth lines right now. Totila may regroup and renew the assault."

"Make your own decision. But with Felix dead, you can no longer claim any reason to be in Rome, official or otherwise. I will allow you to stay in Conon's house for the time being."

Diogenes walked away, passing by shrouded bodies lined up beneath the parapet. He paused and turned. "Don't worry, Lord Chamberlain, we shall see your friend has a proper Christian burial."

A burial proper according to the general's beliefs, rather than Felix's, John thought. Not that Diogenes knew that. No doubt the general was not unhappy to see the last of the emperor's envoy.

John clenched his fists. "Mithra!" The sun was hot. Sweat trickled down his cheek, stung. Putting a hand to his face he felt a long, shallow cut where a blade must have grazed him during the fight. He had come that close to death without realizing it. The blow could have killed him and he would have found himself following Felix up to the stars before he knew what had happened.

"Sir! I'm glad I found you!" It was Cassius. He stood looking at John across Felix's body.

John couldn't control his anger. "You bastard! I left his remains in your hands. What were you thinking of bringing him here?"

Cassius glanced around nervously. He didn't venture to cross to the other side of Felix's corpse. "We meant to drop him over the wall, sir."

"But it's obvious he was killed days ago!"

"Yes, but Diogenes won't be able to retrieve the dead from the base of the wall for quite a while, until he's certain the Goths won't return and by then—"

"You should have followed the original plan."

"We thought his being killed in battle would arouse less suspicion. But before we could do as we intended, my companions were struck down by arrows and then some Goths managed to get over the walls."

John felt his anger waning. Was Cassius right to have tried disposing the body amongst the battle dead or was John suddenly just too exhausted to maintain his anger?

"There's nothing to be done about it," John said. "Anyway, the general seems to want to think Felix was killed today. I'm going home to get some rest, in case the Goths return."

The streets were quiet. The crowds that earlier had poured in a great wave toward the walls trickled back as lone individuals and small groups, some bearing the wounded. The sky darkened as if it were about to release a cleansing rain over the scene of battle but it was merely spreading a pall. No rain fell.

John was greeted at his doorway by Eutuchyus, who informed him that the woman Clementia was waiting in the atrium and wished to see him on a matter of urgency. The steward spat out the word "woman" as if he'd bitten into an apple with a worm in it. John went down the entrance hall, feeling wearier than he had a moment earlier. He was in no mood for visitors.

To his surprise, Clementia was dressed in drab clothing and

wore neither cosmetics nor jewelry, a far cry from the elegant creature he'd met at the senator's mansion. A sack lay by her feet, its dark rough material a contrast to the brilliant colors of the floor mosaic depicting a cornucopia of fruit.

She must have seen the question in John's eyes. "I was afraid the Goths might breach the walls. I thought I would be safer, less conspicuous, dressed like this, if they found me in the street."

She burst into tears and clutched his arm. "I was hoping Felix had returned, sir. That beastly steward only said he wasn't here and tried to make me leave. I'm afraid someone is trying to kill me. Some ruffians tried to get into the house. One of them managed to reach the garden."

"And your guards?" John asked, leading her to a marble bench.

"They drove the men off, but as I told you, I cannot afford to pay them much longer. They will leave soon. If they return at all. They deserted me to defend the walls. I was left alone. I have jewelry to sell. Not much. I think the guards might have made off with some." She gestured at the sack "But there is not much demand for it now, given that anybody with money will buy food, so it will bring in very little."

She glanced down at the cornucopia on the floor. Bunches of grapes spilled from it, purple as the emperor's ink, strawberries whose scarlet outdid the feathers of a flamingo, and pears the delicate green of springtime grass. "A pity we cannot eat that fruit. In the old days my favorite fruit was cherries."

The overcast skies outside sent scanty light through the compluvium, leaving the atrium sunk in a murky, subterranean gloom. John felt almost sorry for the poor creature huddled on the bench, despite his suspicions she had been Felix's last in a long line of mistakes.

"You do not have the demeanor of a servant, Clementia. I noticed that when I visited you."

"I admit I put on airs, sir."

"You put on airs, but you wear them much too well. You are used to being a lady."

He couldn't help smiling at her discomfiture, but it was a kindly smile. She looked up at him and he saw the quick calculation going on behind the glistening eyes. Could she fool this tall stranger with the ascetic appearance?

"I must tell you that I am not the senator's servant," she finally said. "I am his daughter. I posed as a household worker to avoid being taken away by the Goths with the rest of my family. Totila ordered us all into exile or captivity. Our servants, now scattered to the winds, kept my secret. Loyalty of that kind is rare, sir."

"And you came here counting on Felix's loyalty to you?"

"I did. My intention was to ask him for his protection. Your steward told me he has not returned, I now ask I be allowed to stay until he does. Oh, sir, be kind to a woman in distress."

"Felix will not be returning. He is dead."

Clementia hid her face in her hands and wept.

Chapter Fifteen

The next day the Mithran Felix was of necessity given a Christian burial in a patch of ground behind the house he had occupied while in Rome.

To John it seemed a final indignity. He had at least convinced Archdeacon Leon to forgo full rites in favor of a brief blessing. The prelate had been horrified at the suggestion.

John explained that those who died on the battlefield were given brief rites, if any. "It is often the case that men who die at war are buried in mass graves with no rites at all if circumstances do not permit the usual observances. Today Rome is a battlefield."

"But think of his soul."

John did not tell Leon that that was exactly what he was doing, thinking of a soul that did not want to offend its god. "Besides, he is only being buried inside the city temporarily. Later, I will see his remains are returned to Constantinople and properly interred with the ceremonies due to him."

Leon reluctantly agreed. John had the impression he would have preferred to conduct a spectacular burial fit for a general, but that was out of the question anyway. In Constantinople John had witnessed funeral processions for great men involving more mourners than the entire current population of Rome.

Now it was noon and John stood with General Diogenes and Viteric at one side of the shallow grave, Leon in his vestments on the other. Arrayed behind the three men were such members of the garrison who could be spared, with the boy Julius and the rest of the household, including a pale and grim-faced Clementia, at the back. Most of the soldiers were Germans, there to honor Felix's Germanic roots as well as his service. An occasional sob from Eutuchyus sounded theatrical to John, while Clementia remained rigid and silent.

John, outwardly attentive to Leon's measured recital of a lengthy blessing, wordlessly asked Mithra to forgive this blasphemy.

Unmoved by Leon's words, he remembered the man he had known. A man who would have been scornful of the Christian platitudes sounding over his grave. Felix might as well have emerged from the womb sword in hand, and as a military man he had served the empire well. He had also been one of John's oldest and closest friends. A brief smile flickered over John's face when he recollected that practically the first act he had carried out after regaining his freedom was to knock Felix down for his insults during the time John was still enslaved. He also recalled Felix explaining that he had originally come to serve at the palace because he could hardly refuse the emperor's invitation and, besides, it had been a terrible spring in Thracia and he was tired of the mud.

Felix had helped John solve more than a few murders, but he would not be of assistance this time. At least not directly.

John couldn't help thinking the key to the murder lay in Felix's weaknesses. His military career had been affected by those weaknesses, chief among which were penchants for drinking and gambling. He was ambitious and had at last achieved his hope of being appointed a general instead of being what he had once described as a glorified doorkeeper. But he too often forgot the proverbial observation that wine and beautiful women were sweet poison and had engaged in numerous affairs, not least one with Empress Theodora's sister.

Remembering that particular entanglement called to mind the anonymous love letter to Felix. Had he again fallen in with an unsuitable and dangerous woman? The letter had been written by a woman of education, of social position, one of a passionate nature. His gaze moved to plump and pretty Clementia, a senator's daughter.

She had denied any romantic involvement with Felix. Then again, she had lied about being a senator's servant. One of her guards, Gainus, did not recall seeing Felix at Clementia's house, but a guard does not see everything. Besides, she could have easily visited Felix at his own residence. And Eutuchyus, if the steward could be believed, had told John that Clementia and Felix were having an affair.

It could be Felix's murder had nothing to do with Rome. His careless past might have caught up to him. Could Justinian have had Felix killed because of the dalliance with the deceased Theodora's sister? It was unlikely, but the thought reminded John of Justinian's long reach. The emperor's absolute rule over the lives and deaths of his subjects meant nobody, however distant from Constantinople, was safe from harm, including John himself. It would not be many days before Diogenes' messenger returned from Constantinople with the information that John had come to Rome against the emperor's order of exile. John's investigation was likely to end with his own death.

John realized his mind was wandering. The whole tangle seemed hopeless of solution. If he could only find one thread to pull and begin to unravel the mystery. Trying to find that thread in Felix or any other man was a difficult task. We are all larger and more complicated than the most tangled skein of wool, he thought, bringing back his full attention to the closing stages of Felix's committal.

When it was over, Leon fled almost immediately, offering John a few perfunctory words of consolation. The soldiers drifted away, as did the household, Eutuchyus snuffling loudly. Diogenes insincerely muttered the right phrases about being sorry at having lost a fine soldier.

"That's two generals who have died when living here," he went on. "I suppose people will take to calling this the House of the Two Generals."

Left alone, John knelt beside Felix's grave. The smell of earth filled his nostrils, not the rich loam of the countryside but the exhausted stony ground of a city more than a thousand years old. Earth that smelled more of death than life.

He repeated his long-ago oath to Felix to insure he had a proper Mithran funeral in due course. Meantime he would personally conduct a memorial service in the mithraeum that night. After a brief prayer that Felix had by now successfully navigated the seven-runged ladder to Mithra's bright realm, John rose from his knees.

Turning to go back inside he saw that Clementia had remained behind at a distance, standing like a statue, as if frozen by grief, and he vowed again to take revenge on Felix's murderer.

• • ● • •

On the way back to his command post Diogenes questioned Viteric about John.

"I don't trust the man. Did you notice that brief smile of his? It makes me very uneasy when one of the highest officials in the empire arrives, asks too many questions, and then smirks at a murdered general's funeral. More and more I believe he was sent here by Justinian to act as a spy."

"The Lord Chamberlain doesn't strike me as the sort of man who smirks, sir. And is it likely the emperor would send a spy? Justinian knows the intolerable situation you're dealing with, and so far you've prevented the Goths from overrunning the city again."

"What the emperor should send is more troops and money. Do you suppose the emperor suspects me of being overly ambitious?"

"There is no reason for him to think so, sir," Viteric replied.

"But what of it? Before Totila led the Goths they actually offered to make Belisarius king of Italy. He turned them down and still Justinian recalled him."

"Justinian is a cautious man."

"Yes, which is why I suspect the Lord Chamberlain is here to spy on me."

"But surely there is nothing for him to discover that would implicate you in any wrongdoing? All I know is that the Lord Chamberlain acquitted himself well during the Goths' offensive. His sword didn't go thirsty. I'd gladly have him at my side on the battlefield."

"What does that have to do with him being a spy? A spy will fight for his life like any other man."

The streets on the way to the Palantine Hill were emptier than usual, the populace recuperating from its efforts at the walls, resting in case the Goths should renew their attack. A mangy black dog slunk away as the two men approached.

"Well you might hide," Diogenes told it. "If the Goths dig themselves in for a lengthy siege, you'll soon find yourself in someone's pot."

Viteric shuddered.

Diogenes smiled at him. "You haven't been stationed in Rome long enough to taste dog?"

"No, sir."

"You're lucky. A few veterans have enjoyed other sieges here. Go hungry long enough and one wishes the agonizing pains in the belly were from a sword stroke because at least they would end sooner."

Viteric gulped before replying. "About the Lord Chamberlain, sir. As ordered, I try to remain close but he sometimes sends me away under various pretenses and I lose sight of him for a while."

"I'm not surprised. Do your best. You need only to consider his length of service at the imperial court to realize he would be difficult to outwit. A dangerous man. I hope events will not ultimately cause me to address the need to defend my command here as well as directing the defense of the city."

● ● ● ● ●

The dimly lit assembly in the mithraeum was a fever dream of grotesque visages now half-revealed by lamplight, now fading into obscurity as drafts shifted their flames back and forth.

Only a small group of Mithran worshipers had gathered on this night. Many were on extra guard duty in case the Goths should return during the hours of darkness. Even so, from where he stood in front of the altar, John could pick out initiates of three ranks by their parchment and linen ceremonial masks.

Here were Ravens wearing masks painted with feathers and equipped with jutting cruel beaks, and several Lions, faces hidden with magnificent creations faithfully reproducing the proud beast's face, complete with flat noses and rounded ears, haloed by dark manes. A lone Persian was immediately identifiable by his mask featuring wavy beard and hair and high fluted hat. Ceremonial masks and artifacts were stored in a niche from which John had retrieved the mask for his own rank, Runner of the Sun. The bright golden face was surmounted by short spikes representing sun rays.

It had been previously worn by a man who had died on the wall. Now John held the senior rank of those present, the highest of all, Father, being absent from the garrison.

John chose to keep the memorial service for Felix short. It was painful enough to lead opening prayers asking Mithra to be merciful to Felix, but a worse ordeal was now upon him.

Delivering a eulogy to his departed friend.

John's throat felt constricted, and unshed tears shone in the dark eyes looking out from the golden face. "My brothers, we are here to honor General Felix, a man from Germania who served the empire long and well. He attained the rank of Lion and displayed a lion's courage and strength. He fought on the battlefield and rose in the ranks, as all soldiers hope to do. He served as captain of excubitors, one of the highest offices in the empire. Yet what he most wanted was to return to the battlefield and so he sought and was granted a generalship."

His mask seemed to be suffocating him. He tried to control his voice. He blinked his burning eyes but the scene before him dissolved into a watery blur.

I am seeing what Felix saw at the last ceremony he attended, probably on the last night of his life, John thought.

On the low ceiling stars painted on a blue background were dimmed and obscured by a low-hanging fog of lamp smoke. Smoke and shadows roiled around the masked figures on the benches. Was Cassius there? Or even Viteric?

"As his friend and colleague, I will mourn him," John concluded, struggling to find the breath to continue. "As his fellow adept, I celebrate his new life in the presence of Mithra, a home we all strive to reach. May his memory be preserved."

Finally, he allowed himself to weep, silently, grateful that the tears running down his cheeks were hidden by the golden face he wore.

He led a final prayer and waited for the congregants to leave in ones and twos before removing his mask.

Relieved to be free of it, he breathed deeply of the smoky air and looked at the golden face in his hand. He had often felt, while wearing the mask of his rank, that he was becoming something other than himself. That he was actually, for a time, a Runner of the Sun. He had become the mask through which he looked. People became the masks they wore, didn't they?

When the last footsteps had vanished down the passage, John quenched the lamps. Before putting out the final one, he took a look around the chamber.

He saw a gleam on the floor beside and almost behind the altar.

Bending down to pick up the object, he frowned. He was sure he had searched the mithraeum thoroughly upon finding Felix's body nearby. But here lay a silver earring.

Chapter Sixteen

Clementia wandered around the house to which she had fled, peering into many rooms decorated only by spider webs. It didn't surprise her that a house temporarily lodging military men was not kept up as well as the one she had left. Away from the occupied rooms it might have been one of the many houses in the city whose inhabitants had been taken away, its deserted rooms left to gather dust and silence.

And spiders, she reminded herself with a shiver as she brushed away a sticky veil that had attached itself to her face. A scrap of web stuck to her hand. Its dangling architect pulled itself up toward her. She flung the spider away.

Clementia wondered whether she should return home. She'd panicked at the thought of being unguarded there, especially with the Goths at the walls. However, she had expected Felix to protect her. Now that he was dead, could this friend of his, the Lord Chamberlain, be counted on? Was he much like Felix? Still ambitious, despite holding high office? The tall, lean Greek intrigued her. Outwardly he was unlike Felix, controlled and self contained, whereas Felix had been a boisterous, brawling man. But even Felix hid his ambition from those who needed to be kept in the dark.

Had she been too honest with the Lord Chamberlain—with John?

Why had she blurted out her real identity? Because she feared that a man of such stature might not be willing to shelter a mere servant girl, she admitted to herself. At their interview he had struck her as a severe man. If she had been thinking calmly she would have kept her identity concealed. It was too late now, but she resolved to tell him nothing else for the time being.

She emerged into the garden and its deserted animal pens, sadly overgrown with weeds. How different from her own beautiful roses! As she tried to walk a half-obscured path, nettles stung her carelessly swinging hand. She retreated to the peristyle and sucked thoughtfully at itching red wheals swelling on her skin, remembering the previous night, crying for Felix in a strange bed.

Strange because John had taken Felix's room. She was given a room near the kitchen.

She had collapsed at the news of Felix's demise. She was shocked, yet not surprised. It had always been a looming possibility. She had sobbed for a long time, expecting she would eventually cry herself to sleep. In reality, her tears had dried long before sleep came and she lay in silence, planning what to do next.

Clementia was considering how to deal with her new protector John when a rotund man on spindly legs emerged from behind a shaggy, unpruned shrub and stopped abruptly.

"Oh, I beg your pardon. I thought no one was…well…that this was the way out…"

Clementia was poised to run. The man looked more comical than threatening but she remembered the intruder in her own garden. The intruder she had only glimpsed. One needed to be wary of stealthy, uninvited visitors, no matter what they looked like. "Who are you and what are you doing here?"

The man nervously touched the charioteer's helmet he wore. "I am Aurelius. And you must be Clementia."

"What makes you think so?"

"Everyone knows about the senator's servant who's taking care of his house while he's a guest of Totila."

Could it be so? Rome's population had been reduced to the size of a village and the inhabitants, intent on survival, had good reason to find out everything they could about all their neighbors, for who knew when such information would turn out to be useful? "How did you find me here?"

"I asked at the senator's house and the cook directed me here."

Clementia couldn't recall if she'd told the cook where she was going. "And Eutuchyus told you I was in the garden? You did speak to Eutuchyus?"

"Oh, yes, certainly."

Aurelius took two steps toward her.

Clementia tensed. For all she knew this might be the same man who had invaded her house. Before she could decide whether to run or cry for help, another figure came flying out the doorway behind her and flung itself at the unwelcome visitor.

Aurelius went down as his assailant, a thin youngster, beat him with a wooden stave. The charioteer's helmet fell off into a patch of weeds and the boy belabored him on his shiny, bald head.

"Please stop," wailed Aurelius. "I didn't come here to harm anyone!"

The boy relented, stepped back warily brandishing his weapon, allowing Aurelius to crawl around, retrieve his helmet, and sit up holding his head.

"I'm Julius," the boy informed him. "The master asked me to protect the household while he was away."

"And a fine job you've done," John said, stepping out onto the peristyle. "I came as soon as I heard the commotion but I might have been too late. I am familiar with our visitor, Julius. You may leave. You've carried out your duties well."

The boy went away grinning.

John was not grinning. "What are you doing here, Aurelius?"

"Exactly what I've already explained to you, Lord Chamberlain, looking for justice for my daughter."

"What connection does that have with Clementia?"

Clementia stared at Aurelius, trying to hide her chagrin. What kind of trouble was he going to cause? She wished she had ordered the boy to beat him to death.

Aurelius hemmed and hawed and finally said, "She knows Hunulf, sir, the soldier who brought our poor Veneria to ruin. He worked for this woman as a guard."

"Your wife told me you feared Veneria had been killed by a man with whom she was involved but claimed you didn't know his name."

Aurelius looked startled. "Did, I sir? Did I say that? I've been so distraught since Veneria was killed I hardly know what I'm saying. You can understand, I am sure. Besides, I've been investigating further and found out who he was and that he worked for this lady. And anyway I wanted to avenge my daughter's death personally so, well, I kept what I knew to myself."

"So you had a number of reasons for lying to me. Clementia, did a man named Hunulf work for you?"

"He did, Lord Chamberlain."

"What do know about him and Aurelius' daughter?"

"Nothing. I do not delve into the private affairs of my employees."

"But you might have heard talk among the servants?"

"No. I don't eavesdrop on them."

His gaze seemed to drill into her, searching out her secrets. It was a strange feeling. In Clementia's experience, men usually stopped short at the protective shell of her beauty. She noticed that his eyes were rimmed with red. If she didn't know better she might have guessed he had shed tears. "Lord Chamberlain, there are some things I need to retrieve from my house. Would you accompany me?

From a sun-warmed expanse of pavement they climbed an imposing staircase up to the temple of Venus and Roma and passing between a row of white columns, circumferences the height of a man, entered the interior where rows of porphyry columns flanked a nave. Enthroned in a semi-domed apse, the goddess Venus loomed over them, staring resolutely east. In an identical apse, on the other side of a dividing wall, and so invisible from this end of the structure, sat the goddess Roma.

"Do you know," said Clementia, "Roma is amor spelled backwards?"

John had to admit it had never occurred to him.

The ceremony for Felix still fresh in his memory, he had no desire to think about love and considered this visit to the temple an unwarranted detour.

They seemed to be alone, except for silver statues standing along the walls beyond the nave. However John noticed piles of ashes and burnt sticks, the remnants of fires. There was a faint odor of smoke in the air and a stronger odor reminiscent of a public lavatory. He realized that what he had taken for a pile of rags lying at the feet of Venus was actually a beggar, sleeping or dead.

Clementia gave no sign of noticing any of this. She was seeing the temple she had always known, a place of beauty, not a residence for derelicts. "I grew up across the street from this here," she was saying. "Every day I couldn't help but think of Rome and love. The two most important things in the world. I suppose it is why they haven't closed this temple like the others because the statues don't represent pagan goddesses anymore but rather the empire and love. Does that make sense?"

John thought her comments the philosophical musings of a romantic young girl. "I can't say. I'd have to question the emperors and civic authorities who left the temple open to venture an opinion." He was listening carefully. Did he hear whispering or was it just the breeze amid the columns?

"Do you have great temples like this in Constantinople?"

"Not pagan temples. The Great Church is much grander."

Here one was overwhelmed by the size and mass of the architecture, the marble, bronze, gold, and silver. Yet no weight of physical evidence could truly convince one of the presence of the Roman gods because no matter how towering their representations, they were still stone and metal. The immense interior of the Great Church, on the other hand, was filled with an unearthly light. The Christians experienced that light as the essence of their invisible god, whereas John was reminded of his sun god Mithra.

"I dream of visiting Constantinople," Clementia said. "I had hoped…well, Father said we might move there, but then the Goths arrived and they had other plans for us."

"When the war is won your family will be reunited and free to do as they wish."

"If they are still alive."

"Totila won't kill aristocratic hostages."

"You're certain?" John felt her hand on his arm and reflexively flinched. He liked people to keep their distance. "Felix told me you were a close adviser to Emperor Justinian. He said you saw him face-to-face, every day."

"As captain of the palace guard, Felix was also close to the emperor."

"Is it true Justinian's a demon? Did you ever encounter him at night, when it's said he has no face?"

"Those are nothing but nonsensical tales." John edged away but her hand remained fastened to the sleeve of his tunic.

"They say Theodora was very beautiful."

"Not so beautiful, really."

"Prettier than me?" Clementia gave him an unabashedly flirtatious smile.

Looking down at the plump, painted girl, John couldn't help but think of Cornelia, back at home in Greece, her slender, boyish figure browned by working in the sun. Not so much different from the young woman he had loved when he was not much more than a boy.

He could appreciate Clementia's charms, remembering how he felt when young and whole—a blinded man's nostalgia for the blue of a summer sky—but he was no longer susceptible in the way most men would be. That disability had helped him survive the marble jungle of Justinian's court where so many of its traps were disguised in silks and perfume. Yet he did not fault the women who traded on their sex nor the men, like Felix, who succumbed. How could a man who for so many years had lacked the common human weakness judge others? He had adhered without fail to the rigid military morality demanded by Mithra, but what credit was it to him who could not do otherwise? He regretted that he could never know what sort of man he would have been if he had had the choices free to others.

All he said to Clementia was, "I wouldn't say Theodora was prettier than you. At court they jested Justinian had raised the taxes in Egypt to pay for her cosmetics, clothes, and perfumes. But they jested in whispers."

"But she ruled the emperor and whatever men she chose! She didn't do that with cosmetics and silks only, did she?"

John was aware of the girl's perfume. Although he was no connoisseur of fragrances he could tell it was exotic and expensive. A puzzling choice to go with the rough clothes she had donned to flee to Felix. He did not like her clinging to him. It would do no good to tell her he considered himself married, nor would it discourage her to explain he was not interested in an attachment. She would simply decide she needed to try harder to convince him to do whatever it was she wished him to do.

If he told her he was maimed, incapable, then she'd retreat, but he couldn't bring himself to do it. He realized it was false pride. Everyone at the capital had referred to him behind his back as John the Eunuch, and certainly Diogenes and others in Rome knew his history. Clementia gazed up at him with an unsettling mixture of awe and fearlessness, a gladiator about to slay a lion. "Your mansion must have been wonderful."

"People said it was Spartan."

"But you had many servants."

"Two. And I set them free."

She pursed her reddened lips in thought. "So really you're just an old soldier, like Felix."

Her unexpected perspicacity struck him like a dagger.

She added. "You need a woman's touch."

John suggested they proceed to her house, swung around, and walked quickly back the way they'd come, giving her no choice but to follow.

Disconcerted by her obvious advances, already upset over Felix's ceremony, he had forgotten that this place was not unoccupied. He had let his guard down. It was Clementia's faint cry of fear that alerted him to the ragged figures emerging from behind the silver statues.

The men were armed with sharp sticks, broken boards, jagged pieces of masonry. One brandished a chisel. They surrounded John and Clementia and crept forward cautiously, eyes gleaming, like a pack of feral dogs. The man with the chisel was a step ahead of the others.

John put his hand on the sword he carried perpetually in this benighted city. A good weapon was the only advantage he had, aside from the fact that being slender and well dressed, he probably didn't look like a man who would fight.

Glancing at Clementia he saw she had a pathetic little jeweled dagger in her hand. It might have sufficed to peel a small apple. He put his free hand on her arm. "Don't try to fight. There are too many of them. Just run. I'll be right behind you."

Or so I hope, he added to himself.

The pack closed in. No words were spoken. John could hear harsh breathing. He could smell unwashed bodies.

He made a show of backing up and looking around in terror.

Then with a battlefield roar he flew straight at the chisel-wielding leader.

A single blow half-severed the startled man's neck. Blood spurted in an arc as the dying body staggered and fell. John kicked the corpse aside and slashed at the pack, knocking aside boards, crunching into bone. He forced an opening in the ranks.

"Run!" he shouted to Clementia.

She ran, slipped in blood and went sprawling.

A beggar lurched toward her, lifted up the stone he was carrying. She threw her little dagger at him. The hilt hit him on the nose. He stopped, blinked in surprise, and John split his skull open from behind.

John pulled Clementia to her feet. "Hurry, I'll delay them."

She stood frozen looking around. Then she bent over and retrieved her dagger. "I'm not letting them have this. It was my mother's."

John didn't have time to be incredulous. As she ran away he found himself confronting two more assailants.

He disposed of them automatically. He couldn't recall afterwards what kinds of blows he had struck or what wounds he had opened.

After that the pack had had enough. He could have turned his back and strolled out of Clementia's temple of love, but he ran anyway.

John suggested they return to his house but Clementia, clothes bloodied, insisted they complete their mission. Apparently, her silks and cosmetics concealed an iron will.

The senator's house was a short walk away. No guards met them, only the cook who fussed and fretted over Clementia's appearance. When Clementia explained she was moving out of the house, the cook said she would stay with her family for the time being. She would be happy to do so since she didn't feel safe with the guards gone.

"Those ingrates," Clementia complained. "I gave them work and they leave me on my own without so much as a warning."

"Every man with any military experience is staying at the wall in case Totila attacks again. They'll probably return when the danger has passed. If Totila takes the city, there won't be anything for them to guard."

Clementia only sighed. "I can't leave the family valuables in an unguarded house."

To John's surprise she went straight to the garden. At the end of a flagstone path, a thicket of rosebushes concealed a bench flanked by statues of Venus and Roma, miniatures of those in the temple.

Clementia pulled on Roma's hand, opening a door concealed in the statue's back. Behind the door was a box.

"These are special treasures which have always been in the family." Clementia popped open the lid of the box. It contained several religious items including a jeweled cross and a small golden reliquary in the shape of a church, though containing what, she did not reveal.

Apparently satisfied everything was in order, she handed the box to John. He wondered what else she might be hiding.

Only when he was alone that night did John allow himself to think about Felix. Beyond the bedroom window a red, flickering light had replaced darkness. From the distance came shouts and screams. A fire had broken out somewhere, John concluded. He leaned down and picked up a jug from the floor and shook it, then poured the remaining wine into his cup.

He was intoxicated, he admitted to himself. Yes, you are, the voice in his head told him. But tonight Felix is not here to help finish the wine or to sing one of those scurrilous marching songs he loved so much.

John sang a few lines of a particular favorite of Felix's, reciting certain feats of Eros which Theodora allegedly had performed with the cooperation of a number of young servants and mature fowl. Halfway through the second verse John stopped abruptly and threw his cup against the frescoed wall. It bounced off, leaving a bloody stain on the gates of Hades.

He felt foolish as well as angry. He wasn't the sort of man who sang ridiculous songs, except when he was drinking with his friend.

Who was now gone forever.

All lost comrades left gaps in a soldier's world. He had asked Mithra the unanswerable question: why Felix, who had so recently been awarded a generalship? Couldn't he at least have died fighting the Goths?

There came no answer, of course. The commander does not answer to his foot soldiers.

John recalled fighting next to Felix during the riots in Constantinople. The big bear of a man had seemed indomitable. In his memory Felix had held off a whole mob by himself, fending off swords, spears, clubs, axes. It was unimaginable he could have fallen to a single knife.

But the riots had been more than a decade before, difficult as it was to believe. He and John had been that much younger. When does a fighting man's experience no longer compensate for his slowing reflexes and senses? The arm commanded to move does so more slowly. The mind is instructed to remain alert but the ears no longer hear the stealthy footsteps approaching from behind.

It had not been a murderer who had caught up to Felix. It had been age.

And when would John fail to respond quickly enough, either physically or mentally?

He got off the bed unsteadily, retrieved the cup from a corner, and filled it again, ashamed of himself for doing so. Ashamed he wanted to drink himself into oblivion so he didn't have to see Felix's face.

After he had risen to be captain of the excubitors, Felix had been treated with the fear and respect due to the wealthy and powerful. John, too, as Lord Chamberlain, had been feared.

Yet he and Felix were only simple men thrust by fate into complicated lives.

Tears ran down John's face.

Chapter Seventeen

The golden spiked solar crown worn by the colossal bronze statue of the sun god flashed brightly in the morning light as John approached the Flavian Amphitheater. He lowered his eyes and blinked but greenish after-images still tracked across his vision. He was feeling the effects of too much drinking the night before. The intensity of the light made his head throb.

The god's image was breathtakingly tall. Twenty men standing on each other's shoulders would not have been able to look down upon it, yet the oval Amphitheater behind was higher still. Although it had been more than a century since the last of the gladiatorial contests for which it was famous, other events continued to be held there. Wild animal hunts, for example, and, this morning, public executions.

"Diogenes has ordered two of the night watch guards to be executed," Viteric said. "They were caught conspiring to let Goths into the city."

Viteric had not given the great bronze statue a glance. Craning one's neck to look up at it was the mark of a visiting chickpea from the countryside. In John's case it was more an act of veneration, given that to him Sol Invictus represented Mithra.

"The general decided to hold a public execution to improve morale after the attack," Viteric added as he and John passed under one of the many arches leading into the amphitheater.

"He's also managed to round up some Mithrans. As you hear, the decision is popular."

A wave of sound—howling, screaming, cursing—crested and rolled over them as they made their way to the imperial box. Bright sunlight poured down on gleaming walls adorned with niches sheltering statues of gods and emperors.

It looked to John as if the turnout was larger than that for the races. The crowd was concentrated at one end of the arena behind a fence overlooking a row of newly erected gallows.

Diogenes looked up as John and Viteric arrived. "Ah, Lord Chamberlain. Here as an official observer? The emperor will be happy to hear justice was done to these traitors." He gestured to a pair of prisoners held several paces away from the gallows. "And well deserved it is too after violating their oaths of service to commander and emperor."

"Viteric tells me that this—" John paused as he sought the right words, before continuing "—spectacle is intended to improve morale. I take it you mean in the garrison as well as among civilians?"

"But of course! To the garrison we demonstrate that military discipline will be upheld despite the dire circumstances in which we find ourselves, and to others we show not only that those who betray the empire will suffer the harshest consequences but also, and perhaps more importantly, that the defense of the city is safe in our hands."

In addition, John thought, an execution would serve to take the attention of those in the city from their wretched predicament.

"I have taken into account these men's previous service and only for that am I giving them the mercy of a quick death," Diogenes went on.

"Justice tempered with mercy," Viteric ventured.

"Of a kind," Diogenes agreed. "While we are waiting for the preparations to be completed, what brings you to visit me again, Lord Chamberlain?"

"If we could retire out of earshot…?" John responded, glancing at Viteric.

Diogenes instructed a visibly disgruntled Viteric to sit, while he led John to the back of the box. John asked if Diogenes thought Felix might, in addition to his official mission, have been investigating a conspiracy.

"Among my men? I think not. He would surely have mentioned it to me. I don't need such assistance in any event. Do you have any reason to think he might have been investigating a plot?"

John wasn't surprised Diogenes sounded apprehensive. The executions about to be carried out plainly showed that not everyone in the city remained loyal to Rome. "Information I recently discovered could equally apply to any group of people with a common interest, not necessarily a plot."

"Felix never said much about his mission or missions. Perhaps if he had been more forthcoming I could have assisted him to greater effect."

"Perhaps. Do you know a man called Optatus?"

"The name means nothing to me. Is he from a good family?"

"I don't know anything about him. I was wondering if you did."

John went through the rest of Felix's list, omitting Diogenes. The general professed ignorance of Bassus, Junius, Nilus, and Lucinius. Watching the man's shrewd aristocratic face carefully, John believed him.

"What about Sergius?"

"Ah, now that's familiar. He served under my command, I believe." He wrinkled his broad brow and stared towards the gallows where the executioner was testing the ropes. "I don't generally know the names of the individuals in the garrison, unless they come to my attention like those two miscreants out there. Wait, I have it! There was a Sergius killed on a sortie outside the walls several months back."

"Can you tell me anything about him?"

"Except that he was killed? No." A cloud of regret passed over his features. "Soon there will be too many dead for me to remember their names."

"Did Sergius die before or after Felix arrived?"

"I can't recall. It isn't an uncommon name. He probably isn't the man you're looking for in any event. Why do you want to know about these people? Where did you hear about them? I take it these are the people you mentioned who share a common interest."

"I can't say more. It may be nothing."

Diogenes might have pressed John on the matter but a deafening roar rose from the crowd and instead he hurried back to the front of the box as the two traitors were led towards the gallows.

As they mounted the steps to their doom, the vast arena fell eerily quiet. The condemned men maintained discipline to the end. There were no shouts of innocence, no pleas for mercy. Not that they could have been heard. Their final ordeal took place in a cacophony that must have shaken dust off the amphitheater's cornices. One moment they were living, thinking, feeling men, the next lifeless dangling corpses.

John wondered if the two had proceeded to the point of contacting the Goths and if so, how? By what ways had they left the embattled city and to how many others were those ways known? Or had they met spies within the city walls? Or were they in fact guilty of nothing, victims of a miscarriage of justice?

"So right has been upheld," said Diogenes. "And now righteousness will be. Pagans are as dangerous to the empire as traitors, don't you agree, Lord Chamberlain?"

● ● ● ● ●

Cassius looked around uneasily as the condemned Mithrans were brought out to the jeers of the crowd. He had been gathering information on Hunulf and had wanted to tell John what he had learned. Although it seemed useless to him, to the Lord Chamberlain it might mean something.

Was John attending Diogenes' deplorable spectacle?

He couldn't see from his vantage point. The sun was blinding, the crowds blurred into a howling mass, more like a storm raining hatred than a group of individual human beings.

He voiced a prayer to the sun.

Emperors now executed men for worshiping a deity to whom they had once created statues.

Would they execute a Lord Chamberlain if they discovered John's secret?

Cassius wondered if Hunulf had discovered he was seeking information on him.

Sweat ran burning into his eyes and he did his best to blink it away. It would not do for anyone to think he was crying.

There! Wasn't that John with Diogenes?

He was never certain because at that instant the trap door opened under his feet and the rope took his life.

Chapter Eighteen

"You don't need to escort me, Viteric. I can find my way to the wall." John and his companion exited the Flavian Amphitheater with the crowd. While the spectacle had left most spectators boisterous, John felt nauseated. Men he had seen die brutally on the battlefield would have begged for a quick hanging if given the chance. What made him uneasy was his certainty that Cassius had looked directly at him before the trap door dropped. John supposed he had been the last sight of more than one man whose life he had taken but he had not taken Cassius' life. Had Cassius blamed him with his final thoughts?

"I'm certain you can find the wall, sir," Viteric was saying. "You certainly fought well defending it."

"You sound surprised."

"Do I? Well, one does not expect a person such as yourself to be able to handle a sword so well."

"A person such as myself?"

"A courtier, sir. That is to say, a high official or a—"

"I see. You may go about your business."

"Diogenes has ordered me to inspect the walls, sir."

"Is that so? All of the walls or only whatever part I visit?"

Viteric fell silent.

On the ramparts there was no longer a sense of urgency. The more time passed the more unlikely it appeared that Totila would mount another offensive. Blood, broken weapons, and broken bodies had been cleared away. Weary guards did their best to relax at their posts.

The Goths had withdrawn out of sight. The wreckage of their siege engines remained, great piles of charred wood resembling burnt houses. A ram jutted up from the rubble like a giant's thigh bone. The warm wind carried the smell of ashes and the stench of dead horses and oxen and probably men whose remains had been inadvertently left behind to decay.

John went from soldier to soldier, inquiring about the people Felix had written down on his mysterious parchment. Did they know them? Were the men part of the garrison? No one knew anything. Would their memories have improved had they been questioned by someone other than a stranger accompanied by an armed guard?

Viteric must have noted their reticence. "They don't need to bite their tongues, sir. You were just fighting beside them."

"Telling them I'm a high official isn't going to loosen their tongues. It will just make them bite them until they bleed."

Viteric looked abashed.

"No, never heard of any of those fellows," declared a stout, red-faced fellow who took it upon himself to act as spokesman for a knot of visibly uncomfortable men busy repairing a ballista when John arrived.

John asked carefully about Cassius. It was awkward with Viteric at his shoulder. Had he recognized Cassius as one of those whose death on the gallows he had just witnessed?

No one had anything to say about Cassius either.

John turned away and continued along the wall. He was getting nowhere.

During normal times it would have been folly to expect to find anyone in Rome who knew some random person in the city. Now, however, with such a relatively small garrison and an even smaller civilian population, John felt it was worth the attempt.

Given enough time he could have covered the whole city quite thoroughly, but he didn't have time. He had, he calculated, about two more weeks until Diogenes' messenger returned from Constantinople with the information that would seal John's fate.

He noticed one of the men he had seen with Cassius at their first encounter, a short youngster with a furze of blond hair on his pointed chin. He was staring out across the countryside as John approached and when he turned and saw who was confronting him his face hardened and grew pale.

John asked about the people on his list. The young man grunted a curt no to each.

John mentioned seeing him with Cassius a few days ago.

The youngster stared at him as expressionless as the emperor's face on a coin.

"You know he was executed?"

The soldier said nothing.

"How did he come to be arrested?"

The man spit in front of John's boots.

"None of that!" growled Viteric. "This man is an emissary from the emperor. You will answer his questions or Diogenes will know about it!"

"Guards came and dragged him away in the middle of the night. That's all I know," the other responded sullenly.

"You don't know who alerted Diogenes?"

"No. Do you?"

John cursed Viteric's presence silently. Cassius' friend obviously suspected John and it was impossible to convince him otherwise with Viteric listening. Even this brief conversation might strike Viteric as suspicious. He couldn't risk starting to talk about Persians and Lions.

Frustrated, John continued on his way. If he could confirm the identity of anyone on his list he'd need to contrive to question them privately. For the moment he'd have to keep searching, Viteric or not. He didn't have time to waste.

A weathered and scarred fellow who looked stitched together from leather armor considered John's questions with a vacant look in his watery eyes. John expected a perfunctory shake of the head but the fellow surprised him.

"Junius? I fought next to a man called Junius in the last attack."

"Was he a friend of yours?"

"Never met him before."

"Had you ever seen him before?" John wanted to establish whether Junius might have been in the company of a burly German with a big beard, but this time the leathery ancient disappointed him.

"Never saw him until the Goth attack."

"But you're certain his name was Junius?"

"Only reason I know is I heard someone cry out 'Get Junius to the hospital' when he went down."

"So he was carried away to the hospital?"

"To the morgue more likely, with that arrow in his throat."

"Which one is Junius?" The old man with the parchment skin stretched taut over his skull looked out over the crowd of wounded lying on straw pallets covering the floor of the long room.

The big, broad-faced youngster at his side nervously consulted a wax tablet. "There, in the corner, if I'm not mistaken."

The refectory of an empty monastery had been turned into a hospital following the Goth onslaught. As the two men picked their way through the pallets, hands grasped feebly at their robes and voices cried out for aid. The air smelled of death.

"General Diogenes appreciates your agreeing to aid us, Martyrus," said the young man. "We badly need someone with medical skills."

"His Holiness was happy to release me from my duties to help tend to his flock, Decius. But I am an herbalist. It has been many years since I assisted at an infirmary and now with these hands…but I can advise you as you proceed."

Decius glanced around as if searching for an escape route. "I was taking instruction from the garrison's surgeon. He collapsed this morning. Been going without rest dealing with casualties. He insists this man Junius requires an immediate amputation. Life and death, he said."

"Do not fret yourself. Life and death are in the hands of the Lord. Is this the man?"

Decius bent closer to a man snoring loudly and unnaturally. "Yes."

"But he appears to have a neck wound."

"That isn't as bad as it looks. The wound in his leg is worse. The surgeon said it's already infected."

Martyrus undid the bloody dressing. "The leg is to be amputated below the knee?"

"That's right."

Attendants carried Junius into what had been the kitchen and laid him on the wooden table formerly used for chopping vegetables and meat. He moaned and thrashed around like a fish about to be gutted.

"He's waking," Martyrus muttered. "The leg should have been taken off while he was still senseless." A steaming pot and a length of iron sat on a brazier. He inspected the pot. The odor it emitted stung his nose. "The unguents I sent earlier are ready."

Attendants arranged themselves around the table, holding down Junius' arms and legs. His eyes opened. "Wha…wha…?" He made gurgling sounds and his injured neck started to bleed.

"Have you done this before?" Martyrus asked Decius.

"I…I watched…I'm not a medical man, you see. My task is to retrieve the wounded from the battlefield. The surgeon said that at least I know what every kind of wound looks like. As to healing them…"

Martyrus sloshed vinegar from an earthenware jug onto

Junius' bared leg. "To cleanse the wound," he explained. With a knobby finger he traced a ring slightly below the knee. "Cut here. Leave a flap of skin to fasten over the stump."

He tied a leather tourniquet further up the leg. Decius helped him tighten it, then hesitantly picked a scalpel up from a stool beside the table.

Junius struggled and bellowed inarticulately.

"You have an injury of the neck," Martyrus told him. "You cannot speak but as I pray you may accompany me silently."

His prayers were drowned out by Junius' strangled shouts. "Nnn…no…nnnn…" He threw his head back and forth on the table as the attendants struggled to keep him still.

Decius lowered his scalpel toward the quaking leg. His hand trembled more violently than the limb.

"Be quick," Martyrus snapped. "Speed is everything. The Lord will guide your hand."

Blood blossomed around the blade. Decius made a sweeping cut as he'd watched the physician do. He dropped the scalpel, took up a double-edged knife, and ripped apart sinews and muscles.

Junius howled.

Decius grabbed a saw and tried to find the bone in the red gushing ruins of the leg. Spurting blood covered his hands and the saw slipped from his grasp and clattered to the floor. He scrambled to retrieve it.

Junius screamed and screamed. Decius was crying as the fine-toothed blade bit into the bone.

An attendant turned his head away and vomited.

Junius' shrieks were inhuman, matching inhuman pain. He was already a lost soul consumed in the fires of hell.

The saw stuck fast. Decius yanked it free, lost his grip again, and the saw flew out of his hands and skittered across the floor.

Abruptly Junius stopped screaming.

In a panic, Decius jerked the leg upwards and in the sudden

silence the remaining bone cracked like a piece of dry kindling. Decius dropped the leg on the table and recoiled, sobbing. Blood gushed from the ragged stump.

"Ligatures!" shouted Martyrus. "Tie off the vessels!"

Decius stared at him blankly.

Martyrus pushed him aside and grabbing twine from the stool put a gnarled hand into the wound. Blood spattered his face. He blinked it out of his eyes. His hands were clumsy claws. Useless.

"Cauterize it with the hot iron!"

Martyrus wiped his face. The blood-spattered attendants turned away. They no longer needed to restrain Junius. He lay still.

As John approached the former monastery where Junius had been taken he became aware of an almost imperceptible sound, reminding him of the singing which filled the dome of the Great Church and floated out over Constantinople's crowded streets. He glanced toward Viteric but he showed no sign of hearing anything.

As they drew nearer the sound became a dirge and finally resolved itself into the groans, cries, imprecations, and prayers of men in agony.

A harried attendant directed the pair to what had been the former abbot's quarters. The surgeon in charge of the makeshift hospital lay propped up on a cot, addressing an old man spattered with blood. A young soldier sat on a stool against one wall, head lowered, weeping into crimson hands.

"These are Decius and Martyrus," the surgeon said, after John had introduced himself. "Martyrus is an associate of Basilio."

"Holy Father," Martyrus corrected him.

The surgeon ignored him to address John. "What do you want of me, sir?"

"I am seeking a man who might have important information. Junius."

"You are too late. Junius died while my visitors here were attending him."

"I killed him, may the Lord forgive me," sobbed Decius.

Viteric stared at the distraught youngster with unconcealed contempt.

John was speechless. He had allowed himself to hope he had at last found someone on Felix's list. A person who might shed light on Felix's death. "Were you able to have any words with him before he died?" he finally asked Martyrus, who shook his head.

"Nor did I," added the surgeon. "He was unconscious when he was brought in."

Had John missed a vital clue by not racing to the hospital immediately? He was wondering whether there was anything useful to be learned there when a hawk-nosed man appeared in the doorway.

Archdeacon Leon took a step towards Martyrus. "So, it is you, Martyrus. Treacherous blasphemer!" He looked around. "And the meddling Lord Chamberlain is also at hand, I see."

"Have you come to see me?" The surgeon spoke in a harsh whisper. His face had turned white.

Leon went to the cot and advanced his sharp nose to the surgeon's face. "Are you ill? You look as if you've got less blood than there is on the floor of the next room."

"He's exhausted," put in Decius who had gathered himself together. "I'm his assistant. If you need to know anything, ask me. Don't tax him."

"I've only come to inspect the sorry results of General Diogenes' intransigence. I assume you are here for the same reason and will be reporting them back to him, Lord Chamberlain?"

"I came here in search of a man who is now dead," John replied, going on to ask Leon about the names on Felix's list.

"A clergyman meets many people. I don't recall any of those. Will you be asking Diogenes if he is ready to make peace with Totila yet or does he prefer to see more carnage? I remind him

I remain willing to negotiate on his behalf. The Goths will pay attention to a man of God."

Martyrus coughed out a dry laugh. "Man of God? You're a tool of the devil!"

"You have outlived your good sense, Martyrus," Leon snapped. "You should have died before you decided to abandon the church. You will pay for your sins soon enough unless the Lord takes mercy on a foolish old man!"

"This foolish old man is a part of God!"

"According to your ridiculous heresy!"

"Ridiculous? We are told the Holy Spirit dwells within us but truly we are made of the Holy Spirit. As water freezes to ice when thrust into the cold, so the Spirit hardens to flesh when immersed in our physical world."

Now Leon laughed. "That fraud Basilio had plenty of time to meditate on the effects of cold when he was holding down the steps in front of the church he's now occupied. What you say is blasphemy! If true we would all be God, just as the Son is God."

"That is so."

"How can it be? Do you know what God knows? You've seen the maimed men in the next room, bloody, broken, do they look like the Lord to you?"

"Does water flow free when it is frozen? The Spirit is only released when death releases it from this cold world. When that happens the Spirit that is in each of us flows back to God, of which it is a part."

John excused himself. As he went out he noticed Leon had left a trail of red footprints behind him, marking his progress through the abattoir called a hospital.

Theological arguments often led to blood.

Chapter Nineteen

Compared to the stench of the hospital, the smell of dust and horses in the Circus Maximus was refreshing. Under a sky pock-marked with fluffy clouds blown along by a light breeze, two charioteers were practicing tight turns. A sparse crowd scattered around the seating observed them with much lively talk.

As John made his way into the stands, Viteric, exasperatingly, hung close to his shoulder. John wished he could shoo him away as he would a horsefly.

"Who are these people you keep inquiring about, Lord Chamberlain?"

"I was given to understand they were acquaintances of General Felix," John answered, without elaborating. "I intend to find out whether he might have known them from the racetrack. I can approach a stranger and strike up a conversation more easily if I'm alone, so if you'd take a seat, you can keep me in view. I know you have your orders."

Viteric didn't bother to deny it. Looking reluctant, he sat.

John asked onlookers who a newcomer might best consult about the state of racing in the city. A pair of well-dressed men who were discussing the merits of the drivers directed him to a fellow seated alone near the starting gates.

"You'd think he'd followed the races here since the Republic," one of them asserted. "There's nothing and no one he doesn't know."

"And he puts his knowledge to good use when it comes to wagering," added the other. "In fact, he's so lucky everyone calls him Felix."

The name was a common one, but still John found the coincidence disconcerting.

This particular Felix was a lean man whose battered face and missing teeth hinted that in his youth he had been quick with his fists and not very good with them. In fact he turned out to be jovial and friendly. Sitting down next to him, John asked which team he thought was the best.

"The Blues! The Greens will lose their followers a fair bit of money as usual." He pointed to a gray-haired man with a crooked back standing on the spina shouting instructions and upbraiding the practicing charioteers. "See him? Euprepes, that's his name. Used to be a charioteer but now he trains the Greens. He's a fool. Consider his name."

John expressed puzzlement.

"It's not his real name. One day, after he had lost a race by chance when his chariot was clipped by an inept rival, he swore he would change his name to one more pleasing to the gods It was a jest, you understand, made while he had taken too much wine. But when he was sober, he decided to actually do it and being a fool, chose a name which could not do anything but tempt Fate. A famous name in chariot-racing. One every follower of the sport knows as that of a man who won over seven hundred races."

"And did this bring him good fortune?"

"In truth it brought him the sort of fortune he might have expected had he thought further about it. You see, the original Euprepes was executed by Emperor Antoninus for supporting the wrong racing faction. Not very sporting of the emperor, was it? At any rate, the first time the charioteer raced under his new name he was thrown from his chariot, dragged by his horses, run over by his rival's chariot, and his body mangled."

John looked across the track again at the man his companion had pointed out.

"And it didn't end there. No, not at all! He was one of the favored at the time and there were many who had put their money on him. They were not happy. For a while after that few wagered on the Greens, in case his bad luck rubbed off on the entire team. The owners weren't happy either. There was even talk about curse tablets being involved. Racers are a superstitious crowd and the wonder of it is he would take such a name, but so he did and so he remains."

"You and Euprepes were among those who returned to Rome after Belisarius reclaimed the city?"

"That's right. It was a sorry day for the charioteers and their followers when Totila ordered everyone out of the city. You won't find tracks in towns and villages, and racing is what we live for. Many of us came back."

This garrulous fellow was the sort who loved to show off his knowledge. "What would you tell someone like me, new to the city, who might like to place a wager or two?" John asked. "Your name means lucky and I hear you are fortunate in wagering."

Felix laughed. "It's the name I earned, not the one I was given."

"Or gave to yourself, like poor Euprepes?"

"That's so. These days I live up to my name by concentrating on the Blues. As I told you, they are the best team. Forget the Greens. There's not much more to say. The state of racing here is not what it was. The charioteers are amateurs. None are reliable. And the horses aren't of the best. In fact, horses are harder and harder to come by. There are horse buyers here every day."

"The buyers are trying to make sure they have horses to race?"

"Race? No. That's the problem. They want the horses to eat, in case the Goths lay siege until the food supply is gone. They take them home and fatten them up, just in case. So we have a shortage of horses fit to run."

John winced at the idea of such beautiful animals, bred to

race, being served up on a plate instead. He turned the subject back to wagering. "But it is still possible to turn a profit?"

Felix gave him a crooked smile. "You are a businessman? Let me give you some advice, if you intend to wager seriously. A stranger should not allow debts to go unpaid for long. If you lose, paying the same day is the best policy. Some of the men you will deal with are not averse to breaking the odd limb if payment is delayed. Make certain you pay on time and after a while you may well be able to wager without money changing hands immediately. My father once told me that paying a small debt will obtain the payer a lot of credit."

"I sometimes wish I were an aristocrat or a high official. No one worries about lending to them, no matter how slow they are to pay them back."

"That is true. I happen to know several men who extended credit to a general because they thought he would be able to cover higher amounts than they would generally accept as a bet. He lost again and again and now they can't collect what they are owed."

"General Diogenes?"

"No, no. Diogenes settles his debts. I mean General Felix, the man with my name. I knew about all his transactions. Everyone kept telling me about him. They'd say 'he shares your name but not your good fortune.' I got sick of hearing about him. He kept assuring everyone that he would be able to pay soon. He was about to put his hands on some money. Isn't that what they all say?"

"Do you know who the general borrowed money from? How about Junius or Bassus?" John ran through the people Felix had written down.

His loquacious companion suddenly looked suspicious. "I don't know any people going by those names. Why do you ask? Where did you get them anyway?"

"They were given to me by a man I met outside the race track. He said for a few copper coins he'd sell me a list of people who could advance me money on good terms. Was I cheated?"

John's companion gave a gap-toothed grin of relief. "I am afraid you were, but then you did say you were new to Rome."

As he spoke to Felix and studied the man's expressions John was also automatically scanning the stands and race track. Because of this he noticed a movement on the spina and realized that a familiar face had vanished behind an obelisk. A face which had been turned in his direction.

Aurelius apparently did not want John to see him.

All the more reason to talk to him immediately, John decided as he rose and thanked Felix for his assistance. He couldn't bring himself to call the man by the name of his old friend.

When the practice was over and charioteers and workers came off the track, John was watching from near the starting gates. He followed Aurelius out into the street. There was enough of a crowd for him to keep out of his quarry's sight.

Shops and taverns had been built into the side of the stadium under its tiers of seats. Most were boarded up but several remained open. John paid no attention to a fellow who emerged from a shadowy corner offering to take a wager in advance of the next races.

Aurelius hurried into the first latrine he came to. After a long time—long enough that John feared he had taken another way out—he emerged, looking over his shoulder, as John ducked out of sight.

Just as pedestrians started to thin out, Aurelius disappeared through a doorway.

John went after him. He was enveloped in a miasma of cheap perfume and unwashed silks. Several women more or less masked by makeup lounged on worn couches.

A brothel.

"Mithra!" John cursed under his breath. The memory of Felix was following him like a phantom. First there was his friend's namesake and now this brothel, reminding John of Berta, the young prostitute Felix had unwisely planned to marry. That had never happened. Just as his affair with Theodora's sister had come to nothing. Perhaps a good woman from his own social level would have made Felix happy. Now there was no chance of that ever happening.

Aurelius spotted John just as an emaciated blonde, face whitened and lips reddened, laid a hand firmly on top of Aurelius' leather helmet. Caught between two pursuers, he opened his eyes wide in terror and started stuttering. "W...w...w...wait. You d...d..don't understand..."

"Oh, but I do understand, dearie," the blonde purred in the tones of a cat with catarrh. "It's your wife who don't understand."

"I wasn't aware you frequented brothels, Aurelius," John said, brazening his presence out.

"I...I don't." Aurelius grabbed at his helmet and dodged out from under the blonde's hand. "I am here to investigate."

Two of the women on the couches tittered and made rude suggestions as to what he might wish to investigate.

Aurelius threw back his shoulders and tried to look as dignified as was possible for a red-faced, rotund, spindle-legged, sweating man concealing his bald pate under a leather helmet. "I am looking into the murder of my daughter!"

"Murder?" The blonde drew back.

"Why come here?" John asked.

"To look for Hunulf. This is exactly the sort of wretched place I'd expect to find a dog like him!"

"You still think he killed your daughter?"

"I intend to find out."

"Look here," said the blonde. "We don't know any Hunulfs. We don't have anything to do with murder here. If you want to talk about murder do it outside."

Aurelius insisted on describing Hunulf, bringing forth only more vehement denials of knowledge from the woman. "And you, Lord Chamberlain, why are you following me?"

The mention of the title brought the women in the room to their feet. One who had probably been a raven-haired beauty when Theodoric was king of Italy suggested that such an important man could choose to indulge in more pleasurable activities than discussing murders with a common laborer.

John ignored her. "Aurelius, you claim not to indulge in this vice, but what about gambling?"

"Vice," cried raven-hair. "You call us indulgers in vice?"

"I never gamble," said Aurelius. "I've seen the sorry results."

"You work at the racetrack. You'd recognize gamblers, wouldn't you?" John went through his list yet again.

Aurelius insisted he wouldn't know a gambler if he tripped over one. By now he looked so disconcerted John suspected the man was ready to flee, and likely trip over his own feet in doing so.

The blonde stamped her foot. "Murder! Now gambling! If this is your business, gentlemen, take it elsewhere! This is an honest establishment."

An enormous man emerged from a back room. He took a threatening step in John's direction just as Viteric ran in from the street, sword drawn.

Viteric looked around and shook his head. "Lord Chamberlain, you are a difficult man to track."

Chapter Twenty

John came awake in the gray light of morning with the realization that he had already been in Rome for a week. His time for finding Felix's murderer was dwindling quickly. That was what made him anxious. He gave no thought to what might happen after he solved his friend's murder, how he would escape the emperor's wrath, or even if he could.

It must have been later than he guessed from the quality of the light. Eutuchyus was padding around serving breakfast to Viteric, who had invited himself into the dining room.

"Has Diogenes ordered you to take advantage of my hospitality now?"

Viteric chewed thoughtfully on a bit of hard-boiled egg. "The general is adamant that I should give you all possible assistance, and I know how impatient you are to be off and at work the moment you rise."

"Very considerate of you, Viteric."

When they finished their meal—frugal, suiting John's preference as well as the available food—Eutuchyus removed the dishes, silent as a cat. The diners sipped the last of their wine. John added more water than usual. Gloom obscured the weed-overgrown garden on which the dining room looked out. The air in the room felt uncomfortably close.

It was no better on the street. Dark clouds loomed over the city.

"We are going to Hadrian's mausoleum," John answered Viteric's question.

"You intend to question the soldiers about those mysterious names? Perhaps you will have better luck there than you had on the wall."

True, everyone so far questioned had been unable or unwilling to assist, but the presence of Diogenes on the list suggested a strong link with the garrison. It was possible the guards at the mausoleum had heard rumors concerning their general.

Viteric's presence complicated John's investigation. He wondered if he could devise some reason to talk to a soldier or two alone, out of his companion's earshot.

Hadrian's mausoleum, now a fortress, lay on the opposite bank of the Tiber, outside the city wall but connected to it by a bridge. A high, cylindrical tower set atop a base shaped like a cube, the mausoleum was famous as the site of a battle during a previous siege of Rome. The defenders stationed there were famed not only for their bravery but also their unusual weapons when heavily pressed—marble and bronze decorative statues of horses and men torn from their niches and thrown down on the besieging army.

As John and Viteric started across the bridge a chilly breeze announced the imminent arrival of a storm. Viteric glanced upwards apprehensively. "General Diogenes has suggested that Felix may have been killed by someone he was blackmailing."

"That's ridiculous!"

"It's a common motive for murder, sir."

"General Felix would never have engaged in blackmail!"

"He was deeply in debt and found it necessary to obtain funds by any means possible, or so General Diogenes has said. He was always out and about, looking for information, talking to people. Who knows what he might have found out that could have been of use? Besides, he had a high position at court and might have known things about certain current residents of Rome."

"Totila had all the aristocrats deported from the city," John pointed out. "Who is in residence here today who would have any connection to the court at Constantinople except for myself?"

Fat raindrops started pattering down. They felt cold as they hit John's head. His hair was thinner than it used to be. He had not considered Felix might be blackmailing anyone. As absurd as it seemed, Viteric was right. It was a good way for someone desperate for money to get himself killed. John couldn't ignore any possibilities. Perhaps he was getting too old to want to face such an unpleasant fact about a friend.

The pattering turned abruptly into the roar of a downpour, plastering their hair to their heads and soaking their clothing just as they arrived at the end of the bridge.

A grizzled soldier, a veteran of many campaigns, going by the scars on his face and arms, greeted them at the foot of a spiral ramp in the mausoleum's vestibule. "Lord Chamberlain, what brings you to this outpost?"

Unfortunately, John thought, his fame had spread quickly. He noticed the fellow was fighting to suppress a smile at the sodden discomfiture of the visitors.

John instructed Viteric to investigate if there was any wine on the premises since they both needed something to warm them up. As soon as he was out of earshot, John turned to the veteran, whose suppressed smile had turned to unconcealed surprise. "I realize it is highly unlikely wine will be found in a guard post," John told him, "but some conversations are not meant to be heard. I wish to consult you in strict confidence concerning a matter of importance."

The veteran said nothing but gave a brief nod.

"Excellent, a man with discretion. However, what I am seeking is the opposite: a man or men who talk too much, who pass around rumors and gossip."

"Indeed, sir? On what topic?"

"Have you heard anything whispered about Diogenes and let us say a lady friend?"

"No, sir, never, not a word. Such matters soon become common knowledge in a garrison. General Diogenes does not consort with the ladies. He observes the proprieties."

"I find that surprising. Generals do as they please, don't they?"

"Most, yes—the general from Constantinople, for example. We all knew about that. If I may say so, sir, I felt that while the arrangement was private, it also was not conducive to discipline, especially as my men are constantly warned not to get involved with women of the town. A general should set a good example in all ways!"

"General Felix was involved with a particular woman?"

"That is correct. I am making no accusations. I am only telling you what people other than myself have been saying."

"I understand. And what did these others say the name of the woman was?"

"Clementia. A glorified servant, no less!"

Viteric came clattering down the ramp as the veteran finished speaking. He shook rain from his cloak. "Not a drop in the place."

"As it should be, but sometimes is not." John turned away from his informant with a nod of thanks.

"So," Viteric said. "Did you find out what you wanted to know in my absence?"

John couldn't help smiling to himself. Viteric was an adversary but no fool.

They made their way to the top of the mausoleum where sentries stared forlornly into a rising fog as rain sluiced down over them. Most days it afforded a magnificent view of the ancient capital and its surroundings. Today the nearby Church of Saint Peter was nothing more than a ghostly image and the thick mist concealed the city. What remained of once-great Rome might as well have been swallowed up in the vastness of time as, indeed, was the ultimate fate of all cities and men.

John questioned the sentries, learning nothing. Either they were not aware of any rumors concerning Felix or were reluctant to speak out.

"You don't seem to have a large force here," John finally observed.

"No, sir," replied the man addressed. "Most of my colleagues are keeping dry, but there aren't many. We are here to keep an eye on the wall for infiltrators. There are stretches Belisarius did not have time to rebuild entirely. Individuals manage to come and go at will, but the Goths won't be able to hide the movement of an armed band past us."

"Even in this fog?"

"Within the hour this fog will be so dense, I doubt the Goths could even find the wall."

●●●●●

It was still pouring by the time John and Viteric left the fortress and crossed the bridge back into the city. Thunder rolled over the rooftops and an occasional blinding lightning flash forked across a dark sky. To Viteric's relief, John chose to duck into a tavern at the foot of the wall near the bridge.

Viteric took a sip of the wine they were served and grimaced. "This is vinegar, sir. The proprietor must not do business with anyone but men from the fortress. Off duty soldiers will drink anything."

"I have tasted worse."

The tavern resembled a rabbit hole scooped from the city's massive wall. Dim and dingy, it smelled of spilled wine and mold. The monotonous drip from a leak somewhere could be heard over the hiss of rain coming down outside the doorway. John and Viteric were the only customers.

Viteric had grown increasingly curious about the lean, tanned Greek across the table from him. Not in the way Diogenes was, however. "If you've tasted worse than this it must have been on a march," he ventured. "I've heard you were in the military?"

"I was a mercenary."

"I didn't believe it until I saw how you handled yourself when the Goths stormed the walls."

"Why didn't you believe it? Many men are soldiers during their youth."

"Well, but not a Lord Chamberlain," Viteric responded, feeling uncomfortable because that was not the entire explanation for his doubts.

John emptied his cup and filled it again from the jug on their table. "During my military career I developed a taste for cheap Egyptian wine. General Felix often joked about it." He spoke softly, more to himself than his companion.

"He was a good friend, wasn't he?"

"Does Diogenes want to know?"

"No, sir. I was just making an observation."

"You are very observant, Viteric. That is why Diogenes has you spying on me."

"Diogenes assigned me to assist you in your mission, since you're a stranger in the city. He does ask for reports on your progress but—"

"We both know you're spying on me."

"Well, sir, Diogenes sees plotters everywhere. He's read too much about Julius Caesar. He's convinced a conspirator is going to put a dagger into him someday. Of course, General Conon was murdered. So, yes, you could say he's instructed me to spy but I don't want you to think I enjoy the job."

"Don't you?"

Viteric scowled into his cup. "I did. At first."

"Until you saw I could use a sword?"

"I respect a man who can fight."

"And you couldn't respect a...Lord Chamberlain?"

Viteric stared into the rain beyond the doorway to avoid looking into John's eyes. "I'm a soldier, sir. I like simple and straightforward men. I have no use for high officials and aristocrats who resort to lies and cheating rather than steel. General Diogenes was wrong to pick me for this job. He'll regret his choice and make sure I regret it even more."

"He surely realized you weren't going to deceive me. It was obvious from the start what his orders were intended to achieve."

Viteric shrugged. "Soldiers follow orders or pay the consequences. I'm not expecting a promotion any time soon and I have a family to support. Two sons, sir, both fine boys. My wife's father was not happy when we married. As he said, soldiering is a bloody profession and we should not bring our families onto the battlefield with us."

"He was right. Thoughts of them will slow down your reflexes." John paused, gave a thin smile, and continued. "You'd better hope you're retired, living on your own plot of land and a military pension, enjoying your family, and having no further use for fast reflexes when you're my age."

Viteric's gaze wandered around the deserted tavern. "What were you doing at my age, sir?"

"Very often I was sitting in a pestilent tavern just like this one, drinking execrable wine."

"When you weren't in a tavern, I mean, what were you doing as a mercenary? I just thought I might learn something from your experience."

"Young people never learn from the experience of their elders. They only learn from their own experiences. You'll find out in time."

"If I have time, considering we are outnumbered and surrounded by Goths."

John's narrow features were an impenetrable mask but Viteric thought he glimpsed dark depths in the weary eyes. He took another sip of wine and let his thoughts roam back to his wife and children.

Chapter Twenty-one

The beggar Paulus stumbled through the frantic crowd pouring out of the Circus Maximus. He was as wet as Noah on the deck of the ark. The storm boomed and crashed around him. At the first rumblings people had feared the Goths were at the gates again. By now, he thought, most of the population must have convinced themselves the end of the world was at hand.

Seldom had he seen such a storm and he had seen many firsthand, from the unsheltered streets where he made his living.

If he'd had a coin for a cup of wine he would have taken refuge in a tavern but charity had been declining. The city's populace wasn't what it had been and most of those with coins to spare had departed and not returned. To make matters worse, beggars had flocked to the city to take advantage of the free housing offered by its countless empty buildings. The competition on the streets for largess was fierce.

Unfortunately, having claimed a spot near the race track, Paulus found himself far from his lodgings. A cold wind plastered his soaked clothes to his skin. He shuddered.

"There are waterspouts on the Tiber," someone shouted.

"No! There are strange beasts swimming up the river! Demons! The ocean floor has cracked open, all the way down to Hell!"

"It's the Lord's continuing vengeance on a sinful city!"

Paulus was crossing a forum. Everyone appeared to be running, but none seemed to be getting anywhere, because the forum wasn't emptying out. The pavement trembled beneath his feet. He had a vision of the city pulling itself up by its concrete roots and fleeing.

It had become as dark as night. In a flash of lightning he saw a monstrous bull charging at him, eyes blazing, flanks heaving. No, it was only the forum's bronze statue animated by intermittent lightning.

He must get out of the storm.

There was the Church of Saint Minias. He knew it well. Basilio's guards wouldn't let a beggar inside but there were outbuildings close behind it.

He came to a long shed, half brick, half timber, whose door hung off its hinges. It might have been a stable decades ago. Paulus went in and slumped down against a wall, thoroughly soaked and miserable.

From where he sat he could see the back of the church. Saint Minias, Basilio's church.

Basilio, who fancied himself the Holy Father.

Paulus gave a bitter laugh as the rumbling in his empty stomach momentarily distracted him from the thunder outside. To think not so long ago he had battled Basilio for the best place on the church steps.

Basilio had always been a cunning bastard. An Olympian amongst beggars. No matter how piteously Paulus moaned, no matter how pathetically and feebly he shook his cup, no matter that he invented odysseys of woe that would've made Homer proud—still, most people brushed past without a glance, only an occasional passerby flinging a coin distractedly in his direction.

It was the common lot of beggars.

But for Basilio aristocrats halted in their tracks, heeded his message, filled his cup with silver, or so it seemed to Paulus in his envious memory. Why, Basilio even managed to bring tears to the eyes of ladies in fine silks.

And that was before his humors became deranged and he

started spouting theology. Surely he was deranged, rambling on about everyone being the Lord. Paulus certainly didn't feel like the Lord. If he were, he'd be dining on roast duck with the emperor instead of crouching in a gutter gnawing off the edible parts of a half-rotted turnip.

And that was on a good day.

Then again, perhaps Basilio hadn't been mad because look at him now, ensconced in his own warm, dry church while Paulus sat in a shed with water running down the walls.

The awareness of running water made him jump up. He realized his shelter had begun to leak.

He paced around until he found a trapdoor in the floor. Steps led to a basement, much larger than the shed above. Faint light and quantities of water came in through cracks in the ceiling. He made his way through an archway and then along a corridor which suddenly plunged downwards.

He was freezing now. Though he was out of the wind, the air itself felt icy. He had passed through the last dim shaft of light some way back and had to feel his way along.

Eventually he came to a gap in a crumbling brick wall.

Paulus was curious. It was strange how curiosity could temporarily override the desire for food and shelter. He leaned his head into the gap and saw, at a distance, a bobbing light. A torch?

He stepped carefully through the gap and crept towards the light.

As his eyes adjusted he could tell he was in a narrow corridor. The hand he kept on the wall as he advanced felt rough stone. Drawing nearer to the light he could make out plaques bearing engraved names set into the wall.

So he was in the catacombs.

Paulus' heart leapt. He wasn't ready to shelter with the dead.

He pivoted to go back the way he'd come but his entryway was swallowed up in darkness.

Still, he could simply go straight back.

He hadn't turned a corner.

Had he?

The light ahead winked out.

A giant fist of darkness closed around him.

"Help me! Where are you? Don't leave me!" Paulus was shocked when he realized he was shouting aloud and not just in his own mind.

The light reappeared, most likely from around a corner, and floated closer.

Paulus backed away. He should never have drawn attention to himself. He should have just gone back the way he'd come. Who or what would be down here walking in the catacombs anyway? Even if it were just another beggar, Paulus was an elderly man with little chance of defending himself were it to become necessary.

He could discern a shapeless figure carrying a torch.

He couldn't decide whether to remain still and hope it went away or turn and flee.

The figure was hooded, and bent over. It moved forward unnaturally, like a shade. Paulus remembered voices in the street crying that the gates of Hell had opened.

And down here was closer to Hell.

Paulus tried to see the apparition's face but there was nothing within the hood but shadow.

The figure raised a hand and pointed at him.

Its voice was a faint, far off sigh. "Doom," it said. "Doom."

Rain sluiced down the multi-paned windows of the sacristy of the Church of Saint Minias. Thick walls muffled the booming thunder and the aged churchman felt safe and warm. How often had he fled the church steps in search of shelter at the onslaught of storms like this? In memory he could almost feel the cold rain soaking through his clothes straight into his bones and he could almost feel sorry for the wretched beggars who were now suffering the same misery.

Almost, because they had possessed the same chance to elevate themselves as he had, but they had failed by continuing to worship mammon, living for those bits of metal bearing the emperor's face. Out on the streets did they beseech passersby to give up sin and debauchery, to give their lives to the Lord? No, all they asked for was money. It was the work of the Devil.

The work of the Lord, as Basilio had learned, was more pleasurable and it paid better. It was true what Scripture said, that if you gave to Him, He would open Heaven and pour out blessings for you. And Basilio was sure that a dry church to live in and plenty of food and guards to keep him secure were only the beginning.

He was beginning to weave a comfortable sermon out of these rosy musings when there was a terrible pounding and his door burst open.

Several workers stampeded in, dirty and not very fragrant.

"What is this intrusion?" Basilio demanded.

One of them, a man with straggly long hair even dirtier than the rest, pushed to the front of the mob and raised his fist.

Basilio cowered away but the fellow brought his fist down into the palm of his other hand with a sound like a thunderclap. "We're done here, Your Holiness. We come for our pay. None of us is going into them catacombs again. The dead walk there."

"Let's not be hasty! Have you seen that hooded figure again?"

"That we have."

His companions muttered assent, shaking picks.

"I'm sure an extra coin in your next payments will allay your fears." Basilio had no hesitation offering more since he had no idea where their next allotment was coming from anyway.

"Not this time, Your Holiness."

"But you've seen this figure before, or at least thought you saw something," Basilio pointed out.

"What I saw was a shade, floating about. Silent. Escaped out of its tomb," said one man.

"A faceless demon," added another.

"It don't want us prying around down there," said the spokesman. "Just give us what we earned. We're not coming back!"

Lightning flickered, casting a lurid light into the room.

"Heaven hears your blasphemy," Basilio declared. "As if there could be demons anywhere near a church, let alone in a sacred burial place. And why would you fear this spirit in any case? Has it ever harmed you?"

"It hasn't hurt any of us before, your Holiness. But this time it tried to kill a man!"

"A beggar, Holiness. We found him shaking with terror. He said the demon came after him, shouting 'doom'. What else could it mean except it was trying to kill him?"

●●●●●

The downpour continued, turning streets into streams, and forums into lakes. Rain hissed against the pavement and gurgled in the gutters. John had a long wet walk home, warmed on the inside by wine, chilled on the outside. He ordered Viteric to return to the barracks.

On arriving home he expected Eutuchyus to be waiting with dry clothes but the steward was nowhere to be seen. Instead Clementia greeted him, red-cheeked and clothed in a thin tunica. "I've just had a hot bath. You should too. Get the cold of your bones."

"All I need are dry clothes. Where is Eutuchyus?"

"He went to the market before the storm. He's probably taken refuge from the rain somewhere so he doesn't melt." She giggled.

John went to his room and changed.

When he emerged he found Clementia had put cheese, bread, and wine on the dining room table. "I've brought something for us to eat since Maxima won't be able to cook until Eutuchyus gets back."

John sat and eyed the wine dubiously. The relative warmth of the house was making him sleepy. Should he drink more than he already had?

Clementia slid nearer, picked up a piece of cheese and moved it toward his mouth. He intercepted her hand, removed the fragment, and took a bite.

It occurred to him to mention the people on Felix's parchment. He'd been reciting the list all day, from memory. "Are any of them familiar?"

"The general in charge of the garrison here is Diogenes, of course. Aside from that, I have no idea."

"Possibly aristocrats who might have left the city?"

"None of them are familiar names."

He expected her to wonder why he was questioning her but she didn't seem curious. Instead, she squeezed next to him, her hip touching his. "I'm beginning to get chilly," she murmured, putting a hand on his shoulder.

"Was General Felix able to discover news of your family?"

"No, although he kept his promise and listened out for it. You could be my ears now, if you would only be so kind as he was."

John had no desire to replace Felix as her ears or in any other capacity. "Your father was a senator, a well-known man. I would not lose heart. Someone somewhere will know what has become of him."

Clementia made her lips into an exaggerated pout which John pretended not to notice. "If only Justinian had left Italy alone my father would still be serving in the senate. My family would be safe and comfortable. We weren't the only ones Justinian's war destroyed. It destroyed most of the Romans in Italy."

"I would argue the Goths had something to do with it," John said gently.

"When Theodoric was king of the Goths we all prospered. He respected the emperor and admired traditional Roman ways."

"Did he? Surely you weren't even alive when he ruled?"

"I remember his daughter, Queen Amalasuntha. She loved Roman traditions as much as her father did."

"And it was only after she was assassinated that Justinian invaded Rome to save the population," John pointed out, without bothering to outline the vastly complex political situation involved.

Clementia smiled wearily. "I'm certain there was more to it than that. Anyway, do you suppose the Goths are all barbarians? Surely they would not have chosen to dismantle civilization. But when the war started…well, what is war but savagery and destruction? And now look what fourteen years of war have left us."

From his vantage point in the dining room there wasn't much for John to see, aside from a drenched, overgrown garden or the ambitious young lady at his side turning a wistful gaze on him.

He decided to look at the garden.

Chapter Twenty-two

Four sturdy guards carried a litter bearing a corpse down the steps of the Church of Saint Minias behind Basilio's larger, canopied litter. Martyrus and several laborers costumed in clerical garments followed, chanting discordantly. The few who had attended the service just concluded—many of them the same few who attended the services Basilio held every morning—trailed behind.

The procession stopped a short distance from the church, in full view of those leaving Circus Maximus and anyone passing through the Forum of the Bull. The spectacle, if it could be called that, was designed to draw a crowd but the heavens were not cooperating. Chilly winds drove dark clouds across an angry sky and a cold drizzle saturated the air.

Undaunted, Basilio disembarked from his litter and commenced preaching. "We come here today to send a part of God back to Himself."

On cue, guards and laborers sang hymns with all their might, as if their wages depended on it, which they did.

"It saddens me—it saddens the Lord—to see how small our congregation has become," Basilio went on, his voice swallowed up in the windy emptiness of the forum. "And even the faithful have not given according to their means. Woe unto them, I say. Woe unto you who fear the Goths outside the gates but fail to take precautions against the Devil who lurks inside. For, as is said in the Bible, what good are watchmen in the towers when evil stalks the city streets?"

As Basilio continued, workers poured oil on the pile of kindling assembled earlier and when that was done emptied their jugs over the shrouded corpse they then set atop the pile.

Basilio knew that nothing got the attention of Romans more than a good fire.

Except perhaps a mob.

In fact, a small crowd had begun to gather, drawn by the oration, the odd procession, and the intriguing woodpile. And the more who gathered, the more were drawn to the gathering.

Encouraged, Basilio preached on, despite the steadily increasing rain. "Yes, verily I say, evil! Evil right here in Rome! See here a man struck down by demons, practically beneath the church itself. A church fallen into disrepair for lack of what, after all, is only Caesar's, a worldly thing, not to be valued nor hoarded. Woe to you who value gold more than good. Woe to you who spend more time in taverns than in church. If Saint Minias had been full of the faithful this poor wretch would still be alive. The foul fiend that did the deed would have heard the songs and prayers and fled in terror. And had the church been in a good state of repair what hole, what crack, what chink could Satan's minion have crawled in through?"

Basilio thought it would not be politic to mention demons prowling through a Christian burial place, so he left the catacombs out of it, a slight untruth in the service of God's greater good. As the crowd swelled he gave a lengthy, impassioned homily on Christian charity, particularly as it regarded charity towards the church. His unpaid workers supplied hearty amens.

Then a man near the back of the throng shouted, "You're a fraud! Why should we give money to you?"

"The real Holy Father is in Constantinople," someone else cried out.

"Blasphemer!"

"Anti-Christ!"

A ragged woman burst out from the front of the crowd and screamed in Basilio's face. "Where is the bread? My children are hungry!"

"Quick, quick," Basilio admonished his guards. "Get the pyre going!"

It was the smoke that brought John to the Forum of the Bull. Despite the drizzle, he had gone out to walk without any destination, merely to think. Viteric had not arrived at the house as early as usual, leaving him with the solitude he craved when he pondered difficult problems.

He walked up and down the puddled streets, passing by magnificent monuments, baths, and statues, seeing none of them. Why would Felix be carrying a list of people who were all unknown to any of his friends or anyone he dealt with? If they were that important to Felix, surely someone he knew should have recognized at least one.

Unless they were associates he dared not reveal to others, Goth sympathizers perhaps, or opponents of General Diogenes. But that was supposing everyone who had denied any knowledge to John had been truthful, which was almost certainly not the case.

The piercing cries of gulls made him look to the sky and he spotted a column of rising smoke.

He went in that direction. Before he reached the forum he could hear a roar like a storm-driven sea in which there could be discerned angry shouts and yells of pain.

The sound of a riot.

Arriving on the scene, John saw a mob surging this way and that between the Church of Saint Minias and the Circus Maximus. Flanked by guards, Basilio stood in front of a burning pyre, waving his arms, apparently imploring the crowd, his words lost in the rising level of noise. Men cursed and shook their fists, women clutching children to their breasts screamed and wept, babies wailed. On the edges of the tumult one or two bloodied bodies lay unheeded.

There was the sound of breaking glass as stones shattered church windows. Basilio's guards shuffled around uncertainly, as if they wanted to run, trying to prevent the crowd from pushing both them and Basilio into the flames.

The mob grew angrier. A boy attempted to climb through a broken window but was thrown back into the milling mass of enraged faces, disappearing from sight under their feet. A crimson-faced man danced around as if in a fit, finally fell down, and was ignored.

John stooped to help one of the injured who had fought her way from the swirling mass and fallen at his feet. He asked her what had caused the escalating unrest to break out.

Wiping her gaunt, bloody face she leaned on him, gasping, and managed to choke out "We heard rumors there was a funeral and bread would be given out afterwards. But there wasn't any."

"Ignore her," cawed an elderly woman at John's shoulder. "We were all enraged by the blasphemy. We're going to see that fraud burn in his own unholy fire!"

She was gone before John could respond. The younger woman burst into tears and clutched John's tunic. "Oh, sir, what shall I do? I'm hungry and I'm afraid of being killed."

"Order will be restored," John assured her, raising his voice to be heard above the hubbub.

A peal of thunder echoed overhead and raindrops spattered the rioters.

John drew the sword he had taken to keeping with him at all times and forced his way toward the pyre where Basilio and his guards cowered.

The heat was almost unbearable. Basilio was beating at a spark threatening to ignite his elaborate robes as John reached his side. The air was thick with the sickening smell of burning flesh.

"Are you going to stand here and be torn to pieces?" John shouted to the guards. "Get to the church. Use your weapons if you need to."

Shocked by this stranger's sudden appearance they began to move.

John pushed and at times half-carried Basilio through the raging crowd.

Basilio shrieked in anger. Cursed the mob, cursed John, cursed the guards, and even God, then he wept with terror.

A gnarled hand shot out of the melee and fastened itself to Basilio's arm. John whacked the hand away with the flat of his sword. A guard received a flying brick in the face and went down in a shower of blood. Before John could move to his aid someone retrieved the brick and brought it down on the man's skull.

John kicked aside the assailant and stepped over the guard's body.

Rain hissed down on the fire, dampening its flames as John dragged Basilio up the church steps.

Rioters grabbed flaming sticks from the fire and flung them at the church. Many fell short and landing in the crowd set fire to unfortunates who ran screaming or rolled on the ground.

Most of the laborers had fled in the confusion. The guards stumbled up the steps and into the church. As the crowd surged after them, John helped lean against the church door, forcing it shut.

Chapter Twenty-three

Basilio gulped wine from a cup held in shaking hands. The only coloration in his pallid face came from the blossoming bruise on his cheek, the result of a thrown rock. Rain streamed down the windows as thunder shook the church and lightning flared in malignant bursts of brilliance.

"Thank you for coming to my aid, Lord Chamberlain. Has the crowd dispersed?"

John indicated that it had.

"Consider the lesson this storm is teaching the faithful," Basilio said, "that heaven and man protect the church! Imagine that kind of behavior erupting at a funeral. Where is respect for the dead?"

John had no answer. He stared out into the rain. Basilio kept talking.

"Roman honor is dying. And without honor what are we Romans? A man who loses honor is truly destitute, be he wealthy or a pauper. Fighting and bloodshed disrupting such a solemn occasion…may the Lord forgive them." His eyes filled with tears. Genuine tears, John thought.

They were in the room where John had encountered Basilio polishing the silver chalice. The room where a frescoed Thanatos pointed out a painted window at a three-sided structure. The weather outside the painted window was sunny.

"Who was the man you cremated?"

Basilio peered uneasily over the rim of his upraised cup. "I might as well tell you since you'll find out soon enough. It was that rogue we talked about a few days ago, Hunulf."

"Are you certain?"

Basilio's eyes looked unfocused. Recovering from the shock of the riot, he had drunk too much. "Oh, yes. The body was in bad shape when it was found. He'd been dead for days, but I wouldn't mistake a man who was such a troublemaker when he worked for me."

"The body was found where?"

"In the catacombs. My workers discovered it."

"What are your men doing down there?"

"Trimming and refilling lamps and attending to various small tasks to keep the resting places in good order. Just because the dead are buried does not mean they are forgotten."

"Why did it fall to you to conduct the funeral, if you weren't on good terms with the man?" John put it as delicately as he could, but what he meant was who had authorized Hunulf to be cremated publicly by a man most Christians would consider a heretic and imposter?

"He had no family in the city," Basilio replied. "I felt an obligation to conduct his rites, given he had once worked for this church, although I am sorry to say we did not part on friendly terms and even sorrier he came to a truly terrible end."

John inquired in what way.

In the silence that followed the sound of rain thrumming at the windows filled the room. Basilio looked confused. "Didn't I just tell you, Lord Chamberlain? No, I suppose I didn't, in all the excitement. Hunulf was murdered. He had been badly wounded. Stabbed and bled to death. A trail of blood led my men to his body."

There was a certain dark irony in a murdered man being discovered hidden away among the tombs of thousands, and doubtless Basilio considered Hunulf's death sacrilege of the highest order, John thought. To an extent he could sympathize with that point of view.

Basilio gave a wan smile and continued. "My men talk of seeing a shade. Despite my pointing out on more than one occasion that the dead lie in peace and do not casually roam the corridors, such foolish whispers still occur. There has to be an explanation for these supposed sightings. A trick of the eyes, a flickering flame throwing unusual shadows, perhaps even too many cups of wine to fortify the courage before entering the realm of the dead. Not everyone is comfortable working in such proximity to the departed."

"You do not think Hunulf was murdered by a phantom?"

"I don't. My workers, on the other hand…" Basilio's voice trailed off and a look of terror passed over his face. "I saw them fleeing when the fighting broke out. What if they don't return? And my guards…where are they? What will I do?"

A handful of Basilio's guards remained, if only because the church had offered the nearest refuge from the mob. It wasn't difficult for John to find a man willing to talk for a coin or two.

"After that funeral, who's going to come to Saint Minias, let alone fill Basilio's—um, His Holiness'—coffers?"

The guard knew where Hunulf's body had been found. He led John across the cistern and through the catacomb entrance from which John had first emerged into Rome. "Basilio doesn't want us taking strangers into the catacombs, but I'll be needing to search for a new job soon anyway, and since you have been generous…"

He continued around several corners until he arrived at a spot where a dark stain covered the floor. In torchlight it presented a rusty color. Hunulf must have run out of strength here, stopped moving, and bled to death.

Stopped crawling, to be precise, John decided. There were no footprints but only a smeared trail of blood, leading back into darkness. "Where did he come from?"

The guard said he did not know.

"Didn't anybody follow the trail to where it began?"

"Not that I heard of. Not that I can blame them. Who knows who might be waiting at the end of it?"

John wondered if Basilio's men had killed Hunulf for being in the catacombs under the church. But if so, why would they have let him crawl away afterwards? "I'm going to follow this blood. Will you accompany me?"

The guard shook his head and turned away.

"I'll pay you."

"No, sir. It's not worth it. Death stalks these tunnels. From here you can see the last of the torches we keep lit. Follow them back." He indicated the faint glow at the end of the tunnel, then hurried off.

John was left alone. He took a torch and began to follow the trail of blood into the maze. Had Hunulf died before John entered Rome?

He heard the guard's footsteps fade until there was no sound but the ringing in his ears. He was surrounded by a profound silence.

He chided himself aloud for hesitating and commenced retracing Hunulf's route.

The trail ran along the floor, turning up and down corridors in a seemingly random pattern that might have made sense to a mind flickering on the verge of extinction. Judging from the amount of blood, Hunulf had been a dead man at the start of his last journey. Had he realized it, in the Stygian darkness, his wounds invisible? He would have felt his life flooding out of him. It must have been terrible indeed. This was perhaps a fitting place to be buried, but certainly no place to die.

The walls were filled with burial niches, most sealed by marble slabs or terra-cotta tiles with names engraved or carved into them. More than one lay open. The exposed bones had been indifferent to the doomed man struggling past. The dead had not turned vacant-eyed skulls to watch him dragging himself toward the destination they had long ago reached.

Here and there a crimson puddle had stained the floor. Places where Hunulf had paused to rest. How he must have wished to see the light one more time before darkness took him forever.

Suddenly the trail ended. Was this the spot where he had been killed?

Peering around, John realized that wasn't the case because he could see intermittent blood stains beyond. Hunulf must have fallen here after staggering this far.

Following became more difficult. In places bloody handprints on the wall marked where the dying man had steadied himself. He had leaned on the tomb of Gemella who was resting in peace and later on a crude depiction of the Good Shepherd.

John stopped.

He heard a mournful sighing.

No doubt it was just the wind finding its way in through a ventilation shaft. John did not believe in phantoms.

He wondered if he might come to believe in them if he spent enough time down here.

The splotches of blood on walls and floor became less frequent. Hunulf's wounds had bled more as he forced himself to keep moving. From the first, his clothing must have soaked up the flow.

Finally John was forced to bend down, holding the torch low, searching for scattered droplets he would never had noticed if he didn't know they were there to be found.

It appeared that Hunulf had been stabbed and immediately fled, bleeding more and more as he ran, then walked, and finally collapsed and crawled.

But who could have been lurking here, so deep inside the catacombs?

The hooded figure John had followed? But who, or what, was that?

Surely there was no possibility two men could have met by chance in the midst of such a maze.

John continued slowly. His torch illuminated the rough floor and the burial markers in the walls and threw his shadow up onto the low ceiling. He turned a corner and the light unexpectedly spilled out into a larger space.

He straightened and moved the torch around. There couldn't be any doubt. He had arrived, from a different direction, at the mithraeum Cassius had shown to him, not far from the place Felix had been killed.

He turned his attention back to the blood droplets. The trail petered out finally, but not until it had led him almost as far as where Felix's body had been lying. The conclusion seemed inescapable. Hunulf and Felix had both received fatal wounds at almost the same spot. Had they been killed at the same time after attending the same Mithraic ceremony? Or had Hunulf followed Felix's path and fallen into a trap? Had they both been ambushed?

John looked around warily, half afraid he might be the next victim.

There were no telltale sounds from the silent hallways.

He couldn't make sense of it. He could see why the guards and workers wanted to believe in murderous shades. That would be the simplest solution.

Chapter Twenty-four

John returned to his lodgings to find the kitchen occupied by four agitated people. Viteric paced back and forth while Eutuchyus oversaw a bubbling pot of stew. Julius played with a knife at the table. Clementia sat silent in a shadowy corner.

As John stepped through the doorway the others burst forth in a chorus of raised voices. Viteric's emphatic "Lord Chamberlain, I feared you had come to grief!" was loudest. "That boy has been thieving!" was Eutuchyus' contribution, while Julius contented himself by shouting "Liar. It was you!" and throwing the knife at his accuser. It clattered harmlessly to the floor near the brazier at which Eutuchyus stood. Whether Julius had actually intended to hit the steward was unclear.

Clementia sobbed. John passed a weary hand over his face and gestured for silence.

"One at a time," he ordered. "Viteric, as you see I am safe. What has been happening in my absence?"

"But you keep stirring so our meal isn't burnt," Julius ordered Eutuchyus and grinned at John.

"Well, sir," Viteric went on, "when I arrived Julius and Eutuchyus were yelling at each other in one of the bedrooms. I ordered them to be silent and asked your steward to explain."

Eutuchyus took the steaming pot from the brazier, set it aside, and confirmed what Viteric had said. "I happened to see an open door while about my duties, looked in, and caught Julius rummaging through Clementia's possessions. Naturally, I demanded to know what he was doing."

Julius' face turned scarlet with rage. "Liar! It was the other way around! You were in there poking about when I went by. You planned to steal something and blame it on me, didn't you?"

John held up a warning hand. "Continue, Viteric."

Viteric looked uncomfortable. "I ordered both of them into the kitchen so I could keep an eye on them until you returned."

"Does anyone know where the other servants are?"

"Gone, sir, except for the cook and she is so upset she refuses to leave her room." Eutuchyus gave a sniff of disdain. "They said they were afraid of being accused of theft and would not be returning. Their departure is a relief, if I may say so. It has been increasingly hard to feed extra mouths since Julius arrived and, begging your pardon, sir, with Viteric so often joining us for meals."

Clementia finally spoke, her voice cracking. "My beautiful reliquary was broken. The church dome was smashed." She glowered at Julius.

"You all suspect me," Julius shouted before anyone could respond to Clementia. "Yes, I stole food to stay alive. You would do the same if you'd been alone and starving. Some will kill to keep on breathing!" He stormed out.

Julius' expression was so murderous, John thanked Mithra that the boy had already rid himself of his knife.

John gave Viteric a questioning look.

"It seems obvious enough, sir. As the boy admitted, he's a thief."

John headed after Julius. Viteric followed him into the hall.

"Sir! I sense that you dislike Eutuchyus. Still, whose word can you trust? That of a mature servant or a thieving boy? Don't let your judgment be clouded."

John's reply was cold. "Thank you for your advice. Please return to the kitchen and ask Eutuchyus to serve the meal."

He found Julius perched on the broken wall of the half-demolished house next door and sat down beside him. The clear night sky was pocked with stars and in the darkness, out on the street, there was a sense of occasional movement as people passed by unseen.

After a while Julius spoke. "I'm a thief, Lord Chamberlain, but not a liar. My parents taught me to tell the truth." He choked on his words and his voice trailed off.

"Then tell me, on your oath, is what you said the truth?"

"It is. My father's highest compliment was to describe certain close friends as men who could be trusted in the dark. And I say there are people who should not be trusted in the dark—nor daylight either. I don't trust Eutuchyus. More than once I've heard someone shuffling past my room at night. I knew it wasn't you because you have a firm step. It wasn't those two servants who just left either. They always stayed in their rooms."

"How do you know that?"

"They barricaded themselves in. I discovered that because before I found the kitchen on my first visit I tried their doors and couldn't open them. What's more, they burst into prayer when I tried the latches. They're not the sort to go wandering about in the dark."

"You never looked out to see who was passing by your door at night?"

"No," Julius replied. "I was afraid of seeing General Conon's shade. Maybe that was what the servants feared."

John fell silent. Fear of phantoms hadn't kept Julius from stealing food from the house and he was not unaware that capable thieves could also have a talent for lying. It was a talent he had encountered frequently in Constantinople. An innate talent. He had spoken with beggars who were far more plausible than senators.

He felt a sudden rush of pity for the defiant youngster, liar or not. "It would be best if you stayed out of other people's bedrooms from now on, Julius. That way there can be no mis-understandings."

Julius laughed. "That's just the sort of advice my father would have given! And I suppose I should be careful about wandering dark streets and sneaking into houses. What does the emperor's Lord Chamberlain know about what it takes for a poor boy to survive?"

"More than you might imagine, Julius. I ran away from home too."

"How did you live then, without stealing? Did you find work?"

"I became a military man. I was a bit older than you. I wasn't always a Lord Chamberlain, Julius."

Julius looked at him thoughtfully. Maybe, John thought, he was reassessing him. Or maybe John only hoped he was. "In a year or two you will be old enough that the army won't turn you away, if you still want to join. But if you continue to break into houses you will end up a criminal, not a soldier."

Julius jumped down from the wall. "All this excitement has made me hungry. I'm off to try Eutuchyus' latest batch of stew. Let's hope he didn't poison it!"

As they crossed the rubble-strewn space between the two houses John pondered on the events of the past hour. Had Julius been unjustly accused? Or, as Viteric suggested, had his own dislike of Eutuchyus caused him to believe the boy rather than the eunuch?

Now there was another knot to untangle. Was Eutuchyus bartering stolen items for food? That would not only confirm Julius' truthfulness but also explain the steward's unlikely story about finding a pot of honey buried in the ruins of a bakery.

• ● ● ● •

Eutuchyus met the nameless man for the second time as the moon rose that night, shedding a cold light on what remained of a grove of trees. As with others in the city, they had long since been cut down for fuel and the low stumps left now served to display the offerings of those who daily gathered to sell wilted vegetables, expensive eggs, and the occasional scrawny chicken.

Coins had changed hands that morning, and now the steward had arrived to receive the item purchased. The man waiting was stooped and dark of beard, eyes, and skin, speaking with an accent not of Italy. How he came to be in the besieged city was a mystery. He had suddenly appeared in the market selling crusts of bread. On previous visits Eutuchyus had heard whispers about unusual services the man was rumored to provide, matters that would not stand the light of day nor investigation by civil authorities. No one knew where he lived or his name. He refused to give it since to have it meant the ability to exercise power over him.

The moon was balanced over nearby rooftops, giving sufficient light to examine the small sheet of lead he handed to Eutuchyus, who glanced at it and frowned "I do not understand this. What does it say?"

"It is written in the language of my country," came the reply. "We Egyptians are famous for our ability to work magic of great power and you won't find better unless you voyage there, which would be difficult in the current situation. I shall read it to you and then add the names you give me."

He paused for effect and then spoke. "It begins thus: 'Most powerful goddess, lioness-headed Sekhmet, blow your scorching breath on—here's where I left a space for the names…and curse them with every misfortune in this world and the next. Insure they are disowned by their family and their business ventures fail. Afflict them with wasting diseases, to become blind and feeble and reduced to begging in the streets. Cause their sons to emerge from the womb deaf and dumb, their daughters to enter shameful trades, and their loved ones to die terrible deaths. And further, oh Lords of the Dead, after those here named die in agony, when their hearts are weighed against the Feather of Truth on the Great Scales in the Hall of Judgment and there found wanting, order the Eater of Hearts Ammit not to devour those organs thus giving those named a second and final death. Instead cast their souls into dust and darkness to wander, enduring unspeakable torments for all eternity.'" He looked up. "Is that acceptable?"

Eutuchyus nodded. "Most satisfactory."

The other gave a pleased smile, disclosing several gaps in his teeth. He produced a stylus and poised it over the small scrap of lead. "The names?"

"Inscribe it with 'those who have caused me pain,'" came the reply.

The Egyptian looked up. "I have a keen eye, sir, and can guess just who you mean. I have created many curse tablets but never for a man in your sad condition. I do not blame you for seeking revenge on those who maimed you. Be assured this is my most effective curse. I provided the same to a client just a month or so ago. His father had already lived beyond the normal span of years and was in perfect health, expected to live for at least another decade. Now my client is in mourning and the richest man in the city. Yes, depend on it, this is certainly a most powerful curse!" As he spoke he wrote quickly, then rolled up the small tablet and handed the finger-sized artifact to Eutuchyus. "Now you must hide it underground. Drop it down a drain or a well or bury it. The choice is yours but I must stress it is vital for the curse to work, otherwise you've wasted your money."

Chapter Twenty-five

In the dusty gray light of dawn John sat on the bed and stared into his boot. The list was gone. The mysterious parchment he had found on Felix's body, the list whose safety he had insured by carrying it around with him during the day and concealing it in his footwear before retiring for the night, had vanished.

He reached into the boot but his fingers found only grit.

No. Wait. There it was, jammed up into the toe.

He was still fumbling inside the boot when Clementia came into the room. She wore a thin linen tunica suitable only for a lady's private chambers. A necklace glinted weakly in the tired light seeping through the dirty window.

"Lord Chamberlain, I was thinking about what Eutuchyus said and I realize I am an additional burden on the household." She took off the necklace and handed it to John. "I would like you to sell this and use the money to buy food or whatever else is needed. It's worth more than you will be able to obtain for it. A buyer shouldn't be hard to find, though."

John glanced at the necklace. Silver dolphins alternated with amethysts. "A striking design, Clementia. It would go well with a silver fibula and a matching ring made of silver and the same gem, don't you think?"

"I suppose it would. You take an interest in jewelry?"

"No, I found such a ring and fibula among Felix's possessions here. All three were made to be worn together. It's the sort of gift a man gives to a woman with whom he has more than a business relationship. You insisted you did not have a close relationship with Felix."

Clementia looked disconcerted. She sat down on the bed next to John who, himself, was clothed for sleep in a rough tunic. He did not care for her proximity. She put a tentative hand on his shoulder. "One likes to preserve one's privacy. Isn't that true, Lord Chamberlain?"

"True for some."

"I might as well admit it. Felix and I were lovers, yes, but it was certainly nothing to concern anyone else. I didn't know he bought this jewelry for me and wish he hadn't. It seems to be tempting Fate to wear representations of dolphins. After all, isn't it commonly said they take sailors to the afterlife? I never felt comfortable wearing the necklace."

John stood up and threw the necklace down on Felix's desk. "You have lied to me twice now, Clementia. You lied about being a servant rather then a senator's daughter. Think carefully before you answer the question I am about to ask you."

Clementia flushed with anger.

John took the crumpled scrap of parchment out of his boot and showed it to her. "What do you know about this?"

She stared at him. "What is it?"

"A list of names. People I asked you about, if you recall." John watched her demeanor closely. "You didn't seem very curious about the names when I questioned you and you don't look very surprised now. You do know what this list is."

Clementia gave sigh and slumped forward. Not really defeated, John thought, but feigning defeat as a prelude to some fresh subterfuge.

"Yes, I recognize that parchment. I have the contents memorized."

"The question is how and why did Felix come into possession

of this? Who are these people? What connection do they have with Felix?"

"Very well, Lord Chamberlain. I will tell you what I know, though I warn you I only know the half of it. My great-great grandfather was a senator who was instrumental in hiding a number of church treasures just before the Vandals sacked Rome. He passed on a list that he said would point the way to the location of the valuables. But they could only be found by following a specific path and this information was entrusted to someone else who did not know the names. So neither could find the cache without the other. The arrangement had to be kept secret, so secret the details were lost as time passed, as Rome was sacked again and the Goths took control of Italy. We keep searching and hope one day to locate the treasures."

"You say 'we keep searching.' You mean your family? Did your father search before Totila had him taken away or is this a new project you have undertaken?"

John saw from the way Clementia's face clouded that he'd guessed correctly. "And how does Felix fit into all this?" he asked.

"As a high-ranking official, he could go anywhere and ask anyone anything. Rather like yourself, Lord Chamberlain. After I told him the story he agreed to help me search."

"For the enrichment of the church or yourself?"

Clementia met his challenging gaze steadily and said nothing.

Two parts of the extraordinary tale were probably true at least, John thought. Eutuchyus had mentioned even in the worst weather Felix had spent much time out and about. And Leon had lamented that many hidden church possessions had never been recovered.

"Are you sure this is all you know, Clementia, or are you lying to me yet again?"

She leapt from the bed and took hold of John's arm, pressing herself against him. In the chilly room her breath felt hot in his ear. "Lies? How can you accuse me of lying? You, who lived at the imperial court. People like us, who move in the circles of the powerful, must speak discreetly."

John wondered if she had spoken discreetly to Felix. He gently disengaged his arm and stepped away.

"Your friend did everything he could to help me, Lord Chamberlain, because he loved me and I loved him. He would have wanted you to complete his task. And I am sure he would not have objected if you took his place."

"I do not wish to take Felix's place, Clementia. However, to the extent it will help me find his murderer, I will continue to pursue the puzzle of those hidden valuables."

"Thank you, Lord Chamberlain. I can tell you hold me in low regard. When you know me better you might change your mind, as Felix did."

Chapter Twenty-six

John wished to know Clementia better, although not in the manner she proposed. On his way to the Lateran Palace to speak to Leon he wondered what had caused Felix to change his mind about her, provided he had not, in reality, been attracted to her from the first.

Viteric had not arrived at the house early. Nor was John aware of Viteric following him. John had the impression that the young soldier obeying Diogenes' order to keep track of John was not carrying it out as diligently as before.

A guard informed him that Archdeacon Leon could be found in the basilica of the palace this morning. A thin, echoing noise resembling the sound of a small dispirited mob filled the nave. The noise stopped, replaced by the cheerful, melodious song of sparrows flitting through the shadows near the ceiling, occasionally swooping down between the rows of pillars into the light. Then the mournful sound started again.

"They're practicing and they need it," said a stooped fellow who emerged from a side aisle carrying an oil jug. "They used to sound like the angels in heaven. Now they sound like the angels thrown out of heaven, on their way down. Considering the riff raff there is left to choose from now, it's no wonder."

The singers resumed, massed voices rising into a long, sustained moan before petering out.

"I was told I could find Archdeacon Leon here."

"He was here with another man earlier. They have gone to the Holy Stairs. Do you want me to take you to him? I'm not done filling the lamps but my ears would welcome a rest."

His guide led John out of the church and through the palace. "In the old days it was a pleasure to hear them practicing while I worked. Back then they chose only those with fine voices. These days they are lucky if they can find enough voices of any sort. Now there are beggars who sing for coins in the street, actresses and whores, soldiers who sing on the march, and cooks who sing to their pots."

Remembering how his former servant Peter sang dolefully as he cooked, John winced, imagining the Great Church filled to the dome with the singing of dozens of Peters.

They came to a dim hallway. "You'll find him at the far end, sir. Now I must return to work and the infernal racket."

A pudgy, prematurely balding man John recognized as the man who had ushered him into the library where Leon was working on his first visit was staring intently down the stairs. He turned, startled, only when John was almost beside him. "Lord Chamberlain, why—?"

John brushed past him. He could see Leon, who had collapsed near the top of the stairway.

Matthew clutched John's shoulder. "Please, sir, the Holy Stairs may only be ascended on one's knees."

John stopped. Now he could see that the elderly churchman was actually on his knees, robes spread out around him on the steps. As John watched, Leon painfully pulled himself up another step, keeping his eyes down.

"This is the staircase which led to the praetorium of Pontius Pilate in Jerusalem," Matthew went on. "The very stairs on which Christ set his feet."

Leon continued to reenact Christ's fateful climb, wheezing audibly.

As a Mithran, John found it hard to appreciate the Christian desire for abasement and pain. Matthew regarded his suffering superior with reverent approval. John felt embarrassed and sorry for the man.

Finally Leon dragged himself up to the top of the stairs. Too weak to stand he let himself fall back against the nearest wall. Only then did he notice John. He made a feeble gesture of recognition, eyes shut, panting.

"Don't worry," Matthew said. "He will recover shortly. Before the Goths made it impossible, pilgrims used to fill these stairs every day, many of them old and ill, and never once did anyone fail to complete their journey or fare the worse for it. On these sacred stairs the believer is under the Lord's protection."

John was casting around for a comment that was both polite and noncommittal when Leon managed to speak. "Help me up, Matthew. I'm feeling much better."

Before long they were seated in the library where John and the archdeacon had first talked. Leon was still breathless and his eyes resembled half buried embers in his ashen face.

"I anticipated you would visit me again, Lord Chamberlain. How can I assist you this time?"

"I am here in connection with an ecclesiastical matter."

Leon smiled. "You are returning the relic you borrowed? The knife?"

"Not yet. It has not served its purpose. I am here to consult you on another matter concerning the church."

Leon drew his eyebrows together. "This would be…?"

"The preservation of sacred artifacts by concealing them. As you will recall, we spoke briefly of that during my first visit."

"Yes?" Leon sounded uncertain.

Matthew, standing nearby, leaned closer to Leon. "Perhaps you should not try to discuss church matters when you are so exhausted?"

Leon waved the suggestion away. "What is this about concealed artifacts?"

John recounted what Clementia had told him about the joint efforts of the church and senators to keep the church's wealth safe.

"Yes, yes, that is my understanding of the matter, as far as it goes. So those names you were asking me about when we met at the hospital were those on a list handed down in a senator's family?"

John feared for an instant that he had said too much.

Leon smiled wearily. "Don't worry. I was being honest when I said I didn't recognize the names, nor do I have any inkling what the list represents. In fact I do not know what clue it is the church is supposed to have. History is very large and cluttered. It is amazing how quickly things become lost in it. Through the years the church has searched for the lost caches but to no avail. It is perhaps for the best. It is safer to leave them where they are until the time comes when they will no longer have to be hidden."

"Perhaps you should leave now, Lord Chamberlain," put in Matthew. "You have your information."

Ignoring the interruption, John persisted. "And there is no indication where the lost artifacts could be?"

"None. Their location was never written down. The only thing that is said, and I believe it possible it's merely a legend that has grown up over the decades, is that their safekeeping was entrusted to the care of the dead."

As he left the palace John was turning everything Archdeacon Leon had told him over in his mind. He was only vaguely aware of the discordant chants still emanating from the church. As they faded behind him they might have been the faint raucous cries of crows. The harder he thought the faster he walked, a habitual, unconscious action exacerbated by the steep incline of the street leading down off the Caelian Hill. At a corner he almost collided with a curtained litter carried by four slaves.

He stopped and watched the litter and its bearers climb the

hill. Who could be left in this benighted, depopulated city grand enough to be borne in such fashion? And what did it signify to be carried in luxury through empty streets, past vacant buildings, all surrounded by an enemy which might at any hour sweep away what little remained of the city? People would live as they were accustomed to living until the very end.

Having stopped, John realized his calves ached and he was sweating. His swirling thoughts, interrupted, settled and as they did he saw clearly the most important thing Leon had said. That the safekeeping of the church treasures had been entrusted to the care of the dead.

The list Felix had carried with him had to do with the search. John had been searching for those people amongst the living. He should have been searching amongst the dead. And where in Rome were the dead but in the catacombs where Felix had been killed?

John turned and headed in the direction of the city wall.

Although Cassius was no longer alive to guide him, he remembered the way through the armory beneath the tower to the stairs under the grate in the floor. None of the soldiers he encountered challenged him. John looked authoritative and intent on important business. Once in the dark maze of corridors and armed with a torch, he followed the trail of Mithran torchbearers painted on the rough-hewn walls.

No one was at the mithraeum. John said a brief prayer before beginning his search. With only slight hesitation he found the corridor where Felix had been killed. There was little to differentiate it from all the other corridors, so narrow he could touch both walls when he spread his arms. The walls filled with burial niches, each sealed with marble or plaster. Yet this particular spot, where Felix's body had lain, John recalled down to the most insignificant detail and would never forget. The spidery crack in the rock near where Felix had fallen. The marble plaque that was slightly askew. The setting had been carved into his mind. He supposed he would see it in his dreams and hoped he wouldn't.

And why had Felix died here? Because he had attended a Mithran ceremony nearby? But why had he wandered away from the mithraeum afterwards?

To search for those on his list, John reasoned.

The church's treasures must have been sealed in tombs marked with the listed names.

Clementia must have known that and told Felix. But while pretending to explain the list fully, she had withheld that vital information from John until such time as he agreed to cooperate with her.

John began a systematic search. Some of the names were distinct, chiseled into marble in large letters. Others were mere scratches that had been made into wet plaster, or faded marks in red paint and even charcoal. He had to bring the torch so close that sparks cascaded down the wall and smoke obscured the inscriptions further.

The silence was broken only by the sputtering of the flame and the soft tread of his boots. He wondered if there was any other living thing down here. What about the hooded wanderer he had encountered? Or was the wanderer to be counted among the dead as the superstitious would have it?

The catacombs were a world apart from the living world above. There were no maps. They had grown in secret, for reasons other than a city grows. No emperors had decreed grand building projects. There were no streets designed for commerce, no great highways to distant places. The catacombs contained countless thousands of destinations, but each one was final.

John's torchlight caught a glint. The blade of a crescent-shaped knife pressed into the plaster, he saw looking more closely. The inscription next to it said: "Vincentus, who owned the finest shoe shop in the Forum."

Further on a marble slab declared: "Silvanus,who died a soldier, aged nineteen years, three months and twelve days."

How strange to see time marked with such precision. What were twelve days in the face of eternity?

John continued his search. Name after name appeared briefly in his torchlight and was noted. Perhaps for the first time in a century, perhaps for the last time ever.

None matched the ones on Felix's list.

After what seemed hours John blew on his hands to warm them. His fingertips and feet were numb with cold. He felt as if he had covered miles of corridors. If Felix had been on the way to the tombs of the people on his scrap of parchment, he would have had a long walk.

And if Felix had not been in the area where the hidden church property was concealed, but only attending the ceremony, what chance was there of John finding the right tombs in the midst of thousands? The dead beneath Rome far outnumbered the living above.

Reluctantly he started home.

Chapter Twenty-seven

John sat alone in his dining room as the setting sun's orange-gold glare darkened and slanted a red finger tracing a path across the mosaic floor. After those hours spent in the eternal darkness of the catacombs, the sun was a glorious and welcome sight.

The house was eerily quiet. As quiet as the catacombs. If John were superstitious he might easily have believed that as night advanced, Felix's shade would return to point out the path that led to his murderer. Since he was not superstitious he was left to find his own way through the growing shadows.

He filled his cup with red wine from the glass jug before him. He could almost imagine he was back in his study in Constantinople pondering a problem for Justinian while the windows' diamond panes darkened.

If Felix had been helping Clementia to find the church's artifacts was it because he hoped to restore them to the church? John liked to think so. Perhaps it had been part of Felix's attempt to placate Archdeacon Leon, to convince him to stop pressing for peace with Totila.

It was clear Clementia had ulterior motives. She had admitted she was running out of money to pay her guards. Did it matter to her whether she risked putting a blotch on the honor of her absent family? She didn't strike John as a person who cared about honor. It wouldn't buy much. In this world honor is a copper coin and dishonor is gold.

John knew that Felix would do almost anything to please his latest lover. But stealing valuable religious items? He didn't want to believe it. Clementia may well have lied to Felix about her intentions.

At any rate, if Felix had been searching in the catacombs near the mithraeum, he had apparently been searching in the wrong place. Had Hunulf been searching in the wrong place as well? Or had he been there simply because he had attended a ceremony? Clementia's guard Gainus had told John that Hunulf was a Mithran.

Gainus had also hinted that Hunulf had been involved with Clementia. Had she lured him into her hunt, as she had Felix?

The wine John was drinking was of better quality than the raw Egyptian sort he'd favored in Constantinople. Rather than sharpening his senses it dulled them. He also missed his study's wall mosaic, the bucolic scene inhabited by a mosaic girl he had called Zoe. He had carried on innumerable monologues with her. She could have explained the solutions to all the mysteries he had solved, but she was gone now too, like so much of his past, her mosaic a victim of vandals even before John had been forced into exile.

Had he stayed in Constantinople he might have had the mosaic restored, as Basilio was having his church restored. Or so he claimed.

Why had Basilio's workmen found Hunulf's body deep in the catacombs? Would Basilio really want to repair an area of the catacombs so distant from his church? Were they too searching, as well as tending to burial niches? The long lost ecclesiastical artifacts would certainly assist Basilio's efforts to legitimatize his position.

The Church of Saint Minias seemed almost as prominent in the mystery as the catacombs. Hunulf had once worked for Basilio. Then there was Veneria, who had worked at the church before running off with Hunulf, according to Basilio. When found dead she had been wearing expensive jewelry. How had she obtained it? Whatever the explanation, two people involved with the same church were now dead.

Had both of them been searching for the trove? For themselves? For each other? For Basilio?

The personal interconnections were as complex as those of the catacombs. And, John reminded himself, the catacombs were so large and complicated he had already reached the mithraeum by two different routes. Who could say how many routes there were to a possible solution, only one of which could be correct?

Why had Hunulf's trail of blood led John almost to the spot where Felix's body had been found? Had Hunulf murdered Felix after having been mortally wounded by his victim? Why would he have used a ceremonial knife?

Perhaps neither of them had killed the other, but if not, who was responsible?

It certainly opened up another avenue of investigation. As if any others were needed.

Dusk had passed into night and a hanging lamp provided only dim illumination. Who else might have a particular need for the wealth represented by ecclesiastical artifacts?

Vitiges had told him General Diogenes had been hoping Felix would bring funds from the emperor to help pay the garrison, thus stemming the number of desertions. This being so, Diogenes would surely be interested in obtaining money from any source. On the other hand, it would be nigh impossible for Diogenes to find a buyer in secret, even assuming he had somehow located the lost items in the first place. In John's view this alone would have made him the most unlikely suspect, yet the most unlikely people had been found to be culprits in other matters John had investigated, so Diogenes could not be struck entirely from further consideration.

He went to pour another cup of wine and found the jug empty. His mind also felt empty. John was not apt to drink much except, sometimes, when he was thinking too hard.

He reached down and opened the pouch at his belt, sorted through the coins there, and pulled out an irregular bit of glass with a bit of dried plaster stuck to its back. It was a tessera, a piece from a mosaic picked up from what was left on the floor of his study in Constantinople after the unknown intruder or intruders had done their damage. In the mosaic scene it might have served as part of a rock beside a stream, or the spoke of a cart, the shadow under a pine or a cow's hoof. John liked to think it came from one of the mosaic girl's dark and knowing eyes.

"Well, Zoe," John said, "I appear to be lost in the catacombs. Perhaps I should begin Felix's journey from a new starting point."

He would attempt to find out more about Felix's time in this house and then work out from there in ever-widening circles.

"Master, your meal." Maxima, the cook, carried a serving tray into the room. "I regret it is fish again. The price of meat has gone up to the sky since the Goths surrounded the city. Eutuchyus ordered me to spend frugally."

John noticed her gaze had moved to the piece of glass in his open palm. He closed his fist around it. "Quite right. It looks delicious. Which market do you visit?"

"Master, meat is scarce everywhere in the city."

"I wasn't thinking about that, Maxima. I just wondered which you patronized."

Maxima looked confused. Probably because in her experience the master of a house did not concern himself with such trivial details. "I go to the market on the Esquiline Hill."

"Is it a long walk?"

"No. I go up Sandalarius to Subara, which takes you to the gate in the old city wall. The market's right there."

"Has the market been there long?"

"Forever." She hesitated before continuing. "I am certain a man like yourself would get a better price."

"Don't worry, Maxima. I am content with fish."

He dismissed her. He could tell she didn't believe he could be a man of simple tastes, although it was the truth.

• ● •

John could not put the catacombs out of his mind. Though he knew it was his imagination, his clothing felt as if it had soaked up the chill of death. The air in the house was hot and stuffy but John shivered. No matter how many times he brushed at his tunic, dust came off it.

The dust of bones ground to powder by eternity.

He went to the bath, a plain, marble walled chamber with a rectangular basin and a changing room. Since Belisarius had repaired the aqueducts there was ample water. For some reason Totila had not bothered to interfere with the water supply again. Not yet at least. Possibly he thought it unnecessary given his army's overwhelming advantages.

John gratefully stripped off his clothing and left it heaped on a bench. He had descended the steps of the bath until the water came to his knees when he was aware of movement behind him. He turned and saw Clementia coming in his direction, naked as a marble statue of Venus.

Quickly he stepped down into the water, looking away as he did so. His face burned with anger rather than embarrassment.

He heard her coming down the steps and riling the water. Reflections from the lamps on the ledge above the pool swirled around the walls. She put her hand on his shoulder.

"You don't need to be afraid of me," she whispered.

He brushed her hand away and glared at her. "I have no interest in taking my friend's place. Now you have seen me you know I could not take his place even if I wanted to."

"Don't be ashamed, because…" she faltered.

"You should not have come in here!"

"Do you think it matters to me?" Clementia persisted.

"I am married, Clementia." John bent down and splashed water onto his chest and face. "It's all you need to know."

It was easy for him to ignore her advances. Too easy. Painfully easy. What credit did it do him?

"Please, John. Working together we can finish what Felix started. He knew that if we found the church treasure he would be able to pay the garrison and take over from Diogenes."

For a moment John was stunned. Could he believe the woman? Was this yet another lie? "Mutiny? Like those who murdered Conon?"

"Felix thought Justinian would thank him for it. The emperor doesn't want to finance the garrison himself. There is a great deal of wealth to be had if we find what we seek, not to mention power."

"I have had my fill of both."

"Not even to protect yourself and your family?"

"Protect?"

"From whatever the world threatens you with. You don't think your god Mithra will protect you, do you? Or the Christians' god? Or other people? Money and power are the only things you can trust."

John couldn't prevent himself cursing Felix silently. How much had he told Clementia if he had even apparently revealed to her that John shared Felix's religion?

Clementia was scowling at John as if he were a codex written in a language she couldn't read. He supposed she was beautiful in a fleshy sort of way. He preferred Cornelia with her boyish figure and bony, unpainted face.

When John returned to his room he was startled to find Julius there. The boy's purpose didn't appear to be nefarious. He was staring wide-eyed at the fresco of Persephone. According to the artist responsible, the queen of the underworld had worn very little, which John thought unlikely, recalling Theodora's sumptuous wardrobe.

The boy turned from the fresco and looked guiltily at John. "I…I…"

"Never mind, Julius. I suspect General Felix also enjoyed depictions of mythology."

"This was his room?" Julius' gaze went to the codex lying on top of the chest at the foot of the bed.

"Yes. That is what he was reading."

"Reading's no use to a fighting man."

"You think not? General Felix would not agree." John gestured the boy to sit on the bed, picked up the codex, and gave it to him. "This was written by Julius Caesar. You cannot deny he was a fighting man. You told me your parents wanted you to study. I take it you learned to read before you ran off?"

Julius bridled and opened the volume. "I can read, sir! It starts by saying Gaul is a whole divided into three parts."

"I will lend it to you. You'll find it fascinating."

"It can't be very interesting, considering how he begins."

"On the contrary. Scholars say this account is based on dispatches he sent to the senate here in Rome. It describes every detail of his military campaign. You don't think there's anything you can learn from your namesake's writings, Julius?"

"Does he teach you how to use weapons?"

"Generals concern themselves with campaign strategies, not weapon techniques."

"I don't want to be a general. I'd be happy just to swing my sword at whoever the general wants killed." He paused and then blurted out, "Why do you care about it, sir?"

A good question, John thought. He had only known the boy for a few days and one way or another he would need to leave Rome in a few days more. "As I told you, Julius, I ran away to become a mercenary, so I can appreciate your situation."

"Where did you fight?"

"One place was Bretania."

"There were many enemies there?"

"If I and my colleagues were not fighting invaders, we were helping ambitious warlords trying to carve out kingdoms as soon as they'd located enough men to fight for them. Mine was a hired sword and I fought for more than one employer."

Julius was staring at John with evident awe and John uncomfortably realized that the boy's admiration pleased him. He was tempted to describe the terrible exhilaration he had experienced during battle, venting the aimless fury of youth on an enemy. But then he would also have to describe washing the blood of dead comrades from his face, the boredom of freezing, muddy campsites, and a friend who drowned in a swollen creek.

"At one point," John continued, "I sold the service of my sword to Cadwallon. He ruled the kingdom of Gwynedd and his men called him Long Hand."

"And why was that?"

"It was said he had a long reach over his land, ensuring justice and so peace." John was reminded of another ruler with a long reach, one doubtless about to soon stretch out a hand from Constantinople and send him to oblivion. Suddenly he shivered. Though the light was no different it felt as if a shadow had passed through the room.

Julius laughed. "Except when he was fighting. Did you ever meet him?"

"No. His army was large and I only saw his commanders."

"And was the fighting fierce?"

"It was, Julius. There are many stories I could tell you but now we both need to rest. Read this. I read it when I attended Plato's Academy. General Diogenes read it and so did General Felix."

"If I have time, sir. Did you ever fight alongside General Felix?"

"Yes, more than once. I will tell you about that some other day."

After John had gone to bed, his thoughts shifted from his past with Felix to his past with Cornelia. He couldn't help thinking of how it had been when he and Cornelia were lovers in Egypt so long ago. All that was gone. The past had swept it away, as it eventually sweeps away everything and everyone a man has known and finally the man himself and all his memories.

Could that young mercenary who loved Cornelia truly have been John or had the young stranger's memories somehow found a home in John's mind?

His musings were interrupted, mercifully, by the eerie call of an owl.

An owl, in the middle of Rome. What had the city come to? There were plenty of deserted buildings these days for wild creatures.

He passed into sleep wondering if Cornelia was asleep, or lying awake. Whether owls were calling on his estate in Greece and whether she was listening to them.

•●●●●•

Cornelia swung her lantern back and forth as she walked slowly along the ridge overlooking the sea. The ridge remained faintly visible, although dips and hollows were in midnight darkness.

"Over there! Look!"

She peered in the direction Peter indicated. "It's only a bush."

Age had robbed John's former servant of much of his eyesight, although he wouldn't admit it. He was as likely to fall into a hole as to help Cornelia find his lost sheep, but pride prevented him from staying back at his house, as Cornelia well knew.

"Hypatia had no business insisting I ask you to come out tonight, mistress," Peter said. "I told her I could search by the sea while she looked nearer the road."

"I'm glad to help, Peter. We're neighbors, after all."

"I don't know how it happened. I put the sheep out to pasture just before sunrise. It's been so dry, the morning dew makes the grass more palatable. She must have slipped away without my noticing. I would have started searching sooner but I hoped she'd return safely on her own."

The mention of safe return made Cornelia think about John,

who had not yet returned. Perhaps that was good news, meaning he had arrived at Rome without incident.

"When Hypatia got back from the market, did she mention anything about ships arriving from Rome?"

"No, mistress. There has been no news from there. I wish I had accompanied the Lord Chamberlain."

"You have your own place to look after—and a wife." If the truth were told, Hypatia was more and more looking after her considerably older husband. It was only right. Cornelia would have done the same for John. She hoped she would never have to take care of him, not for her own sake but for his.

They continued along the ridge as sky and sea darkened. The lights on a few scattered ships floated in the blackness, stars that had strayed from the flock. Cornelia shone her lantern under bushes and into depressions.

"I hate to think of the Lord Chamberlain off by himself," Peter said. "So far away. And who knows what kind of trouble Felix is drawing him into?"

"He was with Marius, remember? And by now he's with Felix. Those two have been through a lot together." Not that Cornelia hadn't worried over each new adventure.

"I have prayed for him."

"We can't do anything to help John tonight. Let's think about finding your sheep, Peter."

"I prayed for the sheep too. Naturally."

It did not strike Cornelia as at all natural to pray for a sheep. How casually Christians addressed their god about trivialities. She would never have dared trouble the Goddess about a stray sheep nor even weightier matters unless accompanied by an offering.

It was full night by the time their search to and fro brought them to the ruined temple. Peter rested on a fallen column and Cornelia directed her lantern light round the shadowy remains.

A pair of glowing eyes stared at her.

She let out an involuntary cry.

By the time Peter stumbled to her side the eyes were gone but his lantern illuminated the bloody carcass of a sheep. "Wolves!"

As they left an owl called. Turning, Cornelia saw it silhouetted dimly against the stars, perched on a remaining part of what had been the temple's roof.

According to country folk, that was a harbinger of death.

Chapter Twenty-eight

"According to your reports, Viteric, I can only conclude the Lord Chamberlain is in Rome for pleasure and to visit famous places." General Diogenes leaned his elbows on the balustrade of his command post and stared out into the predawn darkness. "Let's see, his itinerary has included the Circus Maximus and Saint Minias' Church, Hadrian's mausoleum and, naturally, a brothel. No traveler leaves Rome without going to a brothel."

"I'm sure he has logical reasons for all of his excursions, sir."

"Are you? Well, people will believe what they wish to be true."

"And you believe he is not to be trusted." Viteric made no attempt to conceal his irritation. He had come to respect John. He was tired of shadowing the former Lord Chamberlain because of Diogenes' unfounded suspicions. There was more urgent work to be done. Beyond the walls the night was filled by lights from the besieging army's camp fires, lamps, and torches. The landscape might have been the floor of an Olympian temple, the starry vault above supported on countless glowing pillars of smoke.

"You say he's been to the papal residence again. To talk to that troublemaker Leon, I suppose. Unless he was just there to see the sights. Are you certain he didn't notice you?"

"I kept a good distance."

"Which is why you lost him after he entered the tower at the wall. The Lord Chamberlain is visiting strange places in his search for word of Felix. If that is indeed what he's up to."

"To find a rabbit, one should look in rabbit holes, sir."

Diogenes shook his head. "Nobody who's met Felix would describe him as a rabbit, and a man who chases two rabbits will catch neither."

"I don't understand."

"It's an old saying."

"Would it not be a plan, sir, to assign an extra man or two to keep watch on the Lord Chamberlain's lodgings during the night hours?"

"It would take more than one man to watch every possible exit. Doors, windows, over the roof, and for all I know, tunneling out or disguising himself! Not to mention while their arrival could be presented as safeguarding an imperial emissary, he would be aware of the real reason they are there."

"Yes, for the same reason I am, as he well knows."

"No matter. By this time my messenger will be almost to Constantinople if he hasn't arrived yet. Let the Lord Chamberlain go where he will for now; we'll soon have the truth of the matter. Meantime, continue to keep an eye on him—even if only a half-blind eye."

Viteric bristled. "Sir, he is extremely adept at—"

"He's a slippery eel. I remember a saying of my father's. He said you can get a hold of an eel's tail but that doesn't mean he's caught."

"And what are my orders if he slips out of my grasp?"

"Our pagan ancestors claimed the gods favored men of action, but in my experience sitting idle in a corner with one's ears open can be more valuable. So if you lose the Lord Chamberlain return to his house and listen to what the servants are telling each other."

Viteric took his leave. Walking to John's lodgings, he did his best to digest the rabbit and eel stew of advice offered by his superior. In his opinion, old sayings were offered as answers by those who had no answers.

Diogenes might have been right about the value of simply

listening, but soon after Viteric entered the kitchen he could tell it would be impossible this morning. No one was talking.

Those sitting at the table were ignoring each other, staring at their plates or into the far corners of the room as they ate. Eutuchyus had provided bread and boiled eggs for the morning meal, and was consuming his own, accompanied by angry looks at John. The boy Julius displayed a surly expression and attacked his food rather than eating it, and Clementia appeared even angrier than Eutuchyus, bolting her meal in a most unladylike manner before jumping to her feet. "You don't mind if I leave immediately, Lord Chamberlain? No, of course you don't!"

The only response to Viteric's arrival was a curt nod from John, so he wandered out into the garden and watched the sky begin to lighten.

After a short time Julius came slinking past and Viteric grabbed his arm. "Why is everyone in a foul humor this morning?"

Julius pulled away and glared up at him. "Eutuchyus is angry because John didn't believe him when he claimed I was looking through Clementia's belongings. I don't know why Clementia's so annoyed. Perhaps she's angry at Eutuchyus and me both, because she doesn't know which of us was the culprit."

"And you?"

"I'm angry because Eutuchyus wants me out of the house."

"Surely that decision is the Lord Chamberlain's?"

"Yes, but who knows what Eutuchyus might get up to when nobody's looking?"

Viteric watched the boy stalk off. He squeezed his eyes shut and took a deep breath. He wasn't much of a spy. He couldn't even keep track of what was happening under John's roof. Perhaps he should put in a request to be returned to duties of a more military nature.

It occurred to him that he had let John out of his sight for too long. As he started back into the house a dark shape moved silently under the garden's peristyle. He thought the Lord Chamberlain was trying to leave unobserved again.

Instead John stepped into the garden and walked over to him. "Viteric. Come with me, we are off to the market."

• ● ● ● •

John and Viteric climbed the Esquiline Hill to the gate in the old city wall. Time had reduced the ancient marketplace to a patch of wasteland but merchants continued to sell their goods there. Numerous structures had been partly demolished or burnt down. The sellers huddled in the shelter of tottering walls against the wind, their offerings laid out on the ground. Feral cats lurked among the tall grass growing against the shells of what had once been prosperous shops, and a small fire in a dry fountain warmed two women whose raucous shouts announced to passersby they had fine jewelry for sale.

Poorly clad children dodged in and out among the thin crowd, hands extended for charitable contributions to no avail. Viteric and John soon attracted several urchins, who scuttled away when Viteric scowled and laid his hand on his sword.

"It's a fair distance for Maxima to walk," John remarked, having said very little during their journey.

"Surely the master of the house shouldn't have to check if the fish are fresh or haggle over eggs, let alone carry them back for his own meal?"

John smiled slightly. "I am here to fish and I may even hatch something."

The goods on sale could be divided into two categories: vegetables of poor quality and everything else that could possibly be purchased or exchanged for something more to the sellers' taste, edible or not. Everything else included every conceivable type of household item, probably stolen from unoccupied homes.

It suddenly struck John that he had just passed by a familiar face. Turning, he scanned the merchants. A gray-haired woman stood beside a cloth on which sat a pitiful collection of chipped lamps, dented cups, and badly tarnished plates.

John walked back to her. "Aren't you Aurelius' wife? We met not long ago."

"So you recognize me, after all, sir." He smile was forlorn, her voice faint. As at their first meeting she gave the impression of having recently returned from the catacombs, not from visiting but from internment. "Have you found my daughter's murderer yet? No, I can see you haven't. Why would a man such as yourself waste his time seeking justice for a poor girl?"

"I have been investigating. Your daughter hasn't been forgotten."

"A good life. She promised us a good life. And now look at me, forced to humiliate myself, selling goods to those who consider themselves my betters."

John thought that anyone who needed a dented cup or a chipped lamp could not be very much better than anyone else. He was about to reply when Viteric tugged at his elbow.

"Look, sir. Those two are selling military equipment." Viteric couldn't conceal his disgust.

John muttered a goodbye to Aurelius' wife and followed Viteric, who was striding in the direction of the malefactors.

John's hand on Viteric's arm restrained him from confronting them. "Not now. Notify Diogenes when you next report," he said in an undertone as they walked past without a glance at the swords and spears shining in inviting fashion in the early morning sun. They pretended not to hear the vilification the duo muttered just loud enough to be heard, and soon fading out of earshot.

John halted in front of a pedestal engraved with the name of the emperor Trajan. Rather than his statue, it now supported a variety of game which, like the emperor, were dead, but not for so long. "Ah, here's what we want. These two charming ladies are selling rabbits."

The younger of the women simpered prettily at John's compliment. She was in the last stages of pregnancy. "'ere you are, sir, freshest rabbits in Rome. The morning dew was on their last meal."

John asked the price. It was high. "In Constantinople you can buy a wild boar for that! However, I'll pay it if you throw in some information along with the rabbits. Were you in the city when General Conon was in charge of the garrison?"

The young woman gave a raucous laugh. "Oh, 'im! I got to know several of 'is soldiers but not 'im personally. Just as well 'cos 'e was bad luck on two legs, Conon was."

The older woman, by her looks clearly the mother of the other, chimed in. "That's right, sir. It was 'im not paying 'is soldiers what led to a lot of people who 'ad nothing to do with fighting getting killed."

"Terrible, it was," agreed the daughter. "Only one servant escaped, but all the others had their throats cut, poor things. Oh, I was glad I'd nothing to do with 'im."

"Did either of you know anyone in Conon's household?" John asked the women.

"Yes. Gabriella. She was 'is cook." The mother looked down thoughtfully at the game on the pedestal. "She told us 'e 'ad a fondness for rabbit and often bought them from us. She also sold things 'ere from time to time. Claimed Conon never noticed when bread or fruit disappeared from the kitchen."

"What happened to her?"

"Last I 'eard she was working in the fields. Serves 'er right too. It's a lot 'arder growing food than stealing it to sell!"

The fields the rabbit-seller described were on the opposite side of the city near the Tiber. Totila's troops had torched the wooden tenements crowded together there, reducing the area to the empty plain it had been before Rome was founded. The Goths had done the Romans a favor. Now that the much-shrunken population was under siege, tillable land inside the walls was more valuable than tenements.

Scattered signs of civilization remained. John and Viteric made

their way through a square surrounded by fire-blackened buildings. Despite the destruction, a statue of Plato stood untouched,
the philosopher's sole student a raven perched on his head. The
bird made John think of the fresco at the church of Saint Minias.
And something else.

Whatever the stray thought had been, it fled as the raven rose
croaking into the sky.

They were at the edge of a field planted with wheat. A heavy-
set man with a round, red face and a dubious expression stood
staring at them, his gaze moving from John to Viteric and the
rabbits he carried.

Exchanging greetings with the two arrivals, the gazer spoke
in a gloomy voice concerning his hopes for the harvest, adding
"Though even at its best t'will be nothing compared to the crops
I grew. The planting was wrong, you see, it was done too soon
for the best results."

"You sound knowledgeable," John observed.

"I oversaw a farm for years. I'm lucky to be standing here
today to tell you. When the Goths arrived I was barely able to
get away and with nothing but the tunic on my back. Happy
to say I've killed a few of the swine in the last couple of assaults
and hope to do the same in future."

"It's good work," Viteric remarked, leaving open whether he
meant growing crops, killing Goths, or both.

"Indeed," came the reply. "You look like men with questions
to ask. What are they?"

"I am looking for a woman," John said. "General Conon's
cook at the time he was murdered by his troops. Gabriella. I've
been told she's working in the fields."

"Oh, her. Yes, I've heard of her. She ran off with her man, and
both of them joined the Goths." He spat on the ground. "Didn't
like getting her hands dirty, so it's said, so when they heard from
a friend who'd already gone over to the other side there was work
for a camp cook, off they went. I suppose both men are fighting
for the Goths now. Traitorous bastards, all three of them."

"'Off they went,' you say. I wouldn't have thought it was easy to get in and out of the city, over the walls and past all the guards. Totila's army hasn't managed yet," John observed.

"A whole army, that's different. Haven't you heard of the Twisted Wall?"

"I'm new to the city. Is it a place where people can leave?"

The farmer's eyes narrowed. "You two wouldn't be thinking about going over to the Goths?"

Viteric glared at the man. "Hardly! There's plenty of work on this side of the wall!"

"If you don't mind not being paid, or so I've been told," the other snapped.

"Tell me about this Twisted Wall," John intervened. "Where is it?"

"It's on the north side of the city, by the Flaminian Gate, not far from the river. The wall split open about halfway down in ancient times. Seems the foundation wasn't right. Part of that stretch of wall leans forward. It's a simple matter to climb up to the gap and pass through."

"Why hasn't it been repaired?" John asked.

"There's no need. In fact, the first time the Goths besieged the city more than ten years ago, General Belisarius wanted to make repairs but the populace wouldn't allow it. You see, it's said the apostle Peter promised the Romans that he would defend the city at that spot. Rebuilding would be an insult to him. Who needs a wall when a saint's protecting you? I don't suppose Peter cares whether a few Romans go over to the Goths."

"That might explain why Diogenes has left part of the northern wall undermanned," Viteric remarked. "He probably heard that tale from Archdeacon Leon. There's not much chance of an attack from the north anyway. There's only a small encampment up there, not what I'd call a fighting force."

John thanked the farmer with one of Viteric's rabbits. He and Viteric continued on until they reached the statue of Plato they had passed by earlier. The raven had not returned.

John stopped and stared at it.

"You have thought of something, sir?" Viteric ventured.

"I'm not certain. It will come to me."

• • ● • •

When John returned home he asked Clementia to accompany him into the garden. "I wish to talk where we won't be overheard," he explained, without adding he would also feel less distracted and disconcerted in the garden than he had in the bath.

Only afterwards had he realized that their conversation in the bath had left important questions unanswered.

He led her to a bench not far from the empty animal pens. Flowering shrubs nearby lent their faint perfume to the twilight. A bird which had nested under the peristyle sang its farewell to the day.

"This must have been a romantic place once, before it was turned into a miniature farm," Clementia remarked. "However, from your manner, I assume you have not brought me out here with a tryst in mind."

"There are some questions I neglected to ask you the other night."

"In the bath? Well, I am glad to know I have some effect on you. Or was it the warm water that fogged your mind?"

"Why didn't you tell me the names on that list represented inscriptions on tombs? That is correct, isn't it?"

"I supposed a man of your perspicacity would have reasoned that out."

"Do you think I believe that?"

"Does it matter? Neither of us possesses the second part of the solution."

"Obviously, otherwise you and Felix would have already taken the treasure, or maybe you and Hunulf, or perhaps you would have just retrieved it for yourself."

"Is that all you have to say?"

John tried to contain his sudden anger. "Why was Felix so intent on finding this treasure?"

"I told you. He thought if he could pay the garrison, Justinian would hand command of it over to him."

"It wasn't because of his gambling debts?"

Clementia laughed. "Felix was gambling heavily because he knew he'd soon be wealthy."

That sounded like Felix, John thought. Always recklessly optimistic. "Felix's ambition was to be a general in the field. Justinian finally gave him his wish. He made him a general and sent him here into the middle of a war. Yet you tell me he wanted more."

"You misunderstand the situation. It was all to do with Anastasia. Felix was convinced Justinian sent him here to keep him away from her. You know Felix was having an affair with Anastasia. Quite improper from a political point of view, of course, with her being the empress' sister and Felix only a lowly Germanic soldier."

"I also know Felix had broken off the relationship."

"Only temporarily."

"Nevertheless, Felix had his generalship."

"He had nothing but a title, Lord Chamberlain. No troops to command, no funds, no real mission except the ridiculous pretense of negotiating with an aging, cowardly churchman. And as soon as Justinian had found a suitable match for Anastasia or the woman herself had found a new man, Felix expected even the title would be taken away."

"Then Justinian did not send him here to replace Diogenes?"

"Of course not, although Diogenes suspected that was the case. Felix was afraid Diogenes would arrange to have him murdered. Perhaps that's why he contacted you. I can't say."

The bird under the peristyle called out and a breeze surrounded John with perfume, whether from the shrubs or from his companion, a shadowy shape in the growing darkness, he could not be certain.

He could understand how Felix might have felt, to be finally made a general but in name only. At his age he would not have another chance. Left to himself he might have come to accept his disappointment, but goaded on by a woman like Clementia his ambition had got the best of him.

Well, John admitted to himself, it wasn't entirely Clementia's fault. Any pretty woman could have turned Felix's head. "We'll go inside now, Clementia. The breeze is turning chilly."

Chapter Twenty-nine

John searched the servants' quarters at his house. The rooms that had belonged to Conon's servants had been left untouched. A woman's tunic lay across a bed, ready to be put on at the beginning of a workday which had never come. A necklace with a wooden cross still sat on a table.

Finally John found what he was looking for, a pair of breeches and a short tunic. Laborer's clothing. The clothing was ill-fitting as well as shabby. It wasn't surprising, given few were as tall as John. Its appearance and condition made his disguise look more authentic.

He had waited until he was certain the members of the household were asleep before creeping through darkened hallways on his mission. Exiting the city was best done in the middle of the night and would also insure Viteric didn't follow. In this case John was more concerned with Viteric's safety than about what he might report back to Diogenes. A soldier apprehended on the way in or out of Rome would likely be executed for desertion or spying. A peasant, as John now appeared to be, would have a better chance.

He made his way quietly through the house, avoiding the room occupied by Eutuchyus, whom he regarded as stealthy and cunning as a rat approaching a cupboard. A cloud of perfume hung outside Clementia's doorway. It reminded him of passing by a flowering shrub in a dark garden. A shaft of moonlight slanting through the compluvium illuminated the atrium as John slunk catlike along the walls.

When he was finally outside he went north. A spectral moon turned the city into a nightmare landscape of stark black and white. The shadows in the streets might have been bottomless pits. The leaning wooden tenements resembled towering marble mausoleums. It was as if the monstrous moon had drained all color and life out of the world below.

John considered his plan. Once he was beyond the wall he could hire a boat or steal one if necessary to cross the Tiber to the Goth camp. He had his blade and a money pouch, prepared for any eventuality.

There was a scuffling from behind. Faint but unmistakable.

The sound of a footstep sliding over an uneven patch in the ground.

He turned. The street was empty. There was no flicker of light from any window. Doors to deserted buildings hung open. The few people who had returned to Rome had mainly settled nearer the Palantine Hill. There were not even feral dogs or cats prowling, there being nothing for them to scavenge.

It struck him that this was how a dead city looked. Bleached bones in the moonlight. All of Rome would look like this one day, and Constantinople too. For cities died as surely as people did.

He resumed walking.

There came another footstep.

He pivoted and sprinted back the way he'd come. A figure jumped out of the shadows into a patch of moonlight and vanished again into darkness.

John raced after it, closing ground quickly.

He lunged, grabbed, felt fabric in his fist. The figure fell, yelled. "It's only me, Julius!"

John kept his grip on the boy's tunic and yanked him to his feet. "Why are you following me?"

The boy's eyes looked big and shiny in the moonlight. His gaze moved to John's blade, which also looked very big and shiny. "I only wanted to kill some Goths."

John released him. "Explain."

"I overheard you and Viteric talking when you arrived back today. You're going over the wall, aren't you? Into Goth territory. Well, when I tried to join the military they told me I wasn't old enough to kill Goths, but now we'll see about that!"

John sighed. "I don't intend to kill anyone, Julius. I want to find and interview someone."

Julius brought out his own knife. "But you'll need to kill Goths to do that, won't you?"

"I hope not."

Julius looked dubious. "You hope not? But why?"

"Violent death tends to be messy and noisy, Julius. What I'm doing requires secrecy."

"Spying?"

"If you will, yes. And spies work alone. Return to the house."

"What, go back there all alone, at this time of night? Who knows what's lying in wait?"

"You are probably the most dangerous menace lurking between here and the house, Julius."

"But, sir…"

Although John believed what he'd told the boy was true, what if he were mistaken? Could he take the chance the boy would not attempt to follow him despite orders and bring disaster on them both? "All right. Come with me. But remember, you're under my command and you will follow orders."

They went along a straight street parallel to the Tiber, the moon following. He could make out guards at the gate.

Leaving the street, John and Julius angled away from the river, passing mostly ruined buildings, until they came to a wide open space filled with rank vegetation. Charred foundations and occasional statuary indicated that the area had once been gardens where private villas backed up against the city's northern wall.

The Twisted Wall was clearly visible. Uneven and bulging, it gave the impression of a great beast dozing in the pale moonlight.

"We'll know soon enough if Diogenes posted guards here," John muttered. As he started through the overgrown gardens he felt Julius' grasp on his tunic.

"No, sir, don't go any further." The boy's voice came out in a whimper.

"What's the matter, Julius? You're not frightened, are you?" The boy's reaction struck John as out of character.

"You didn't say you were going to the Evil Wall!"

"Evil Wall? I thought this is called the Twisted Wall."

"That too! This is where they buried robbers and cutthroats. Their shades haunt the place."

John took hold of Julius' hand and pulled him into the dark vegetation. "Not so loud! We can't be certain there are no guards around!"

"Let's go back, sir. Goths don't frighten me. They can be killed but you can't kill somebody already dead."

"I remember you mentioned being frightened that Conon's shade might haunt the house."

"Oh, that was just silly talk. The Evil Wall is real."

John didn't stop to argue. He pushed on. One shrub clawed at his tunic, another drove thorns into his ankles. A patch of nettles set his hands afire. No phantoms or armed men appeared.

"They say Nero's tomb is nearby," Julius went on. "I wouldn't want to meet him!"

"Yet you say you're not afraid of Goths and the Goths burnt more of Rome than Nero did," John snapped.

Julius fell silent.

The tangle of vegetation ran right to the base of the wall. John glanced up and down its length, searching for a gap. In the moonlight the uneven masonry formed a bewildering patchwork of black and white, every bright block accompanied by its own inky shadow.

So far as John could see, the wall here was in poor repair and barely half the height it should have been, but still unscalable. He forced his way through the brush and vines.

Julius screamed.

The shade swooped down on John before he could react.

Not a shade, he realized almost instantly, but a shadow, followed by a heavy body.

He was driven down but as he hit the ground he brought his knee up into his assailant's belly.

Rolling away, he saw that Julius had leapt on the assailant's back, pummeling and scratching like a starved cat fighting for a rat run over by a cart.

The man bellowed in alarm. "Stop! I give up! I didn't know there was another one!"

John pulled Julius away, taking a flailing fist in the eye in the process. He was relieved the boy hadn't had time to use his knife. The attacker was a shabby man, considerably overweight. With John looming over him displaying his blade, the fellow got shakily to his feet, rubbing at his bottom. "You pushed me right onto them thistles," he said reproachfully.

"You ambushed us. You're lucky to be alive."

"I thought you was a guard."

"What are you doing here?"

"Same as you, I suppose. Visiting friends outside Rome."

John didn't inquire whether the visit related to business or pleasure. "So it's true it's possible to get out through the wall here?"

"Oh, yes. If I can, anyone can." The man patted his ample belly and winced. "See how that bit of the wall leans forward? Scramble up until you reach where the next section sags in the opposite direction. It makes a sort of fold you can climb down." He went on to attribute the fact the Goths had not entered the same way to the protection of Peter, finally pointing out that the saint would not allow Rome's enemies to discover a breach in the city defenses.

John had no answer to that. He would have thought the saint had better things to do than put in sentry duty at a weak spot in the wall of the city in which he'd been imprisoned and executed.

"Off with you now," John ordered. "And keep your mouth shut about meeting us."

"At once, sir." The man took a few careful steps away, rubbing first his sore belly and then his stinging backside. "Just don't set your little demon on me again!"

Julius grinned so broadly at the compliment John could see his teeth shining in the moonlight.

Chapter Thirty

Cornelia sat on a bench in the courtyard by the house and tried to enjoy the morning sunshine as she plucked a chicken whose erstwhile companions scratched around in the dirt. She told herself she was relaxing, not waiting, not tense with anticipation. But in fact she was waiting as she did every day and her heart missed a beat when the flock scattered with a burst of outraged cluckings and she saw Hypatia returning from the market in Megara.

Would there be news from Italy? News of John?

"Would you like to dine with us tonight?" Hypatia asked before Cornelia could say anything. "I've enough mussels for everyone. I intend to cook them in raisin wine the way Peter likes them. The merchant I bought them from swore Poseidon himself could not have fresher. They had to be tied down to prevent them jumping back into the sea, or so he claimed."

Hypatia sounded almost too cheerful. Cornelia put aside her bird's pallid carcass and brushed stray feathers from her lap. "You must have purchased them from old Silver Tongue."

He was a notorious tongue-wagger, distributing news along with what he liked to call the bounty of the sea.

"That's right."

"Did he have anything to say about the situation in Italy?"

A cloud passed over Hypatia's smiling face. "No, but he did

tell me that a fellow who bought a basket of sprats said everyone at the docks is talking about a man, newly arrived, who claims to be a courier from Rome with urgent imperial business in Constantinople."

Cornelia felt her mouth go dry. Was it possible the man had business in Megara too? Business concerning a former Lord Chamberlain? Or his family? "Did you learn anything more?"

Hypatia's lips narrowed and she frowned.

"I can see you don't want to tell me."

"It's only rumors."

"Rumors sometimes turn out to be true."

"But if they're not true you'll be worried for no reason."

"I already worry."

Hypatia sighed. "I was hoping I could put it off to later, but since you insist…According to Silver Tongue's source, this man was in the tavern across from the stairs leading down to the docks drinking and talking too much. He was angry because his ship, the *Nika*, needed to come into port for repairs and he'd been looking forward to a swift trip both ways."

"Both ways?" Cornelia said thoughtfully. "It must have been very important business indeed to rush back to Rome. Do you think it has anything to do with whatever Felix was so worried about? Whatever it was that took John to Rome?"

"It's possible. There's no way to know."

The chickens were emerging from the weeds around the yard to resume their scratching, oblivious to their deceased companion.

"The ship probably won't be able to sail until tomorrow at the earliest," Cornelia said. "I think I'll walk down there and see if I can find that fellow. He must know what's going on in Rome, if nothing else."

"He certainly can tell you about that. He seems to know a great deal. In fact, according to Silver Tongue this traveler mentioned Justinian's Lord Chamberlain had arrived in Rome."

"John!"

Hypatia looked ready to cry. "There's more. The loose-lipped stranger said the man he was talking about was a fraud and he'd be unmasked as soon as Justinian heard about it."

"When Justinian finds out John has left Megara…"

Hypatia put her arm around Cornelia, who pushed her away, suddenly furious. "You weren't going to tell me!"

"No. I was, but I wanted time to think about how I could. There's probably no truth in it. Just drunken talk. Besides, there's nothing we can do."

Cornelia walked away without a word. In the room she shared with John she opened a plain wooden chest at the foot of the bed and dug down through the clothing stored there until she found a linen bundle tied with twine. Inside was a dagger with a copper blade riveted to an ivory handle.

It was Egyptian. She had carried it with her all her life on the road, until she stopped traveling, left the dangerous city of Constantinople, and settled here in the peaceful Greek country-side. She had thought she would never need it again.

Running her finger along the blade she remembered John giving it to her when they were young lovers.

"I will always protect you," he had told her. "But if I am not by your side this will protect you."

That had been long ago, but the blade was still sharp.

John and Julius hid their rowboat in a patch of reeds and waded through foul-smelling mud to the riverbank. To Julius' disgust, John had not stolen the boat but purchased it, rousing its owner by pounding at the door of a ramshackle riverside hut. The bleary-eyed fisherman had looked frightened, then suspicious, but the price offered allayed his concerns. John explained that it was easier to put a coin into a man's hand than hit him over the head. It wasn't a lesson Julius wanted to hear.

John didn't like the impetuous boy tagging along but didn't want to put off his visit to the Goth encampment. "We're going to obtain information, not to fight," he explained to his companion a dozen times.

The air was clammy with mist. As they scraped the mud off their boots, birds sang, anticipating the sun. Voices and the squeak and rattle of carts led them to a road. The sun was up by the time they reached a procession of farmers bringing supplies to the Goth encampment. Evidently, they had traveled from beyond the ravaged area around the city. In addition to carts piled with vegetables, there were men leading cattle and sheep. A slightly built middle-aged woman marched resolutely along, weighed down by a big crate of squawking chickens, leaving a trail of feathers in her wake.

John strode up to her and took hold of the cage. "That must be heavy. Let me help you."

For a moment the woman looked alarmed, fearing a robbery, but she relaxed when John and Julius fell into stride beside her. The bored guard at the camp entrance paid no attention to a farm family delivering chickens.

John wandered through the crowd of soldiers and farmers haggling and unloading goods. In many ways life in Italy went on normally—that is to say normally, as established by more than a decade of continuous war. By now the unpredictable movement of armies was simply endured like bad weather.

Julius' gaze darted back and forth, taking in Goth soldiers. His fists clenched, he looked barely able to contain his anger. "How will we find the kitchens, sir? Will you force it out of someone?"

"We're almost there, Julius. Notice the smell of cooking?"

Not far away, cooks worked over rows of huge braziers. John asked a fellow who seemed to be overseeing the work about Gabriella.

"That one! You won't find her here. She didn't like getting her hands greasy. You might try Captain Oduulf's tent. She took up with him shortly after arriving."

No one challenged a tall, rustic fellow with a boy as they tramped past tents, stopping occasionally to ask directions. Totila's army had nothing to fear from Roman farmers and the farmers were happy to trade with either the Goths or the Romans as they alternated control of the countryside. Whether Rome fell to the Goths again was a matter of indifference to farmers who had no inclination to move to the city. The outcome of the war, John thought, mattered mostly to Totila and Justinian and the fighters in their pay.

When they found Oduulf's tent John realized there was no good excuse for a strange peasant to burst in on the captain, so he sat on the back of an empty cart and waited. Julius produced a handful of bacon he'd somehow stolen without any of the cooks or John noticing.

John accepted some to the boy's apparent surprise. "If only you'd pilfered some wine."

"If you want, sir, I'll—"

"I was jesting, Julius."

John thought it would be ironic if this bacon had come from one of the swine Marius and he had been hauling to the city when the Goths apprehended them.

Before long the tent flaps opened and a young woman dressed in fine silks emerged, a vision from a jumbled dream. She might have been transported from the imperial court by a playful pagan god and set down here amidst rough tents, dirt, smoke, and the stink of horse droppings.

John sprang up and went over to her. "Gabriella?"

Her eyes widened in terror, her face turned white. John blocked her path back to the tent.

"Don't worry," John said. "I haven't come to harm you." The coin in his hand vouched for his truthfulness. But it was also a denomination a man of his current appearance would never have glimpsed in his lifetime, much less carried on his person.

"Who are you?"

"It doesn't matter. You recently cooked for General Conon?"

"Who says so?"

"As I said, I'm not here to hurt you or take you back to Rome."

Gabriella turned the gold coin around in her hand. She was dark-haired and dark-eyed. The coin gradually soothed her. "They killed all the servants when they came for the general. I was afraid…"

"The rebels have all been dealt with, Gabriella. You don't need to fear them. How did you escape?"

"By the grace of God. Only by the grace of God. They crept into the house in the middle of night. Normally, I would have been sleeping so I would never have woken up. Or do you wake up for an instant when your throat's slit? Anyway, there was a terrible yowling. Cats fighting in the garden. I got up to chase them away and spotted the intruders before they saw me. I laid down in the bushes in the dark and stayed hidden until they were gone. What I heard…the screams…sounds I never thought a person could make, it was like someone had cracked open the door to Hell. Afterwards, I went into the house to see what had happened. I wish I hadn't. I'd pay this coin, pay a whole bag of gold, if I could forget what I saw."

John questioned her gently. She had fled and never returned. She knew nothing about what had transpired at the house after the slaughter, nothing of Felix. All the servants except for herself had been murdered, even James, whom she described as elderly and crippled.

"He had less chance to escape than anyone," she went on. "He was our steward, and his room was apart from the rest of us. The noise must have awakened him because I came across his body in his doorway. There was no reason for them to do to him what they did."

"But surely the steward was Eutuchyus and he escaped death?"

Gabriella frowned. "Who?"

"Eutuchyus. A eunuch."

"No. I never heard of him. Oh, James limped badly and was forever losing his balance and clinging to us, his poor old hands flying everywhere. Terrified of falling, or so he pretended. None of us girls could be angry with him, he was so pitiful, but certainly not one of those creatures."

Chapter Thirty-one

As she strode toward the tavern Cornelia's fingers momentarily brushed the hilt of the dagger concealed beneath her clothes. The whitewashed building displayed a badly rendered eagle indicating that hospitality was available within. However, the stout red-faced man who emerged from the doorway was demonstrating a decided lack of hospitality to the struggling girl in his grasp. He threw her to the ground and kicked her in the ribs.

"Don't let me catch you coming in here again taking my trade away." He kicked the girl in the face before going back inside.

Furious, Cornelia rushed to the girl's side and helped her up. If she hadn't come here on other business she'd have been tempted to use her dagger on the red-faced bully.

"Don't try doing business in there," the girl mumbled through a bloody split lip. "Got his own girls, deny it though he may. He must make more from them than his watered-down wine. You'll have better luck on the docks, chickpea." She turned and walked in their direction.

A burst of screaming and coarse laughter drew Cornelia's attention to the open door. She could see another girl being manhandled and then pulled out of sight under a table while patrons offered oaths and filthy suggestions.

She hesitated before entering. It wasn't that she feared for her safety. She'd traveled the empire's roads for years with a troupe of entertainers. She was used to inns and taverns like this and much worse. She could take care of herself. And yet the thought of entering into that vile atmosphere, dirtying herself, repulsed her.

How fastidious you've become, she thought, stepping through the doorway.

No one was paying attention to her because the tavern owner had just swooped down, reached under a table, dragged a man out, and flung him into the sunshine. "Too bad you didn't get your money's worth!" he shouted. "And you won't get it back either. Next time, drink after you've used a girl!"

A fat man sitting half-concealed by the open door leered in Cornelia's direction. "These Greeks are a rude race," he croaked. "They could learn the finer points of etiquette from the lowest beggar in Rome."

"You're not Greek? You're from Rome?"

"Born there. Would you like to hear the latest scandals, pretty lady? I've just come from there. I'm on my way to Constantinople on important imperial business." He winked at her.

Cornelia sat down on a stool next to him. The way he looked at her made her feel like a freshly cooked leg of lamb. Or maybe a big, succulent fly considering the fellow's resemblance to a bloated toad. "More wine," he cried out, "for me and my lovely lady friend."

Cornelia had guessed correctly that it wouldn't be difficult to find the braggart Hypatia had described. She again felt for the dagger concealed in her clothing, reassuring herself it was still there. "I hear the situation in Rome is not good."

He shook his head, waggling his jowls. "Who can be sure? The Goths are at the gates, it's true, but General Diogenes is a shrewd man. Did I mention I am going to Constantinople on his behalf?"

She gritted her teeth and let the loathsome creature paw her arm. After all the villains John had brought to justice, after emerging unscathed from Justinian's court, that gold-and jewel-encrusted den of vipers, was he to be brought down by this intoxicated fool?

It was possible, for the fool was on the way to the capital, on what he described as important imperial business involving a general in charge of the garrison. A general John would have had to meet.

She accepted the cup he thrust at her and pretended to sip.

The noisy tavern stank of stale wine, sweat, and vomit. Time and dirt had long since obscured most of the frescoes on its walls. Cornelia stared at the painting behind them. Here a bare leg emerged from the grime, there a bare arm. From what little could still be seen the fresco was of the sort usually found in brothels.

"The general trusts me, you see, because I have worked for him in the past." The man's chubby hand continuing to run up and down Cornelia's arm. "Drink, drink," he urged. "I can feel you're tense."

She debated whether she should stab him. Where they sat was shadowed enough she might be able to do so without being noticed. Or should she lure him away, give her a better chance at escape by eliminating him in private? What if something went wrong and she never got the chance? Now, while seated within arm's length she had the opportunity to make sure he never reached Constantinople, let alone return to Rome with John's death sentence.

She grasped his roaming hand. "There's talk you are going to Constantinople to unmask a fraud."

"What's that?"

"A man arrived in Rome, claiming he'd come from the emperor."

"Yes, that's true."

"And General Diogenes expects Justinian will deny sending him."

"Yes. That's what is being said." He leaned toward her, breathing noxious fumes in her face. "Perhaps we could discuss the matter in a less public place?"

All around inebriated patrons talked, quarreled, arranged assignations. Who would have noticed her arrival, or remember later what she looked like? Who could even vouch afterwards that she had been sitting beside this particular man when he suddenly collapsed? Who, in fact, would even notice that he had slumped forward, head on the table, like any other intoxicated man, while blood from his lacerated heart leaked out into his voluminous clothes and ran down his legs to the filthy floor?

By the time he was discovered Cornelia would be back on the estate. Who would believe she was the kind of woman who frequented low taverns, let alone murdered strangers in them?

With one hand she withdrew her weapon from its hiding place. With the other she grasped the man's tunic near his shoulder and pulled him forward, so she could whisper in his ear before driving the dagger upwards into his heart. "You expect the emperor to tell you this man is not in Rome on his orders and then you intend to take this information straight back to Diogenes?"

"Tell me? Not me! I'm no messenger. I only heard the rumors."

Cornelia held the poised blade in check. "You weren't sent to see the emperor?"

"Perhaps we should talk about this in my cabin?"

"Then what's your business in Constantinople?"

"Well…boots, actually. I have a supplier, you see. He gives me a good price and Diogenes' men have been wearing the same boots for a long time. There's a fortune to be made! I only hope the Goths don't overrun Rome before I can return."

Cornelia pushed him away. "So that's why you're in such a hurry?"

She got to her feet, feeling light-headed. She had almost murdered a man for no reason. Now she wouldn't need to kill.

Nor could she save John.

Chapter Thirty-two

Eutuchyus had not been Conon's steward. He had arrived at the house after Felix was in residence, posing as the former steward. Why had he lied?

John and Julius sat in a pine copse outside the Goth camp, roasting a chicken which, according to Julius, had happened to cross the road to place itself in his hands. The boy had a knack for finding food and under the circumstances John was not about to complain.

They were waiting until dark to recross the river. After eating, they rested. The day was warm. There was a soft cushion of fallen needles beneath the pines.

"Why do you care so much about Eutuchyus to risk coming here?" Julius asked.

"A good question. There's something about him that bothers me."

From the start there was something that didn't ring true. John had an instinct for such things. He could feel the need to investigate a person further without understanding why.

Or was John only flattering himself that he had been suspicious from the start? Wasn't it that he had taken a dislike to the creature immediately, for reasons having nothing to do with suspicions?

It didn't matter now, though. John knew Eutuchyus had

insinuated himself into Felix's household under false pretenses. Why? Had Diogenes put him there to spy on Felix? The general was fond of spying on presumed enemies. Had Felix been involved in a struggle for power? Was that why he had summoned John?

John had wracked his brain over the mysterious list and the church artifacts. It was possible that Felix had indeed been seeking the latter but that it had nothing to do with a different problem. His friend was perfectly capable of getting into more than one scrape at the same time. Had John erred in attempting to conflate separate situations?

He realized Julius was sitting with his back to a tree, chewing on a long piece of grass, staring intently at him.

"What is it, Julius?"

"Well, sir, you think harder than anyone I've ever seen."

John let his clenched features relax and smiled. "You should have seen the lecturers at Plato's Academy."

A raven called from the top of a pine. Since he'd been thinking about philosophers he remembered the raven perched on the statue of the philosopher he'd seen in the square. And having just been pondering Felix's list and the hidden valuables, it came to him what had been nibbling at the edges of his thoughts since then.

The key to the list.

Again John realized that while it was necessary to think hard, revelations often came only after one was done thinking.

That night John and Julius overslept. When they woke, nearer to dawn than John had planned, they slipped away to the boat concealed in the reeds. Wading through the muck they freed it and pushed it toward open water. John feared deep water, and as the reeds thinned and the river rose past his ankles, past his knees to his waist, he felt his heart start to pound and decided they were sufficiently to the river's main channel to get aboard.

It was a mistake.

There was a screech and the boat rocked as it grated against a rock.

Then they were free and being carried downriver in the current.

"My oar! I've lost my oar!" Julius stared over the stern. The water glimmered faintly in the light of the newly risen moon. John could make out the bobbing oar rapidly receding.

He looked down to see if there was another oar and realized the boat was leaking. The rock must have pierced the hull.

He cursed himself for allowing his fear to cloud his judgment. There was no enemy more deadly or treacherous than one's own fear.

But knowing that didn't stop the panic from rising in his chest faster than the water rising in the boat.

He and Julius leaned over the sides and paddled at the water with their hands, trying to direct the boat toward the shore.

In truth, Julius was doing more than John.

As John put his hands into the water he could see the moon reflected a hundred times in the ripples and he could sense, beneath the bejeweled surface, the darkness, deep as death, waiting to embrace him. "Mithra!"

Julius glanced at him, puzzled and alarmed, but kept paddling.

The boat sank lower and lower and finally ground to a stop on the river bottom, where the water was shallow enough to wade ashore.

White eddies of mist had begun to rise over the river as John and Julius emerged from under the bridge connecting Hadrian's tomb to the city. A trio of armed guards met them. Fortunately for the bedraggled pair their leader was the grizzled veteran whom John had consulted on his previous visit.

"It seems we are fated to meet when I am soaked to the skin. This time I have brought along a different companion who is, however, just as wet." John shivered. As his terror ebbed he felt the cold wind that was dispersing the tendrils of mist on the water.

"Indeed," came the reply with a hint of a smile and a quick dismissal of the guards. "Do you require assistance? Blankets?"

John shook his head and, gesturing to Julius, struck out at a fast pace for their lodgings.

Although he was cold, his face burned with shame. He hoped the boy hadn't noticed his fear.

"That water was cold enough to invite death to creep into your bones," the boy muttered.

It was an accurate comment, but John didn't like hearing it put that way.

They walked rapidly, trying to keep warm, through streets becoming peopled, if sparsely, by ill-clad residents emerging to curse the new day. None looked surprised at the sight of a man and boy squelching along in waterlogged clothing except a passerby who followed them for a short way. John turned, hand on blade, and glared at him until he slunk down an alley that was merely a cleft between two buildings.

"It's our clothing, sir," Julius told him. "We're better clad than many, and men have been murdered for a pair of boots before now."

John wondered if Julius was speaking from experience and glanced down at his companion's footwear. The boy caught the look and flushed. "Took them off a dead man I found in a ruined church," he mumbled. "He didn't need them anymore and I did."

• ● ● ● •

Viteric would not be needing to don his boots, given he would not be walking for a while.

If he survived.

That was the thought that flashed through John's mind as he stared at the young soldier lying facedown in the hallway near the kitchen. Clementia sat beside him, pale and shaking, valiantly attempting to staunch the flow of blood from his back.

It was strange. John couldn't remember entering the house or even spotting the gravely wounded man whom John had particularly wanted to prevent following him to the Goth encampment, partly to keep the young soldier safe.

No, try as he might, John could not recall the moments prior to his standing there, looking down at Viteric and Clementia.

Eutuchyus lurked nearby, exuding the impression of someone wringing his hands and shaking without actually doing so. John noticed Julius staring fixedly at the steward with undisguised hatred.

"Julius, run as fast as you can and inform General Diogenes about this. He'll send a physician so Viteric may yet be saved. He's lost a lot of blood." John's voice sounded far away to himself. "Clementia, I'll take over."

He knelt down, ripped Viteric's tunic open, folded its sides into a pad to cover the wound, and applied pressure to stop the bleeding.

The boy ran off.

"It was him!" said Eutuchyus in a high, whining tone. "Crept up to Viteric in the dark and stabbed him. He's the sort who would kill his mother for a couple of coins. You saw him throw his knife at me not so long ago!"

"You saw the boy attacking Viteric, Eutuchyus?" John grunted with the effort he was making.

"Not exactly, but—"

"I should think not, because Julius was with me!"

Eutuchyus shrank back and now John was certain the creature really was trembling.

As he worked over the unconscious man, John began to consider those who had been in the house while he and Julius were away. Eutuchyus, Clementia, and the cook Maxima.

Not to mention whoever might have accompanied Viteric here or followed him. Or an intruder who had managed to get into the house before or after Viteric arrived to look for John.

If Viteric had, in fact, arrived for John before dawn.

Why else would he have come here, alone or with another?

And did the attack have anything to do with whatever Felix had been seeking, or with the matter that had brought Felix to Rome in the first place? Or both?

Footsteps clattering down the hall announced the arrival of the garrison physician who worked with efficiency and speed. Extra layers of padding were bandaged tightly in place, the blanket he had brought thrown over Viteric, and the four husky soldiers who arrived with him were instructed to carry the wounded man in their sling as gently as possible.

John watched them go, Clementia at his side. As they stood there, a number of possibilities rushed through John's mind. For an instant he was back on the battlefield, in the middle of a bloody chaos in which he somehow was aware of the smallest of details simultaneously, the flash of a sword, a shattered helmet flying through the air, one fighter struggling against two, a man falling in a shower of blood, individual screams and oaths.

"I found him like that, John." Clementia's voice shook.

John glared at her. "A blade is often a woman's weapon. Easy to conceal and even a weak woman can kill with it if it's inserted in the right spot. I know you own a dagger. You used it when we were attacked in the temple, although not very well."

All he had seen and learned during the previous days, puzzling details, seemingly unrelated matters and his endless ponderings, often vague and contradictory, seemed to be coalescing. He could not have explained how, could not have forced the process. It was more than placing one fact after another into an evolving mosaic. The connections took place in some deep part of his mind that remained as mysterious to him as to any stranger.

He glanced down at the ceremonial knife tucked in his belt. "I removed this from Felix's chest."

"What's that to do with me?"

"You see how Zeus' thunderbolt on the hilt has been overlaid with a cross? Archdeacon Leon considers this to be a holy relic, the sort of sacred artifact your family helped to conceal many years ago. Perhaps one of your ancestors helped himself to an item or two in the process? That reliquary that was broken, for instance. What is that, if not to house a relic?"

"The church doesn't own every relic. The devout can buy them too, as you well know. And what about that knife? You are carrying it with you. I couldn't have stabbed Viteric with it."

"But you could have left it in Felix's chest. Not far from where he died I found this." John produced a silver earring from which hung a miniature dolphin of the same precious metal.

"So I stand condemned by an earring? The jewelry Felix gave me betrayed our relationship to you. But this earring isn't mine! I'm not the only woman in Rome who wears earrings!"

"If we were to investigate your jewelry, do you suppose we would find a matching earring?"

"I tell you it's not mine!" she responded, her voice rising in panic.

John disregarded her protests. "Women are forbidden to set foot where I discovered it. But you could easily have passed for a man while wearing a mask."

"Mask?" Clementia was puzzled. "Where would I obtain a mask? And for what reason? Only actors wear masks and I have had nothing to do with the theater."

"You knew that Felix was a Mithran. You were close to him. Men tell their lovers everything. Knowing Felix, he probably told you exactly where the mithraeum is located. Secret, but not to you. Did you insist he take you to a ceremony or follow him without his knowledge?"

John silently asked Mithra to forgive him for impugning Felix's honor by suggesting such a shocking betrayal of their religion's beliefs. Yet it was necessary to gather enough information to find Felix's murderer.

Then he would consider the matter of the attack on Viteric.

"I can see you don't believe a word I say. I have owned a great deal of jewelry and I can't immediately remember every item. A number of possessions were stolen from my house, including jewelry. But consider this. If I wanted to disguise myself as a man by wearing a mask, would I be so stupid as to also wear earrings?"

No, she wouldn't be that stupid, John thought. Not Clementia. Yet under stress, people often acted without thinking. In a rush to follow Felix she might well have forgotten. The solution John had been certain was coalescing was suddenly fading instead. Whatever inexplicable deductive processes had been at work came to a wrenching halt.

Clementia smiled.

Before John could speak again Julius burst into the room.

"Sir, Diogenes is sending men to arrest you!"

Chapter Thirty-three

"When I got to his command post, Diogenes immediately ordered the physician be sent," Julius said, panting and holding his side. "I was just leaving when I overheard his second order that several soldiers be dispatched separately to arrest you for stabbing Viteric."

"I'll leave by the back way," John told him. "See if you can distract them."

"Where will you go, sir? Are you leaving the city?"

"No."

Clementia grabbed John's arm. "I'm coming with you."

"No." He tried to pull away but she clung desperately.

"What if they kill everyone in the house again? I must come with you!"

"As a senator's daughter you should be safe. Julius, hurry!" John pushed Clementia's hand away while Eutuchyus looked on in apparent terror.

Clementia followed John down the hall. "I'm coming with you. I haven't come this far to fall at the final turn!"

The ragged denizens of the city sided with the man and woman fleeing the authorities through the dawn-lit streets. Children threw rocks at the pursuers and three ill-dressed women blocked the entrance to an alley after John and Clementia ducked into it. That afforded a short delay before the soldiers pushed through the little group using the flats of their swords as persuasion, enough time for the pair to turn down an even narrower passageway at the point where three converged.

"How close are we to the Forum of the Bull?" John risked a glance back as they continued to run. There was no sign of their pursuers for the moment.

"Not far!" Clementia was breathing hard. She had managed to keep up with John, aided by his grasp on her wrist and shortened strides, but looked near the end of her endurance.

John wondered whether he was protecting Viteric's attacker but there was no time to consider the question now. Once he had agreed to take Clementia with him he felt obligated to keep her safe.

He slackened his pace as they approached daylight spilling into the end of the narrow way, halted at its mouth, and peered out. A giant bronze bull stood not far off. A thin man with straggling red hair perched on the statue's shoulders, haranguing a small crowd.

"Walk slowly," John muttered. "We don't want to draw attention." He forced himself to cross the open space at a snail's pace. They ducked into the Church of Saint Minias just as the first of the soldiers emerged from the alley. No one tried to stop them. Apparently, Basilio had not managed to pay his guards after all.

John remembered the way down to the cistern where he had first emerged into Rome. They descended stairs and passed through the archway flanked by a pair of mismatched granite lions. The clatter of boots not far behind echoed in the dim, cavernous space.

Clementia glanced around fearfully. "Where are we going? We'll be trapped here!"

"There's an entrance to the catacombs. Unfortunately, it's on the other side of the cistern."

He yanked her forward to one of the walkways that led through the forest of columns. On both sides lay inky black water. A blackness one could sink into for eternity. John had to force himself to continue.

Their way was faintly illuminated by light falling from above—by design or on account of damage to the vaulted roof, it was impossible to say. They heard shouting and could see torches moving along the water's edge as their pursuers searched for some sign of their prey. Reverberating around the vast space, the voices could be made out with disconcerting clarity, sounding nearer than they were.

"There must be another way out," someone said. "Search the walls on all sides."

Clementia squeezed John's hand. "They'll have the entrance blocked by the time we get there."

"It's not in a wall. It's concealed in a column. Almost impossible to find unless you know where it is."

As they crept along, John glanced up occasionally. Watery reflections trembled in the vaulted ceiling, revealing the variegated capitals of columns scavenged from celebrated public buildings and temples for this humble and invisible work.

They came to a place where impenetrable shadows fell. John slowed. He had to feel his way along with his foot.

Suddenly, shockingly, he brought his foot down on empty space.

He fell forward, pulling Clementia with him.

He was going into the water!

Then he realized he was lying on the walkway, Clementia prone beside him.

He took several deep breaths. Calmer, he groped around in the darkness until his fingers found water, then broken concrete. "Part of the walkway's crumbled but it's still crossable. The water barely covers it."

He shuddered and ordered himself to crawl forward. For John, it was hellish, aware of Clementia's now desperately grasping one of his boots, knowing if she panicked they would both fall into the greedy waiting water.

But which of them was more likely to panic, he wondered grimly?

Once his hand slipped and his face fell forward into the shallow water covering the damaged masonry. He jerked his head back up, blinking blind eyes, sputtering, stifling a scream.

By concentrating on their slow progress and constantly whispering reassurances he pretended were solely for Clementia but were as much for himself, John guided them safely across the broken stretch.

Clementia refused to get back to her feet. "I have to rest. I just can't go on."

Reluctantly John sat with her against a column.

He listened to the voices of their pursuers. Luckily, none of Basilio's men were at work. Had they abandoned him for lack of pay too?

Clementia squeezed his hand. "It won't be long until they realize we're in the middle of the cistern. What then?"

"We'll be in the catacombs."

He heard her sharply indrawn breath.

"And how will you get out without walking right into the arms of Diogenes' men? Are we supposed to hide until we've starved to death?"

"The catacombs run beyond the city walls. That's how I entered Rome in the first place."

"Your plan is for us to escape the city?"

A wavering ray of light flickered across the spot where they sat. He noticed she was peering at him quizzically. Or was her gaze calculating?

"You're an intelligent man," she continued. "What Felix was seeking…is it in the catacombs? Is that why you've brought us here? You've found the key to the list, haven't you?"

She was right. The church above them held the key to the location of the missing artifacts rather than the items themselves. Not surprisingly, Basilio had guessed that piece of the puzzle wrongly. It was amazing how swiftly family histories became distorted. The poor man had been looking at the key every day without grasping its significance.

The truth had begun to come to John the day he and Viteric saw the raven perched on the philosopher's statue. It had reminded him of something, but he couldn't say what. He only remembered later, thanks to the raven in the pines he and Julius had camped beneath. There were those who said that seeing a single raven meant sorrow. But for John two solitary birds had meant revelation.

When John spoke to Basilio in the sacristy of his church he had noted a curious fresco depicting Solomon's reception hall. A statue of Thanatos with a raven on his shoulder sat on a gilded column near the throne. The god was pointing out a not-quite rectangular window towards what the painter had rendered as a structure with only three sides.

The combination of Solomon and a pagan god would have been unusual anywhere but particularly so in a church. Solomon had been a wise man. Was he offering an answer? The raven represented a Mithraic rank. Thanatos was the Greek god of death. The three-sided structure was not a crude depiction of a four-sided building but rather an accurate painting of a pyramid.

John had entered a mausoleum of that shape while fleeing pursuit on his way to Rome. Inside the pyramid lay an entrance to the catacombs, the land of Thanatos. Just outside the entrance sat a sarcophagus on which was carved an image of Mithra. He had seen other Mithraic imagery on burial plaques during his flight.

Archdeacon Leon had mentioned a story he believed to be mere legend to the effect that the ecclesiastical possessions hidden from the Goths had been entrusted to the care of the dead. John had guessed that Felix's list might consist of names on the tombs in which the artifacts had been hidden. But the catacombs which contained the tombs—countless thousands of them—formed a seemingly endless maze, impossible to fully search.

Thanatos was pointing the way into the section of the catacombs where the appropriate tombs could be found. Pointing to the entrance to ancient Mithran catacombs.

Under the guise of making repairs, Basilio must have ordered his workers to search, thinking the valuables had been concealed in the church or the catacombs beneath. He had learned of the secret door into the catacombs from the cistern and assumed the treasure must be hidden nearby. He was mistaken. The catacombs stretched far away from the church, as far as the Appian Way.

John recalled that Basilio had told him how he had found Veneria, the chariot-mender's daughter, and Hunulf, the man with whom she was involved, pretending to examine the fresco of Thanatos. According to Basilio it had been a pretense, given the embarrassing state in which he came upon the couple. But had they also grasped they should be looking in the catacombs near a mithraeum while not fathoming the meaning of the pyramid? Certainly Hunulf had been attacked near the mithraeum where he and Felix worshiped, as evidenced by his trail of blood.

"What are you thinking, John?"

"We must start moving."

"But—" Clementia leapt to her feet, screaming, shaking her hand. A dark shape flew off into the water. "A rat! A rat!"

Even after her screams stopped they continued echoing as if she had awakened the legions of Hell.

John grabbed her hand and ran as he scanned the tops of the columns.

A pair of demonic eyes met his own. What looked like a gigantic toad stared down from an elaborate capital.

They had arrived at the entrance to their salvation, the world of the dead.

Chapter Thirty-four

"Did you hear that? They're right behind us!" Clutching John's hand, Clementia spoke in a whisper verging on a muffled scream.

"The soldiers wouldn't have followed us this far. They'd never find their way out." The corridor was as black as the bottom of a grave.

"How will we find our way out?"

"I've passed through this part of the catacombs before, when I entered the city. I was following someone but I made gouges in the wall at every turn, in case I had to come back this way."

He continued to feel his way along carefully. The marks he had made were not deep and he didn't dare miss one, a fact he did not mention to his panicked companion.

"There, John, that slithering sound! Are there snakes down here?"

"I don't see what they could eat." The faint noises Clementia was hearing might be the settling of earth, a draft weirdly magnified, or more probably just her imagination.

"Where are we?"

"Somewhere between the cistern and an entrance to this catacomb on the Appian Way."

He sat down, back to the wall, to rest and gather his thoughts. His hand was slippery with blood from groping along the rough rock. "You are from an old family, Clementia. Your ancestors must have been pagans a long time ago. Does your family have an ancient mausoleum along the Appian Way?"

"Not that I have heard. My father never spoke about our oldest ancestors. As you say, they were probably pagans."

Had the pyramidal monument belonged to one of the families involved in concealing the treasure? Had it offered a convenient entrance to the underground maze or had the valuables been transported from the church of Saint Minias? The latter seemed more likely since Basilio had the idea the hiding spot was in the church. In fact there was only a doorway to the catacombs under the church. The giant pyramid, however, was an entrance easily identified in a fresco.

"Did your family have any special connection with the church of Saint Minias?"

"No."

"Nothing was ever said about gifts to the church? About funding for beautification, for instance? Did anyone ever mention a fresco?"

"No, never. Why are you asking all these questions?"

Apparently the aristocrats and church had indeed each possessed only half of the information necessary to find the missing artifacts. One of the aristocrats had made up the list and someone connected with the church had commissioned the fresco. The details were now likely unknowable. Both parties to the scheme had done their best to make sure their part of the secret was preserved.

John stared into the darkness, seeing nothing but what the dead see. "Are you ready to go on?" He helped Clementia up.

She stood, a faint presence of rustling robes and perfume. He wished she had stayed behind. He wondered again about the earring in the mithraeum. He could believe it had been stolen from her. Hunulf had reputedly stolen certain items when he left her employment. But if she hadn't been in the mithraeum, who had?

They went on, burrowing through the darkness.

The fresco had pointed him toward the location in the catacombs where the ecclesiastical trove was hidden. Felix had not known about the fresco. He only knew he was searching for burial chambers bearing certain names. Why not search near the mithraeum after a ceremony? He was killed in a side corridor where those coming and going from the mithraeum would have had no reason to venture, allowing his body to go undiscovered for days.

Hunulf, another Mithran, must have been keeping an eye on Felix, who had stolen his mistress. So Hunulf followed Felix and caught up to him.

It wasn't a stretch to imagine the two men had fought. Hunulf had killed Felix and, mortally wounded, crawled away leaving a trail of blood. Was that how it had happened?

John was aware of the ceremonial knife hanging from his belt, lying against his thigh.

It did not seem the sort of weapon a fighting man like Hunulf would choose to employ against a formidable opponent.

What if the two men had been followed by another of the masked celebrants?

The earring suggested a woman's presence and the knife used to murder Felix, a knife identified as a relic by Archdeacon Leon, again brought to mind Clementia's possession of a reliquary and John's suspicion concerning her family's possible thefts from the church treasure they had helped to hide. But if Clementia had attended the ceremony disguised by a mask and wielded the knife, why hadn't John noticed the earring the first time he searched the mithraeum following Felix's death?

There were any number of possibilities.

His thoughts were interrupted by furtive noises behind them. Almost imperceptible. Fabric brushing rock, a shoe scuffing. Or did he only think he heard something? When a man couldn't see, his other senses were free to play tricks.

Besides, anyone following John and Clementia would have to depend on similarly vague sounds. Would it be possible?

Clementia squeezed his hand and he was aware of her perfume as she leaned closer. "There is something following us! There is!"

Something, she said. Not someone.

John recalled Basilio telling him how his workers insisted that a shade roamed the catacombs. He had followed a hooded figure out of the tunnels but he was certain it had been a human being. Albeit someone who knew the maze well.

"We're almost at our destination," he reassured Clementia, although he had long since lost any track of time or any notion of how near to their goal they might be.

John told himself he didn't believe in phantoms. But if there were phantoms, if there was a Hades, perhaps this was what they experienced, endlessly feeling their way along in the dark, unable to see, no expectation of ever reaching any goal. Simply wandering.

Then, abruptly, John saw light ahead. "Someone keeps torches burning near the entrance from the pyramid," John said. "The family must still visit their ancestor."

They entered the chamber where the massive sarcophagus sat, its marble sides sculpted into bas-reliefs of Roman and Egyptian gods and the tell-tale depiction of Mithra slaying the sacred bull.

John took a torch from the wall and shone it back into the corridor through which they'd come, saw no one, no movement. In the light the suspicion they had been followed through the Stygian hallways seemed foolish.

"We'll start looking here." John indicated the nearest tunnel.

Neither needed to consult the list. Both knew it by heart.

Clementia began to examine the plaques lining the walls. Her eyes glittered and her face was flushed.

The search didn't take long.

"Lucinius!" she called out triumphantly. "Lucinius, my friend! I've been looking for you for so long!"

The name was engraved on a thin marble slab closing off a burial niche.

John handed the torch to Clementia, got out his blade, and chipped at the plaster holding the slab in place.

Torchlight flared and shook as John worked. Clementia clenched and unclenched her fist on the torch's shaft. "Finally, finally," she murmured.

Yes, John thought, finally. After Felix had died trying to find this place.

And what did it really matter what the niche contained since it wouldn't bring his friend back to life?

"Look out!"

The plaque came loose and fell before John could catch it. The sound of it hitting the floor was deafening in the narrow corridor. Clementia stepped out of the way, then rushed past John and thrust the torch into the opening revealed.

She screamed.

John stepped forward and peered inside. Typically the spaces were only large enough to contain a body. This one stretched back and back and was empty save for a thick coating of bone-colored dust, the distillation of time.

By the time John had taken the torch, illuminated every corner of the space, felt around, and satisfied himself that there was nothing there, no trace of a treasure, no secret panels, Clementia had calmed down. Her face, though, was pale as that of a corpse. Something in her eyes seemed to have gone out.

"Let's examine the rest of them," John told her.

But both knew what they would find behind the carved names stretching in a line from where Lucinius pointed the way.

Nothing.

John's hand went to the ceremonial knife he carried. Archdeacon Leon suspected some of the church's valuables had been stolen by those trusted to hide them in darkness and obscurity. The religious items possessed by Clementia's family, for example. In fact, it appeared that none of those artifacts had ever been safely hidden. All of them had been stolen.

And so in the end this was what Felix had died for? A fruitless quest?

Then again, was any amount of money worth dying for? Did it matter that he had been searching for nothing?

Now what?

Clementia had begun to sob. John was trying to think of what to say to her when there was an inhuman wail and a robed and hooded figure came flying at him.

John swung the torch at his attacker, who knocked it out of his grasp and clawed at his eyes. The torch spun across the floor and came to rest, filling the corridor with long, jagged, crazily leaping shadows. John caught a glint of wild eyes and bared teeth.

For an instant the face was that of Eutuchyus. Then as it pulled a dagger from its belt it became a woman, shrieking "You cheated me! You all cheated me! Hunulf, the bastard, deserted me! He paid for that!"

John's assailant continued to shriek at him. "Now, you'll die too, you meddling creature! Oh, I've kept an eye on you, I have!" The figure pivoted toward Clementia, who cowered against the wall. "And you, you miserable whore! You stole Hunulf and you and this half-man meant to steal what the church had hidden, but now you'll pay for that as well."

John leapt forward. He drove the slight body back and down to the floor.

It lay still.

John crouched down and extracted the ceremonial knife from the body at his feet.

The knife he had yanked from Felix's chest and vowed to use to avenge his friend's murder. But would Felix have wished him to kill a young woman?

The creature had called itself Eutuchyus, but the unguarded features were clearly female. A woman he had never seen except when she was posing as his steward but now a mosaic of deductions began to fit together.

"This woman must be Veneria," John said.

Epilogue

"Why should you regret killing the woman?" Cornelia asked. "She was trying to kill you."

She and John walked along the ridge at the edge of their estate. It was a hot, cloudy August day. The sea and sky seemed to be frowning at each other.

"I could have overcome her without killing her," John replied without hesitation. While traveling back to Greece he had thought often about what had happened in the catacombs.

"Then you would have regretted not avenging Felix, as you promised him."

"She was hardly more than a child, Cornelia."

"A child? Plotting and killing in cold blood, trying to lay her crimes at other peoples' doors?" She clutched his arm. "What if you had got back to the house an hour later? Diogenes' men would have been waiting to arrest you for that murderous assault on Viteric and you wouldn't be here now!"

John had been recounting what had happened in Rome. He had arrived home the previous day but only after a night's sleep had he agreed to talk. He would have preferred never to speak of Rome again, but Cornelia wanted to know. Had to know, she insisted. There was no arguing with her.

He had explained Veneria's quest for both the hidden church treasures and revenge on Hunulf after he deserted her for Clementia. While working at the church of Saint Minias, Veneria had learned about the secret entrance and used it to visit the catacombs. She had been the hooded and robed shade seen roaming their passages, returning again and again in her futile search, even during her time posing as Eutuchyus.

When John was lost on his first day in Rome, her father Aurelius had brought him to Felix's house, mentioning how well he knew the area in which it was located. In light of subsequent events, it seemed more than likely his familiarity with it was because he visited his daughter there.

"Fortuna smiled on me, Cornelia," John had continued. "Veneria did not know Julius and I were away from the house at the time Viteric was attacked. She had to be there when he was discovered but in order for her plan to succeed, someone had to notify Diogenes, so it's a good wager her father was there and involved with Viteric's stabbing."

"Hoping you would be arrested for it, thus removing you from the household," Cornelia replied thoughtfully.

"That's my conclusion. After all, who was living there? A timid steward with no reason to hate Viteric, a boy, two women—Clementia and the cook—and myself, the obvious culprit, given Diogenes' already aroused suspicions and my habit of shaking off Viteric's company. After all, a man with nothing to hide does not fear a companion."

"And Viteric, did he die?"

John shook his head. "No, although according to the physician it was a close fight to prevent Viteric from setting off on his final journey."

He went on to describe Julius accusing Veneria of investigating Clementia's possessions. "Rather than stealing, I believe she intended to place among them the twin of the earring left in the mithraeum, so as to point a finger at Clementia as responsible for Hunulf's death. Veneria stole the earrings from Felix's room after his death and before my arrival. Obviously intended to match the necklace Clementia already had, it's not surprising she vehemently denied ownership in a panic upon hearing where it had been found and what that could mean for her."

"Speaking of jewelry," he continued after a pause to collect his thoughts "while I was playing knucklebones with Gainus—"

"Who's he, John?"

"One of Clementia's guards, and before you ask, I won. In any event, during that game Gainus told me he thought Hunulf had pilfered a number of valuable items when he left Clementia's employment and she herself confirmed some of her possessions, including jewelry, had disappeared."

John continued talking, idly swinging a stick as they walked. "Basilio, the man in charge of the church of Saint Minias, referred to Veneria wearing expensive jewelry while working there, and also told me that even after Hunulf left the employment of the church, he continued to visit her there."

"And you think Hunulf gave Veneria jewelry stolen from Clementia?"

"Indeed. Veneria's parents must have taken a piece of it to the mortuary, where they pretended to find it on an unclaimed body to claim it as proof their daughter was dead, thus freeing her to assume the identity of Eutuchyus. How likely is it anything valuable on a body would still be with it when arriving at the mortuary? So even while Aurelius shouted that he wanted justice for his supposedly deceased daughter, he had been helping her."

"And not only that," he went on, "there is the question of the weapon Basilio identified as a relic. Clementia's family had been involved in hiding the ecclesiastical artifacts and, coupled with her possession of a reliquary, I have no doubt the family also stole the knife which, being valuable, Hunulf stole and gave to Veneria.

"As for Felix's death, I can only surmise he met Veneria as she searched near the mithraeum and had to be silenced since he recognized her. She killed Hunulf in a jealous rage near the same spot while they looked for the missing artifacts together."

"From your description those catacombs are as black as the humors of a sinner," Cornelia observed. "How could Veneria follow you and Clementia on your flight through them?"

"We heard the noise of her pursuit once or twice, showing she could hear us and follow. Given the maze we were passing through, it was a highly dangerous pursuit. I would admire her courage, had it not been driven by murderous intent."

Cornelia was silent, considering what John had told her. Finally she expressed puzzlement. "But why such an elaborate subterfuge in the first place, pretending to be a steward?"

"Hunulf knew about Clementia's search, having become involved in it during his time as her lover, and what Hunulf knew, Veneria soon knew, including the fact Clementia had begun an affair with Felix. Veneria therefore presented herself to Felix as Conon's household steward, claiming to have escaped death when the rest of the servants were murdered. This gave her an opportunity to eavesdrop on their conversations in hopes of overhearing useful information."

Cornelia frowned. "Given the sort of woman she was, I've no doubt she also gloated over being able to observe an unsuspecting Clementia, given she intended to kill her."

John had also talked about Basilio. How in retrospect, despite his dismissal of what he called a legend, it was possible the catacomb repairs he had ordered undertaken were an excuse concealing his own search for the lost artifacts reputed to have been entrusted to the care of the dead. "If so, no doubt he's still looking," he concluded.

Cornelia, ever practical, had wondered about the hidden doorway to the catacombs under Basilio's church.

"The early Christians were resourceful," John replied. "They had to be to practice a proscribed religion. They were continually enlarging the catacombs to entomb their dead so it's not surprising one branch passed beneath a temple. Possibly they inadvertently broke into the cistern area and decided to use the place as a secret exit to be used if needed. There's no way of knowing."

"I won't suggest you return to Rome to solve that particular mystery, John! What do you think will happen to Basilio, now it seems he has little hope of recovering the missing items?"

"He will need to subsist on what he can earn from his religion, if he can. As to religious matters, before I left Rome there was much talk about a mystery Basilio will never solve. What happened to the body of the general buried behind the house in which I lived for a while?"

Cornelia's initial puzzled look changed to a smile. "Could it be Felix was moved to the Mithran catacombs under cover of darkness?"

"Yes, and appropriate rites were performed. There was something else. He was exhumed with the assistance of a couple of adepts from the garrison. One of them evidently told Gainus, the gambler I just mentioned, since he also arrived to help with the task. He was not happy to be the one who uncovered a curse tablet just below the surface of Felix's grave."

"But who could have put it there?"

"That's another mystery. It is written in the language of Egypt—"

"Which you always use when you curse!" Cornelia pointed out.

John gave a rueful smile. "Indeed. I suspect Eutuchyus was responsible because he, or rather she, came from a family with strong connections to racing so not only knew about such curse tablets but quite possibly had seen one, since they're occasionally dug up at racetracks. Not to mention she was on the spot to bury it. Perhaps she decided to invoke supernatural aid for her revenge on Clementia and Hunulf. In any event, I destroyed it by dropping it into the kitchen brazier. Whatever the truth of the matter, Gainus was quite upset about his discovery. Gamblers are as superstitious as racers, it seems, and he viewed it as a very bad omen."

A sturdy dog came bounding up the hill. It rubbed its head against Cornelia's thigh and turned reproachful eyes on John.

"Wolves were raiding the sheep so I bought him from that butcher who keeps a shop by the marketplace in Megara," Cornelia explained.

"What is he called?"

"The dog? Leucon."

"And he is, as he is called, white-haired. I see he has wandered away from his charges," John pointed out.

Cornelia scratched the dog's ears. "What will happen to the boy Julius?"

"He decided to take my advice and remain in Rome until he's old enough to join the army. In the meantime Diogenes has given him work carrying out errands for the garrison."

"And Aurelius and his wife?"

"Vanished. Diogenes has had men searching but when I left the city they hadn't been found. I am certain they are both far from Rome. When it came to accounting for his own misdeeds Aurelius is obviously not so insistent on justice being served."

"What about the senator's friendly daughter? But let me guess. She already has her eye on Diogenes?"

"I believe you are correct. She no longer needs to pretend to be a servant, which makes matters easier for her right now, but if the city should fall to the Goths, she will be carried off as a captive. Which was why she was posing as a servant in the first place."

"Do you think Rome will fall?"

"Not this time. Diogenes is a competent commander."

A brisk wind raised whitecaps on the sea and rocked seabirds, feathered jetsam floating on the choppy water.

"You haven't mentioned the most important matter, John. What will become of us now that Justinian knows you left and went to Rome? The penalty for leaving exile…"

John put his arm around her shoulders. "I have left that for last because…because I am afraid you will be sorely troubled by what I have to tell you."

"Oh, John…" She put her head on his shoulder and he saw tears come. "But you did him a service! You found his emissary's murderer! Does that not count for something?"

"Yes, but you know how fickle the emperor can be. I had to stay in Rome while Diogenes and Justinian exchanged communications. Diogenes' messenger returned from Constantinople not long after I solved Felix's murder. Justinian made it clear he had not sent me to Rome and, without going into details, let us say he was not pleased. However, rather than immediately carrying out the emperor's orders with regards to me, Diogenes sent a second messenger, explaining what had transpired. I was confined to my house, under guard, while waiting for the reply. In the end the emperor allowed me to return home, but he will be sending a ship from Constantinople for me."

Cornelia put her arms around him. "How long do we have?"

"That's in the hands of Fortuna, isn't it? But, please, don't cry anymore when I tell you…I know it isn't what you would want, Cornelia, but Justinian has ordered me back to the capital to resume my imperial service."

Afterword

During the years 535 to 554, the Eastern Roman Emperor Justinian I carried out a military campaign which successfully, although temporarily, reclaimed Italy from the Goths. Italy was left depopulated and devastated. Ironically, the Roman culture and governmental institutions which had survived largely intact under the Gothic king Theodoric the Great were destroyed.

During the war, the efforts of General Belisarius were hampered by the emperor's refusal to make sufficient resources available and Belisarius returned to Constantinople during the 549 to 550 siege of Rome. Previously, the commander of the Roman garrison, General Conon, had been killed by his own soldiers, who had not been paid for some time. The siege ended when members of the Roman garrison, still disgruntled at lack of pay and afraid of starving, opened the gates to Totila. Much of the population was slaughtered. It is said that General Diogenes was one of the few to escape but this is the last known of him.

During the sixth century the pope still lived within the city walls rather than the area that was to become the Vatican in later years. Pope Vigilius, however, was detained in Constantinople from 546 to 555, due to a dispute with Justinian over religious doctrine. Archdeacon Leon is a fictional character, inspired by Pelagius, who remained in Rome as Vigilius' representative. Pelagius later became pope in his own right.

Catacombs are commonly associated with Christian burials. However, pagans also constructed subterranean galleries of tombs and evidence of their presence, including paintings connected with the worship of Mithra, have been found in Rome's catacombs, possibly because fossors digging new tunnels sometimes inadvertently broke into private pagan areas.

For structures and locations we have used the names by which they were known during the sixth century. These names often differ from those used in classical or modern times. For instance, the famous Colosseum was in the sixth century the Flavian Amphitheater.

The pyramid tomb we have erected beside the Appian Way is our invention and should not be confused with the similarly shaped tomb of Caius Cestius. Built around 15 BC, it was later incorporated into the city wall and remains a popular tourist attraction.

Glossary

AMALASUNTHA (r 526-534)

Daughter of THEODORIC, she ruled first as regent for his grandson Athalaric and then as queen after Athalaric's early death. Her assassination by a faction opposed to a closer association with the Eastern Roman Empire led JUSTINIAN I to invade Italy.

ATRIUM

Central area of a Roman house. The COMPLUVIUM, a square opening in the roof, provided light and air to surrounding rooms. Rain falling through the compluvium was collected for household use in an IMPLUVIUM, a shallow cistern or pool.

BELISARIUS

General whose exploits included halting the Persian advance in the eastern part of the empire and recapturing northern Africa from the Vandals. His campaign against the Goths in Italy was hampered by Justinian's failure to supply adequate resources and he was recalled before the war ended.

BLUES

Supporters of the Blue chariot team. Like the GREENS,

they took their name from the racing colors of the team they favored.

CADWALLON (fl 6th century)

King of Gwneydd in Wales. His nickname Lawhir (Long Hand or Long Arm) has been interpreted to refer to his widespread authority. Some three hundred years after Cadwallon's death a writer offered an unlikely alternative explanation: Cadwallon could pick up a stone without bending, because his arms reached the ground.

CEREBERUS

Three-headed dog whose role was to guard the entrance to Hades.

CHURCH OF SAINT PETER

Familiar name for the basilica of Saint Peter. Erected in the fourth century and demolished in the sixteenth, it was the predecessor of the present Saint Peter's Basilica in Vatican City.

COMPLUVIUM

See ATRIUM

CONCRETE

Roman concrete was formed from a mixture of lime and volcanic ash.

CURSE TABLETS

Rolled or folded sheets of thin lead inscribed with imprecations believed to cause harm to the persons named in them.

FLAVIAN AMPITHEATER

Commonly known today as the Colosseum. Dedicated in 80 CE, it was the site of gladiatorial contests, executions, and other public spectacles. The name "Colosseum" was derived from the nearby colossal statue of Nero. By the sixth century Nero's head had been replaced by that of the Sun God.

GREENS
See BLUES

GREAT CHURCH
Colloquial name for the Hagia Sophia (Church of the Holy Wisdom). Completed in 537, it still stands in Istanbul.

JUSTINIAN I (r 527-565)
Byzantine emperor whose ambition was to restore the Roman Empire to its former glory. His accomplishments included codifying Roman law and an extensive building program in Constantinople. He was married to THEODORA.

MESE
Main thoroughfare of Constantinople. Enriched with columns, arches, statuary depicting secular, military, imperial, and religious subjects, fountains, religious establishments, monuments, emporiums, public baths, and private dwellings, it was a perfect mirror of the heavily populated and densely built city it traversed.

MITHRA
Sun God usually depicted wearing a tunic and Phrygian cap, his cloak flying out behind him, while in the act of slaying the Great Bull. Also known as Mithras, his worship spread throughout the Roman Empire via his followers in the military.

MITHRAEUM
Underground temple dedicated to MITHRA.

PLATO'S ACADEMY
Greek philosopher Plato founded his academy in 387 BCE. The academy and other pagan schools were closed in 529 CE by order of JUSTINIAN I.

PRAETORIUM
In Roman times commonly denoting a military headquarters but used in the Bible to refer to Pilate's residence.

SPINA
Low platform separating the two arms of a U-shaped racetrack. It was often decorated with sculptures and monuments.

TEMPLE OF ROME
Originally named the Basilica of Constantine, by the sixth century it was known as the Temple of Rome.

TESSERAE
Small cubes, usually stone or glass, utilized in the creation of mosaics.

THEODORA
Byzantine empress. When the Nika riots broke out in Constantinople in 532, she is said to have urged her husband JUSTINIAN I to remain in the city, thus saving his throne. She died in 548.

THEODORIC (r 493-526)
Gothic king who conquered and ruled Italy, he was known as Theodoric the Great for the peace and prosperity of his long reign. He was the father of AMALASUNTHA.

TOTILA (r 541-552)
Gothic king who enjoyed considerable success against the Eastern Roman Empire. He was killed in battle in 552.

TUNICA

Undergarment.

VIGILIUS

Pope from 537 to 555. From 546 to 555 he was detained in Constantinople by JUSTINIAN I as the result of theological controversy. He was finally permitted to leave but died before reaching Rome.

To see more Poisoned Pen Press titles:

Visit our website:
poisonedpenpress.com
Request a digital catalog:
info@poisonedpenpress.com